W9-ACU-496

The Saturday Evening Girls Club

Center Point
Large Print

**This Large Print Book carries the
Seal of Approval of N.A.V.H.**

The
Saturday Evening
Girls Club

JANE HEALEY

JRVLS
105 3 ST SE
JAMESTOWN ND 58401

WITHDRAWN

CENTER POINT LARGE PRINT
THORNDIKE, MAINE

This Center Point Large Print edition
is published in the year 2019 by arrangement with
Amazon Publishing, www.apub.com.

Copyright © 2017 by Jane Healey.

All rights reserved.

This is a work of fiction. Names, characters, organizations,
places, events, and incidents are either products of the
author's imagination or are used fictitiously.

The text of this Large Print edition is unabridged.
In other aspects, this book may vary
from the original edition.
Printed in the United States of America
on permanent paper.
Set in 16-point Times New Roman type.

ISBN: 978-1-64358-296-2

Library of Congress Cataloging-in-Publication Data

The Library of Congress has cataloged this record
under Library of Congress Control Number: 2019942053

For Ellie and Madeleine,
my very own Saturday evening girls

CHAPTER 1

Saturday, September 26, 1908
Boston, Massachusetts

Every morning, as long as the weather was fair, I would come up to the rooftop of our building with my coffee cup and stand among my mother's tomato plants. I would sip my coffee and look across the vastness of Boston Harbor. I never tired of the view. There was always something new to see.

Today the most striking thing about the harbor, more than the schooners and merchant ships traveling to and from imagined destinations, or the hodgepodge of buildings fighting for space on the waterfront, was the fog. The clouds of mist danced on the surface of the water, and the morning sunlight gave them a glistening, ethereal glow that was so stunning it almost hypnotized me.

Was this the type of glorious autumn morning that had greeted my parents when they came here from Italy twenty-four years ago? Had they woken up on that crowded, rancid-smelling ship and seen this type of daybreak over Boston? And if they had, were they then filled with the kind of hope that filled my heart now?

My parents had come to America dreaming of a better life than they had in their peasant village back in Sicily. When I stood on our rooftop on mornings like this, I dreamed of a distinctly *American* life, better than what my parents had today.

My quiet reverie was interrupted by a screechy-voiced woman hollering out of one of the top-floor windows to her husband on the street below, and I realized that it was time to catch the streetcar to go to work. I took one more glance at the fog on the harbor's surface before I hurried toward the stairs.

I stopped at the fifth floor and ran down the hall to drop my coffee mug at home before I left. I heard the Castellano baby crying; Mrs. Mineo yelling out the window to her son, Luigi; and five-year-old Anita Pirandello's horrible coughing. This was life on the fifth floor of 53 Charter Street. Doors were always open. Everyone helped each other. And everyone knew everyone else's business.

"I'm going to my club meeting right after work, so I won't be home for dinner," I said to my mother as I entered our family's tiny kitchen. My mother was sitting at the kitchen table with a pile of clothing from my father's tailor shop next to her. She was stitching the hem of a pair of navy-blue pants.

"Oh, Caprice, I thought you left with Fabbia

and Vita," she said to me in Italian as she looked up. "Here, this is an onion sandwich you can have for lunch."

She picked up a brown sack on the table and handed it to me.

"*Grazie*," I said, thanking her. I kissed her on both cheeks, looking at her crinkly, espresso-brown eyes and the deep creases marking her round, pink cheeks. It was like looking in a mirror years from now. I was okay with this. My mother was a pretty woman. I only wished I had been born with her shiny black hair instead of my own odd-colored auburn. I'd always felt God picked the wrong color hair for me.

I was about to shut the door when I heard her call out, "Oh, Caprice?"

"Yes?" I answered, peeking back inside.

"Your father has invited over Enrico Zummo for dessert tomorrow night," she said. "He's the son of Joey, the shoemaker."

"Mama, no. *No!* Why does Papa continue to do this? You know I—" My mother held up her hand to stop me, and I clenched my jaw and felt the warmth of anger creep up my cheeks.

"Caprice, please be patient with your father," she answered in Italian. This was our language tarantella—we danced back and forth between my English and her Italian. "Please. He's only trying to do what he thinks is best for his oldest daughter."

I sighed and realized that I didn't have time to argue or I would risk being late for work. That was probably why she had decided to warn me about the shoemaker's son today; she just wanted me to know ahead of time, to try to keep the peace in our house.

"I will try to be patient," I said. "I've got to go."

"And you never know, you may like this Enrico, no?" she said, giving me a tiny shrug, her eyebrows raised.

"Yes, you never know, Mama," I replied. I was a twenty-year-old woman. I would rather die than have my parents arrange a marriage to a Sicilian stranger. Not that my mother would ever understand. She had married my father at sixteen after meeting him *once*.

I left our building and hurried down to Hanover Street to catch the streetcar to Madame DuPont's Millinery, my place of employment since I had graduated high school three years ago. It was 7:30 a.m., but the streets of the North End already hummed. Shopkeepers washed windows and rearranged their wares on the sidewalks. I saw several pounds of macaroni drying in the Caroli family's pasta shop. Headless yellow chickens and enormous cuts of blood-red beef were hanging in the windows of the shop owned by Mr. Tomei, the butcher.

This morning, the unsavory smells of the North

End streets—of horse manure and rotting trash—
were muted by the smell of strong Italian coffee
wafting from many of the windows and the slight
salty breeze coming off the harbor.

I broke into a run and jumped onto the streetcar
just as the doors were about to close. I sank into
an open seat in the back and breathed a sigh of
relief. Thank God, I would not be late for work.
Madame DuPont didn't need another reason to
berate me. My being Italian appeared to be all
the reason she needed.

As usual, the ride to Washington Street seemed
far too short. I felt my stomach tighten as I waved
good-bye to the streetcar driver and walked down
the clean, quiet street toward Madame DuPont's.
I glanced into the gleaming shop windows that
displayed exquisite leather shoes and the latest
dresses in taffeta and silk shantung. A woman
strolled by me wearing large diamond earrings
and a gorgeous deep-green cashmere cloak.
Feeling self-conscious of the frayed cuffs and
missing button I had yet to replace, I pulled my
own coat a little tighter around me. These were
things that I never thought about in the North End.

The women who visited Madame DuPont's
shop would never set foot in the North End. Why
would they, when they could shop and live in this
pristine part of Boston? The Washington Street
shops catered to the society ladies of the city.
Women who would happily pay thirteen dollars

for a new fall hat knew nothing about what it was like to live in a place where you shared a bathroom with several families. I had not spent thirteen dollars combined on clothing in the past year, much less on one hat.

I opened the door to Madame DuPont's and smelled the familiar sweet-and-sour scent of new fabric. The walls were painted a soothing cream color, and the ceiling was covered in shiny copper. On either side of the shop were chocolate-brown built-in wooden shelves. All of our latest creations adorned them—turban-style hats made of chiffon and velvet in gray or black, Milan straw hats with velvet trim and silk rosebuds.

Madame was sitting at her desk going over the books and didn't even acknowledge my arrival. My Irish coworkers from South Boston glanced up briefly, only to return to their work when they realized it was just me.

I walked over and sat at my lonely little table at the back of the shop and started to organize the supplies I needed for the day. I didn't like working for Madame DuPont very much, but I did love my job as the shop's sole trimmer. I had been promoted to the position last year. Once the shop's makers shaped the hats, it was my task to make them beautiful by adorning them with unique combinations of flowers, ribbons, feathers, and lace.

We worked in silence for about an hour. When it was quiet like this, I often imagined that I was sitting at my own shop in the North End, selling gorgeous, *affordable* hats to the women of my neighborhood. I envisioned an impeccable little storefront on Hanover Street. The ivory-colored paint trim would be spotless, and the windows would always gleam. My finest creations would be displayed in the front glass window.

My own hat shop: Caprice's Millinery. It was what I wanted more than anything in the world. And tomorrow I would finally have a discussion with my parents about paying board so I would no longer have to hand over every penny I earned to them. I needed to save my own money and finally *do something* about opening my hat shop instead of just dreaming about it.

Suddenly Madame DuPont bolted out of her seat, walked to the middle of the room, and announced in her haughty French accent, "We will have a short meeting at noon today after I distribute your pay envelopes for the week."

All of us looked around, although no one met my glance. We had never had a meeting in all of the time I had worked for Madame. I had no idea why we would start now.

Madame ignored our reactions and walked over to Bridget, one of the makers, while taking her silver reading glasses off her long pale nose. "Bridget!" she said in that jarring tone that cut right through you. "That hat looks terrible." She clucked her tongue and shook her head. "Your work is still so sloppy. Sometimes I wonder if you've learned anything from me. Here, hand it to me; I will fix it."

Bridget's face turned crimson, and she stared at the floor while Madame DuPont tried to fix the mess of a hat. Madame was right; Bridget's work was terrible. I stroked the fluffy ostrich feather I was holding and tried to concentrate on the work in front of me, but my body was so tense that I couldn't focus. Whenever Madame yelled at one of the girls, it was just a reminder that sooner or later it would be my turn again.

There was a time when I had walked to the streetcar with the South Boston girls at the end of the workday. We would joke about who had endured the worst of Madame's harassment and would take turns imitating her French accent. It had made working for Madame a little more tolerable.

All of that ended when the shop's former trimmer had left to have a baby a year ago. When Madame DuPont had chosen me to train as her replacement, the South Boston girls stopped talking to me. They had all worked for Madame at least a year longer than I had, and they had resented my promotion.

By the end of each week, I could barely stand it anymore. After six days working in that icy atmosphere, I couldn't wait for the comfort of my weekly Saturday Evening Girls meeting.

I had been a part of the Saturday Evening Girls club, or the *S.E.G.* as we all called it, since I was thirteen. We were not young girls anymore, but the club's name remained the same. At the S.E.G., we had educational speakers and discussed literature and listened to music. But what I loved most about our weekly meetings was sitting in the back of the room with Thea, Maria, and Ada, my best friends, talking to each other about whatever was on our minds that week. The S.E.G. meeting was not only the best part of my week—it was the best part of *vita mia*, my life.

A couple of women visited the shop in the course of the morning, and each time Madame DuPont transformed into the vivacious French shop owner. Her small blue eyes glistened and her faux smile warmed as she told a short, stout woman named Mrs. Cabot how wonderful she looked in a gray turban. The hat was all wrong for her. It made her look like a jar of olives about to explode.

Getting lost in the art of making hats was the only thing that got me through the days—that and the pay, of course.

At noon, I was anxious to hear Madame's news, thinking that it must be something quite important to call a meeting for the first time. She quickly passed out our pay envelopes and stood at the front of the shop, facing all of us at our worktables.

"As of next week, I am closing the shop and moving to New York. My husband has been offered a new job at a bank in New York City, so I am bringing my business there. Boston is second class to New York when it comes to fashion, anyway." She said this to us in an icy, stiff voice, staring above our heads so she didn't have to look any of us in the eye. Smoothing her skirt, she informed us, as casually as if she were talking about the weather, "This is your last day of employment at the shop."

We all sat in stunned silence. A hot, queasy feeling washed over me, and I was afraid I might have to run out to the street to be sick.

My dream started to evaporate into the air around me. I couldn't believe this was happening. No job. No *pay*. My family couldn't afford to have me living at home and not working, not while Fabbia and Vita were still in school. I would be forced to get a horrible factory job like my friend Thea. And my father would be more determined than ever to marry me off.

"So, that's it then?" I heard someone say in an Irish brogue, anger and tears choking the voice. "You're just turning us out onto the street? Just like that?"

Madame DuPont looked down her nose. Her eyes revealed no sign of sympathy. "Well, yes, I

16

suppose I am," she said, adding with a wave of her hand, "but I have trained you all well. This is one of the most well-regarded shops in Boston. You should—well, most of you should—be able to find other jobs."

With this, one of the girls grabbed her things and stormed out of the shop. A few others followed her. I gathered up my coat and hat in a daze, the sick feeling getting worse as I stood up. Bridget exited without saying good-bye; I heard her sniffling as she slammed the shop's door behind her. I was anxious to leave too, especially now that I was alone with Madame.

"Caprice," she said as I was about to run for the door. I looked up at her, wanting to scream at her for the way she had dismissed us all with no recourse, for all of the harsh comments and treatment over the past three years. But instead, I just met her gaze, my eyes as cold as hers. I would not let her see me cry.

"You are a very talented trimmer, Caprice," she said, squeezing her hands together. "Very talented. Perhaps one of the best I have ever had work for me. Still . . . good luck. You'll need it."

For a brief moment, I couldn't move. I was taken aback by her words. On my last day of employment, Madame DuPont had given me genuine praise. Something I had been waiting to hear since I had started working for her three years ago. But she had to ruin it by wishing me luck. *"You'll need it."* *Why? Because I'm Italian?* That was what she didn't say.

There was an awkward pause as I stood there, blinking back tears. I took a deep breath and answered in a harsh whisper, "Good-bye, Madame."

I bowed my head and rushed toward the door, not daring to look back for fear she'd see me weeping.

CHAPTER 2

A shared trouble is half joy.
—Italian proverb

It was still drizzling when I arrived at the headquarters of the Saturday Evening Girls on Hull Street in the North End. I realized I must look like a fright, but I didn't care. I had spent the afternoon wandering the streets of Boston, not wanting to go home to face my family but not having anywhere to go until the S.E.G. meeting started.

I entered Hull House through the basement, which was now the storefront of the newly opened pottery shop, the business that supported the club's activities. I walked through the shop and up the basement stairs, then climbed one flight past the first-floor pottery workroom and one of the meeting rooms, up to the second-floor assembly room. It was a large, welcoming space with an enormous marble fireplace. The fire was blazing and the room was warm, the smell of wood smoke mingling with the dry, toasty scent of the pottery kilns two floors below.

I saw Ada, Thea, and Maria sitting on our usual seats in the far back of the room. Ada had a book on her lap as always, her petite hands

19

flying as she told Thea and Maria a story. Maria's enormous blue eyes widened, and she burst out giggling at whatever Ada was saying. Thea was facing away from me so all I could see was her haphazard chignon of honey-brown hair, but her laughter was so loud it echoed against the assembly room walls.

I walked over to where they were sitting, nodding and saying hi to some of the other club members as I passed by them.

"Hello, ladies," I said as I came up behind Thea's chair.

"Jesus, Mary, and Joseph! Caprice, what happened to you?" Maria asked, jumping up to pull over a seat for me. "Sit down; you look awful."

"Oh, Caprice, you're soaked to the bone," said Thea, taking my coat and hat from me as I removed them.

"Are you okay?" Ada said, grabbing my hand.

"I'm so glad to finally see you all," I said, sinking into the chair Maria had brought over. "It's been a horrible day."

I told them what had transpired at Madame DuPont's that morning. They sat around me in a circle, and despite my troubles, the familiar happiness I felt when the four of us were together washed over me. How many times and in how many places had we sat like this, trying to find answers to the problems in our lives? Too many to count.

Gazing at them today, I still saw remnants of the girls we once were when we had met seven years ago. Tiny, five-foot-tall Ada with her shiny black braids and dimpled cheeks, studied me intently with her dark eyes. Maria pulled at one of her platinum-blonde curls, her alabaster skin growing pink with anger as I got to the part about Madame closing the shop. Chubby, freckle-faced Thea smiled and her green eyes filled with pride for me when I told them that Madame called me one of the most talented trimmers she had ever known.

"That witch!" Maria exclaimed as I finished my story. "I can't believe she would just turn you all out onto the street." She said it loud enough that a few girls in the assembly room turned to look at us.

"Maria," Ada said, her voice low, "I'm sure Caprice doesn't need the whole club to know what happened just yet."

"No, please! Not yet," I said, holding up my hand. "My family doesn't even know yet. Oh, yes—if that weren't bad enough, my mother told me my father is bringing another potential husband over for dessert tomorrow night. Enrico Zummo, the shoemaker's son."

The three of them groaned when they heard this. They were well aware of my father's match-making attempts.

"So," I added, throwing my hands up in disgust

and slouching in a very unladylike manner in my chair. "My dream of opening my own hat shop—the dream you have all listened to me talk about for the past *year*—seems very out of reach at the moment. I was planning to ask my parents tomorrow about paying board. But of course that won't happen now. I don't know what in God's name I'm going to do next. I may get some advice from Miss Guerrier . . . or Mrs. Storrow, if she's here tonight."

"Yes, she's coming," said Ada with a nod. "Fanny Goldstein just told me that she was."

Miss Guerrier was the head librarian at the North End library and the founder of the S.E.G. Mrs. Storrow was a prominent member of Boston society who had taken an interest in the club years ago and had helped support it ever since.

"I bet one of them can help you," said Thea. "You have skills—you're a beautiful milliner. Your hats are exquisite. Look at me, I have no real skills at all—outside of assembling boxes—and they were able to find me a *much* better job."

"Oh, Thea, they really did?" I asked. "Congratulations, that's wonderful news. No more box-cutting factory?"

"No more box-cutting factory. And no more hemorrhoids from sitting all day long on that horrible stool . . . well, at least hopefully they'll clear up now," Thea said, turning crimson. "And no more boss who curses all day. Mrs. Storrow found me a job with an interior decorator downtown named Mrs. Thatcher. And I'm going to be working on Gainsborough Street, right near the dress shop Maria works at, so we can take the streetcar together. Oh . . . but, Caprice, I'm sorry, I don't mean to sound like I'm gloating."

"Not at all, Thea," I said with a smile. "I'm thrilled for you. And your parents?" I asked, hope in my voice. "Are they happy for you too?"

"They're the same as ever," said Thea, her tone resigned. "They still barely acknowledge me unless it's to give orders to cook or clean something. Since my sister's baby, David, was born, it's gotten even worse." Thea shrugged.

All of us nodded. There was nothing to say. Thea's parents had been cold and indifferent to her for years.

"Thea, you know I understand how *that* feels," Maria said. "Although my poor mother acknowledges me, of course, it's my father who I think would rather I wasn't around. He never came home from work today, so you know that means he's going to stumble home in the middle of the night horribly drunk."

Thea, Ada, and I just waited for her to continue. We had heard many variations of this story.

"Antonetta is here with me tonight. Honestly, if we could, I would stay overnight here with her. Last Saturday, he came home at two in the morning, dragged my mother out of bed, and told her to make him something to eat." Maria bit her lip and gave us a mischievous look. "I sent her back to bed and made him a cheese sandwich—but I made sure to spit into it before I gave it to him."

We all gasped.

"Maria, you didn't!" I said, hand over my mouth.

"Oh, but I *did,*" she said, crossing her arms in front of her. "And I don't feel one bit sorry about it."

"Did he notice?" asked Ada, grimacing.

"Oh, please, ladies. If I had served him horse manure, he probably wouldn't have realized it," said Maria, her mouth twisted with bitterness. "But enough talk about my father. You've heard it all before. Ada, you had started telling us about your college classes before Caprice got here."

"Yes, I love them," she answered, smiling. "They're going so well, and my father doesn't suspect a thing."

"Do you think you and your mother will be able to keep it that way?" I asked.

"I really think so. As long as we're careful," Ada said with a nod. "That reminds me—do you think Frankie or Dominic might be able to walk me home from the streetcar on the nights I have class? It's too risky having anyone from our building walk me—people talk too much."

"I'm sure one of them will, Ada. I'll ask them," I answered.

Last month, Mrs. Storrow had told Ada she had found a scholarship fund so that Ada could attend Simmons College at night. Ada's mother had agreed to let her attend the night classes, but they had decided not to tell Ada's father. Ada's father believed that higher education should not be wasted on a woman.

"I'll mention it to Frankie and Dominic tomorrow at dinner." I said. "What time do you—"

"Good evening, ladies." Miss Guerrier's voice boomed across the room.

Miss Guerrier was wearing the simple charcoal-gray wool skirt and plain white shirtwaist she always wore. Her reading glasses were forever on a chain around her neck, and her graying, dark-brown hair was in a neat bun. She looked across the room, smiling at all of us, waiting a beat until we were quiet enough for her to speak again.

I looked out across the crowd, and it seemed everyone was in attendance tonight. Since the S.E.G. began so many years ago, it had grown to forty members. Like Maria and me, some of us were from Italian immigrant families. Our parents had come over from peasant villages in Sicily or Parma or Avellino. Others were from Jewish immigrant families who had come over from market towns in Russia called *shtetels*. Ada and Thea's families had come from the same town near the Black Sea.

"Good evening," Miss Guerrier said again when everyone had finally stopped talking. "Welcome. I hope all of you had an enjoyable workweek. We have altered the planned agenda for tonight. We have postponed our scheduled speaker, Professor Johnson, until further notice. Instead, after some brief pottery shop updates from me, Mrs. Storrow has a very exciting announcement."

The room started humming as to what this announcement might be, and Miss Guerrier paused before continuing. "After discussion surrounding this announcement, we will have refreshments and, if there's time, some folk dancing. First, some updates from the pottery shop . . ."

I half listened to what Miss Guerrier was saying; I was too preoccupied thinking about the events of the day and how my conversation with Mrs. Storrow and Miss Guerrier would go. Would they be able to help me find another job? What would my family have to go without this week if I didn't bring home a pay envelope?

"And now for the good news and the bad news," Miss Guerrier said with a smile. "The good news is that our wonderful pottery shop sales clerk, Concetta Leone, has been accepted to the nursing program at St. Elizabeth's Hospital in Brighton!"

The room erupted into applause, and I spotted a blushing Concetta a few rows in front of me as she gave a small wave and nod of thanks.

Miss Guerrier continued. "The bad news is that she will no longer be able to work at the pottery shop because she will be working as a nurse's aide at the hospital. Thank you for all of your hard work, Concetta. We wish you luck in this exciting new chapter in your life."

With this last bit of news, Ada and Thea both elbowed me at the same time and Maria leaned over in her seat, her eyes bright with excitement.

"Caprice, this is perfect," whispered Ada. "You have to talk to them about working at the pottery shop—I bet they're going to want someone else to start right away."

"Ada, they may already have someone lined up," I whispered back, trying not to sound too hopeful.

We stopped talking because now Mrs. Storrow was at the front of the assembly room, and we were all curious to hear what she had to say. In truth, I had felt a tiny surge of hope when Miss Guerrier said Concetta was leaving. Could I work at the pottery shop? Even temporarily?

Tonight, Mrs. Storrow was radiant in a navy-blue silk dress with a cream-colored yoke. The outfit complemented her lovely pale complexion and chestnut hair perfectly. Maria craned her neck to see her and gave a little sigh when she got a full view of what Mrs. Storrow was wearing.

"Good evening, ladies," said Mrs. Storrow, looking around the room with a warm smile. "Now for the big announcement that you've been waiting for." She paused for dramatic effect. "I'm pleased to announce that we will do one more performance of *The Merchant of Venice* this year. Mrs. Jack Gardner has invited our group to perform at her gorgeous home, Fenway Court, three weeks from today, to help raise funds for the S.E.G. The patronesses attending will be some of the most prominent ladies of Boston society!"

Maria and Ada, who both had lead roles in the play, nearly jumped out of their seats. Gasps and chatter filled the room.

"This is going to be quite different than performing for a bunch of sniffling, yawning schoolchildren," said Maria with a smile, tossing her hair over her shoulder.

"Okay, ladies, we have chocolate almond biscotti, coffee, and lemonade for refreshments," said Miss Guerrier, nearly yelling above the buzz of chatter and laughter. She glanced down at her watch and with a laugh said, "And in lieu of folk dancing, how about some socializing?"

As soon as she said this, I was already out of my chair, and it was all I could do not to run to the front of the room to where Miss Guerrier and Mrs. Storrow were standing.

"Hello, Miss Guerrier, Mrs. Storrow."

"Hello, Caprice, how are you?" Mrs. Storrow said, giving me a warm smile that made her eyes crinkle at the edges. "And how is the lovely Madame DuPont?" She asked this with the smallest hint of sarcasm in her voice. "I haven't been by the shop lately."

"Well," I said, my jaw clenching at the thought of my former employer. "Unfortunately you won't be able to visit the shop again. Madame has decided to close it and move to New York. I lost my job today."

Mrs. Storrow and Miss Guerrier both gasped as Miss Guerrier reached out and put her hand on my elbow.

"Come, let's sit and talk." Mrs. Storrow gently put her arm around my shoulder, and the three of us walked over to some chairs in the corner where we could talk quietly and actually hear each other.

We sat down, and again I described what had transpired at Madame DuPont's.

"The most frustrating part of this is . . . I was planning on having a discussion with my parents about paying board, to start saving so I can open my own hat shop here in the North End. Mrs. Storrow, you put the idea in my head a year ago, and I think about it all the time. But it's a little difficult to talk to my family about paying board when I don't even have a job."

"Caprice, I don't blame you for being so upset,

of course," Miss Guerrier said, polishing her reading glasses as she spoke. "But don't lose heart. You are a gifted milliner, and if you want to open a hat shop someday in the North End, I have no doubt you will achieve it."

"Caprice, I wouldn't have suggested opening your own shop someday if I didn't think it was an actual possibility," added Mrs. Storrow, leaning over and patting my hand. "You must know enough about me by now to know that I'm not one to ever give people false hopes."

"Well, thank you both for listening," I said, realizing that since I had arrived at Hull House tonight, the queasiness in my stomach had disappeared.

"Now there's the issue of what you're going to do for work," said Miss Guerrier. And then, giving me a sly smile she added, "At least in the short term, I know of a certain pottery shop that needs a new sales clerk."

"Yes, of course," said Mrs. Storrow, clapping her hands together. "Oh, good thinking, Edith. That works out perfectly. You can start work Monday; that way you won't even miss a week's pay. But Miss Guerrier is right; it would only be for the short term, for the next few months or so. The pottery shop is still not making the money I had hoped it would, and this spring I'm going to have to eliminate a couple of positions, including sales clerk."

"I understand completely," I said. "Short term is enough time to help me figure out what I'm going to do in the long term. I can't tell you how relieved that would make me if I could take it—as you said, even if it's just for now."

"Of course you can," said Miss Guerrier. "You can meet me here early Monday morning, and I'll show you what you need to know."

"Oh, thank you! Thank you both so much." I jumped up and hugged them. "This is the best news I've had all day."

"Thank you, Caprice—I'm just as relieved I won't have to take Concetta's place," said Miss Guerrier.

I searched the back of the room, looking for my friends. Thea, Maria, and Ada were standing in the corner talking with a few other people, but all three of them had their eyes on me. I gave them my widest smile and nodded. Maria and Ada started to clap, and Thea ran over and embraced me. It was a most unexpected and happy ending to my day.

CHAPTER 3

*Don't be sweet, lest you be eaten up; don't
be bitter, lest you be spewed out.*
—Jewish proverb

Sunday, September 27, 1908

"*Benedicat vos omnipotens Deus, Pater et Filius
et Spiritus Sanctus.*"
    "*Amen.*"
"*Ite, missa est.*"
"*Deo gratias.*"
The entire congregation made the sign of the
cross as Father Catalano uttered the last words of
Sunday Mass at St. Leonard's Church. I turned
to file out of the pew with my family, relieved
to not have to sit on the uncomfortable wooden
bench any longer. My mother and father went
first, followed by Frankie, then me, then Fabbia
and Vita. Every week we sat in the same pew,
five rows back on the right. Every week my
aunt Cecilia, uncle Arthur, and cousin Dominic
sat behind us in the sixth row. If Dominic's
brothers and their wives were in town from New
Hampshire, then they sat behind us too. There
were not supposed to be assigned seats at Mass,

and yet there were. The name *Russo* should have been etched on the back of our pews.

I spotted Maria walking out not too far in front of me, holding her sister Antonetta's hand. Maria's mother and brother were walking with them. The Santuccis sat on the left side of the church in the last row. But I couldn't recall the last time Maria's father had been at church.

The September sun blinded me when I first stepped outside, and I took a deep breath of air that smelled clean and delicious after the stuffy, incense-infused interior of St. Leonard's.

"I'll go pick up the chicken at that new butcher shop on Salem Street. Maria will walk with me," I said to my parents.

"Okay, Caprice, but don't be too long," my father said, putting his hat on and buttoning his coat around the wide expanse of his stomach. "Arthur and Cecilia are coming over with Dominic in a little while."

"Yes, we need to cook that chicken shortly," my mother added.

"Of course, I'll be home soon," I said, rolling my eyes as I walked away. At times they still talked to me as if I were a child. I started looking for Maria again. I glanced over at my sisters, Fabbia and Vita. Though two years apart at fourteen and twelve, respectively, with their dark-brown braids and matching sailor dresses, they could have been mistaken for twins. Fabbia was small for her age, so Vita was nearly the same height. They were too busy talking with their friends to notice me, which was a relief. I just wanted a little time with my friend before spending the whole day with family.

I saw Maria and walked over to her. She gave me a nod and whispered in Antonetta's ear. Antonetta skipped by me to join Vita and Fabbia.

"Butcher shop?" asked Maria with a smile.

"Yes, the new one at Salem and Stillman," I said. "Do you want to . . . ?"

"Do you even have to ask?" she said, laughing. "Anything to stay outside a little longer; it's a gorgeous day. Richie has already taken my mother home."

Hanover Street bustled with families dressed in their Sunday best, picking up bread or a bit of meat for dinner. People stopped in the middle of the street to talk and laugh with one another, grateful to have this one day of rest after the drudgery of the week's work. The enticing smells of onions cooking, of gravies and fresh-baked bread, wafted through the neighborhood, a hint of the meals that would begin in a few hours.

We walked by a street performer who was sitting playing a fiddle. He was a grubby older man with deep wrinkles in his cheeks and curly, matted gray hair under a well-worn, dusty brown hat. A small, scruffy black-and-white dog was lying next to him. The performer had written a song just for Maria called "Maria *Tesoro*"— "Maria Sweetheart." He started singing it when we passed by, just as he did every time he saw her. Maria gave him a coy smile, linked arms with me, and practically started skipping down the street, laughing.

We passed by a group of young men I recognized as being a couple of years younger than us, and they all stopped talking and stared. Only one of them was polite enough to tip his hat and say hello. Another whistled under his breath, and I heard a third whisper something about "that Santucci girl." Maria pretended not to notice.

Men had been watching Maria since we turned thirteen years old. Her beauty was unrivaled in the North End. With her tumbling blonde curls, enormous pale-blue eyes, and regal cheekbones, she would stand out anywhere, but in a neighborhood where most people were dark-haired Russian Jews and olive-skinned Italians, she stood out even more.

And even though Maria often pretended not to notice all the male attention she received, we knew she was well aware of it. It was obvious to Ada, Thea, and me that Maria basked in the adoration.

"Did you tell your parents about working at the pottery shop?" Maria asked as we rounded the corner onto Salem Street.

"Not yet," I answered. "My father will no doubt

think I was fired because I'm Italian. My mother will probably just shrug her shoulders and be happy I'm still making money. I was going to tell them at dinner, but now I'm thinking I might wait until tomorrow morning before I leave for work. Why should I bring the whole family into the conversation tonight?"

"Oh, I agree," Maria said, nodding. "And if you tell them tomorrow morning, there'll be less time for your father to start an argument about it—because you can't be late for work, right?"

"Exactly," I said with a smile. She knew my father well. I opened my mouth to ask how her father had behaved last night but thought better of it. "How are things at the dress shop? You haven't said much about Miss Weld lately."

"I must say, Miss Weld may *finally* be starting to trust me. It only took her four years," Maria answered, her voice tinged with sarcasm.

"Really? But honestly, it's about time, Maria. It's not like you haven't been a good seamstress for her."

"Agreed," Maria said with a nod. "I think she's realized that I'm the best dressmaker she's got by far, maybe even better than her. In just the past couple of months, she's stopped constantly looking over my shoulder and nagging me about finishing work or timeliness or anything else that she can think of. A couple of new girls just started; she's trying to train them, but they can barely thread a needle. It's pathetic, really.

"I make beautiful, well-fitted dresses for all of her rich customers. And I do it on time and without wasting a bit of material." Maria shrugged. "The truth is, she'd be lost without me."

"Of course she would," I answered. "I'm glad she's finally started treating you like she knows that."

"Maria! Maria Santucci!" We heard a voice yelling behind us and stopped walking.

We turned to see a short bald man walking toward us. He was dressed in a navy-blue three-piece suit and wearing a charcoal-gray hat. As he got closer, I noticed his squinty dark eyes and flushed complexion. I guessed he was around thirty years old. I knew him from around the neighborhood but couldn't remember who he was until Maria said his name.

"Oh, Mr. Toscanini, uh . . . hello," Maria said, her voice nervous as she glanced sideways at me. "This is my friend Caprice Russo."

He gave me a slight tip of his hat and looked back at Maria. "I need to speak to you," he said. "It's about your father's, er . . . situation. I spoke to my father about it, and . . . well, let's just say I think I can take care of it."

"Oh?" Maria said in a soft voice. And I realized she had turned very pale since this man had started talking.

"Yes, just this one time," he said. "We can make special arrangements."

"Well, I don't know how I . . . I can certainly—"

Mr. Toscanini interrupted Maria before she finished speaking. "I will stop by that pottery shop to see you this week," he said nonchalantly. "We can discuss it more then."

"Okay." Maria nodded. "We can discuss it then. Thank you, Mr. Toscanini."

"Maria, I told you, please call me Mark," he said, giving her a smile that made me want to drag Maria away from him as quickly as possible. "Nice to meet you, Clarice."

"It's Caprice," Maria and I said at the same time.

"Right," he said, tipping his hat and walking away.

"What was that about, Maria?" I asked. "Is your father okay?"

"Well of course he's not okay—he's a drunk. But if that weren't bad enough, now I've discovered he's gotten himself in trouble with some gambling debts too," she answered, still pale and fidgeting with her dress.

"Oh, Maria, no! I'm so sorry," I answered. "But I'm sure you've heard what I've heard about the Toscaninis. My father always says that one day Mark Toscanini Senior barely had a nickel in his pocket, and the next day he was the owner of that enormous chocolate factory. He believes the factory is mostly just a front for illegal activities . . . like gambling, apparently? Otherwise, how would your father owe *them?*"

Maria sighed. "Yes, it seems the family is somehow involved with some local gambling, Caprice. I don't really know the details. I just know my father owes them money."

"Well, it sounds like they might forgive the debt somehow then. Or . . . ?" I wasn't even sure what more to ask her.

"I don't know," Maria said. "I'm sure Mr.—I'm sure Mark will tell me more when we talk next. I don't know what 'special arrangements' he's talking about. But please don't tell anyone about this, okay? Not your parents, not even Thea and Ada. It's mortifying enough already, and I'm sure people in our building are already gossiping."

"Of course, I promise," I said softly, worried for my friend. I leaned into her and squeezed her arm.

We were quiet as we approached the new little butcher shop on the corner of Salem and Stillman Streets. The outside had been freshly painted white, and the windows revealed a meticulously clean interior. There was a small spotless case displaying carefully arranged fresh meats of all cuts and prices. A few chickens were hanging above it.

"I'll be right out," I said to Maria. I felt a pang of awkward embarrassment. My family was fortunate enough to be able to afford meat for Sunday dinner a couple of times a month. I was certain Christmas was the only day of the entire year that Maria's family had a chicken or a roast. For the hundredth time I wished I had enough money to buy something for her family, though her pride would have never allowed it.

I walked in, and a tiny bell rang at the top of the door. I inspected the meats in the case and the blackboard on the wall listing the day's specials.

"I'll be out in just a minute! Just cleaning up in here," a deep voice called from the back room.

"Okay!" I yelled back.

A few seconds later, a young man emerged. He had black hair cut very short, light-brown eyes, and rosy-apple cheeks on dark-olive skin. He looked vaguely familiar. I guessed that he was probably in his late twenties. I couldn't decide if I thought he was handsome or not.

"Um . . . hello. What can I do for you, miss?" he asked, his eyes sparkling with mild amusement. My stomach did a little flip.

"Oh, hello. My mother ordered a chicken earlier this week," I answered, feeling my face grow warm. I took off my turban-style hat and started smoothing out my hair. "She sent me to pick it up. She likes your new shop because it's so clean—and you gave her a good price on ground meat last week."

"Well, I give all of my many customers good

prices," he said, a touch of arrogance in his voice. "Who is your mother?"

"Rosina Russo," I answered. "I'm Caprice."

"Ah, yes, how could I forget a name as musical as Rosina Russo?" he said. "It's nice to meet you, Caprice. I'm Salvatore Valenti. This is my first butcher shop, but I plan to open many more," he said, spreading his giant arms out wide as if he planned to own the world.

"Well, uh . . . congratulations and nice to meet you," I answered, raising my eyebrows because I wasn't sure what else to say. This guy was what my friends and I liked to call a *barrone cacozza*, Italian for squash baron. Someone who thought he was on the make.

"I will wrap your chicken, Caprice-with-the-pretty-red-hair," he said with a wink, and now I decided that he was definitely a *barrone cacozza* because he brought up my hair color, the thing I was most self-conscious about in the world. I immediately shoved my hat back on my head.

"Um . . . thank you," I stammered, ignoring his comment as I tried to get the words out quickly. "And I also need to order a roast that I'll pick up after Mass next Sunday."

"No problem, I would be happy to do that for you," he answered. He bowed his head and gave me another smile followed by a wink.

He got one of the chickens from above the case, and as he was putting it on the scale, he asked,

"How is your cousin, Vincent? I went to school with him; I haven't seen him in a while."

"He's doing well, living in New Hampshire," I answered, referring to Dominic's older brother. That meant this squash baron was around twenty-six years old. "His wife is having a baby this spring."

"Ah, wonderful," he said as he wrapped up the chicken in white paper. "Please send him my regards."

"I will." I paid him for the chicken. Our fingers brushed as I took the package from him, and I quickly pulled my hand back as if I had touched a burning stove. This young man with his grand dreams and little butcher shop was annoying me for some reason.

"Thank you," I said with a nod. "I'll pick up the roast after nine-thirty Mass next Sunday."

"It was very nice meeting you, Miss Russo," he said. "I hope I'll see you again soon. Tell your friend outside that she's welcome to come in next time and have a cup of coffee. *Arrivederci.*" He had that same bemused look on his face, like he knew what I was thinking.

I felt my cheeks grow red. I nervously smoothed out my skirt and held the chicken in front of my chest.

"Thank you, Mr. Valenti." I nodded at him. "I'll see you next Sunday."

The bell tinkled, and the door slammed shut

behind me. Maria started laughing, her cheeks returning to their usual rosy-pink hue.

"Caprice," she said. "You're holding that package of chicken like a shield. And you look flushed. Was it very hot in there?"

"No, it was fine," I answered as I started to walk. "Just fine."

"That new butcher is Salvatore Valenti, right?" Maria asked. "He's a few years older than us— your cousin Vincent's class, I think."

"Yes, that was him," I said. "He's a bit of a *barrone cacozza*."

"I don't know about that, but he does have *another* reputation," said Maria. "He's quite the Lothario. He's left a trail of broken hearts through the North End."

"Really?" I said. I pictured young women all over the neighborhood crying into their handkerchiefs.

"Really," Maria said with authority. "He's twenty-six, and it seems he's committed to being a lifelong bachelor. Still, he is handsome, don't you think?" Maria prodded, hooking arms with me again.

"Oh, I don't know . . ."

"Caprice, please, I know you thought he was. I could tell by the color of your face when you walked out of the shop."

"Well, okay, maybe I thought he was a little bit handsome." I felt my cheeks start glowing again.

"His family is from Avellino," said Maria. "They live on the other side of Hanover Street. He has a couple of brothers older than him. His latest broken heart was a girl named Louisa Covello. She's still devastated over him apparently. Her father would like to string him up."

I looked at Maria in surprise. "How the heck do *you* know all of these things about him?"

She shrugged her shoulders and tucked a tendril of hair behind her ear. "Remember, Mrs. Orzo lives on my floor—she's the biggest gossip in the North End. She tells me everything."

"Ah, yes, I forgot," I said, and changing the subject, I added, "Well, my father believes I may be meeting my future husband, Enrico the shoemaker's son, late this afternoon."

"Oh, yes," said Maria. "About that Enrico . . ."

"Now what about Enrico?" I stopped walking and unhooked arms with Maria, balancing the chicken on my hip. We were just a couple of doors down from our building. "What do you know about him that I don't? Something else Mrs. Orzo told you?"

"Caprice, has your father actually ever *met* Enrico, or does he just know Enrico's father?" Maria asked, frowning.

"Um . . . no, I don't believe he's met him personally yet," I answered, wondering what in the world she was talking about.

"You'll see for yourself, but I don't think it's

going to be the match your father was hoping for," said Maria with a sly grin.

"Wait, what do you—oh, never mind." I wanted to ask more questions but decided it wasn't worth it. Maria was enjoying this too much. And I had my family's Sunday dinner tucked under my arm. We headed into our building, and I hurried up the stairs to help my mother prepare the meal.

I loved my mother's chicken dinner on Sundays. She cooked it with lots of garlic and onions, and the tender meat and crusty skin just melted in your mouth. And it made our home smell like delicious, garlicky chicken for the rest of the evening.

As we finished up the meal, I was dreading the arrival of Enrico. My family was crowded around our kitchen table—my parents, Fabbia, Vita, Frankie, Aunt Cecilia, Uncle Arthur, and Dominic. Our home was a four-room, cold-water flat. On Sundays, we moved the kitchen table to the sitting room, which also served as my brother's bedroom. My parents' room and the room that I shared with Fabbia and Vita were both off of the sitting room.

My aunt Cecilia and my mother took turns hosting Sunday dinner every week. Since my mother was cooking this week, Aunt and Uncle brought the extra chairs and dessert.

"Oh, Frankie, Dominic," I said to them,

interrupting their conversation about the Red Sox. "I've been meaning to ask you. Ada was hoping you two might be able to take turns walking her from the streetcar after her Simmons classes on Tuesday and Thursday nights."

"Why can't one of the guys from her building do it?" Frankie said with a sneer, running his fingers through his hair.

With his thick, shiny black hair and clear tan skin, my brother was that terrible combination of handsome and obnoxious. Just eighteen months older than me, we were close in age but definitely not close as siblings.

"Frankie, her father doesn't even know that she's taking college classes," I said, already annoyed at him. "If someone in her building walked her, within a week every one of her neighbors would know."

"Caprice, I'll do it," said Dominic. "Ada Levy is so tiny she looks like a ten-year-old. She should not be walking anywhere alone at night."

"Oh, Dominic, thank you," I said. "She'll be so relieved. So will her mother."

"It's no problem," Dominic said with a shrug. "It's not a long walk, and I sometimes head down to the Sicilian Club at night to play cards anyway."

My cousin Dominic and I were just two months apart in age. Like Frankie, he was also quite handsome in his own way—very tall, with

47

curly blackish-brown hair, and a strong Roman nose. But unlike my brother, Dominic was not a *gavone*.

Dominic and Frankie got back into their heated discussion about the Red Sox, and Fabbia and Vita started to clear the table so they could go play checkers. As usual, when my uncle and my father were at the same table, the conversation turned to the small tailor shop that they owned together. I got up and helped my mother and aunt clean up.

"Oh, Caprice, do you have your pay envelope?" my mother asked me as we were bringing dishes into the kitchen.

"Yes, let me go get it." I went into my room and took the pay out of my coat. I stared at the thin white envelope in my hands and realized it was the last one I would ever receive from Madame DuPont's.

"Here's my board for the week, Mama," I heard Frankie say as I walked out of my room. I clenched my jaw to keep myself from saying something I would later regret.

I quietly handed my envelope to my mother, and she put Frankie's board money in it and stuffed it into her brassiere.

It made me crazy. I had to hand over my *entire* pay for the week while Frankie gave them *half* of his. Because I was a daughter and not a son, I was a servant to my family. No money of my own. No chance for any sort of independence. I needed this to change. Soon.

"Caprice, Enrico should be here soon for dessert," my mother whispered to me as she made coffee. Warmth crept up my cheeks as my frustration built, and I clenched my teeth so hard I felt my jaw might crack.

She gave me a sympathetic look and said, "Now, please, for your father's sake, just try to be sweet."

As if on cue there was a knock at the door, which was only partially open. I heard a rather high-pitched man's voice say, "Hello?"

Frankie opened the door, shook Enrico's hand, and offered to take his coat. Enrico was wearing a pristine white shirt and black pants. The first thing I noticed was that he was extremely skinny. He looked like Jack Sprat. My skirt would fall off of him, his waist was so small.

My father got up and walked over and introduced himself, and I was furious that he would try to set me up with a young man that none of us had even met before. Again I swallowed my aggravation and attempted to smile politely as I brushed the crumbs off my skirt and smoothed my hair.

"This is my daughter Caprice," my father said, bringing Enrico over to meet me.

"Hello, Caprice, it's nice to meet you," Enrico said.

"Hello, nice to meet you," I said, shaking his very slim hand. "Let me introduce you to the rest of my family."

Fabbia and Vita giggled shyly as they were introduced and then retreated to our bedroom to continue their checker game. My aunt and uncle were their usual warm and welcoming selves. Dominic shook Enrico's hand politely, then raised his eyebrows at me when Enrico turned away from him.

We all sat down again at the table for dessert. There was a bit of an awkward silence as we passed around the biscotti that Enrico had brought from his mother.

"Enrico, don't you sing in the choir at Sacred Heart?" Aunt Cecilia asked, politely breaking the silence. God love her.

"Yes!" Enrico said, smiling and clapping his hands together and waving them about as he spoke. "I *do*. I absolutely love singing in the choir. I'm a soprano; I sing several solos. Father Tassone thinks I could be a professional singer—" He stopped himself, paused, and looked at me before he added, "But I will probably take over my papa's business."

Aunt Cecilia nodded her head at him and gave him a close-lipped smile. Uncle Arthur, never one to hide his emotions, looked like he was going to burst out laughing, and I said a silent prayer to the Virgin Mary that he wouldn't. My mother got up to put on more coffee. I looked over at my father, and he was sitting very stiffly in his chair, avoiding my gaze by studying a nonexistent bug on the floor.

I glanced across the table at Dominic and Frankie, but they were looking at Enrico as if they were incredibly interested in his potential singing career. I didn't know whether to hug them or kill them.

"What are some of your favorite hymns?" asked Frankie, his hand under his chin. Ugh. So obnoxious. I tried to kick him under the table.

"Well, 'Ave Maria,' of course, and 'Corde Natus Ex Parentis,' but I also love . . ." And I stopped listening as Enrico started rambling about his favorite hymns and his various musical abilities.

Enrico was what my brother Frankie called— well, what all Italians called—a *finocchio*. He was not interested in me as a potential wife. He would never be interested in *any* girls. Ever.

I took a bite of chocolate almond biscotti and a big gulp of red wine and gave Enrico a grimace as he continued to talk about life in the choir. He winked at me and gave me a quick, sympathetic glance in return, and I realized that he understood my pain. And it suddenly occurred to me that it was not only the young women my age who thought arranged marriages were antiquated. Many young men felt the exact same way.

I decided to join Enrico's conversation with my brother and cousin. I turned to him, gave him a genuine, grateful smile, and asked him about his family. I took comfort in the fact that the two of us were in this predicament together: going along with our parents' old-fashioned matchmaking attempts but knowing in our hearts that nothing would ever come of it.

So for tonight I was relieved, but no doubt my father would have some other young man knocking at our door next Sunday, or the Sunday after that. I took another sip of wine and clenched my jaw at the thought of facing more suitors of *his* choosing, not mine. It was going to be a very long winter.

CHAPTER 4

*Don't open a shop unless you know
how to smile.*
—Jewish proverb

Monday, September 28, 1908

"It's because you're Italian. That's why she let you go, isn't it?" My father asked me this for the third time in as many minutes, leaning forward and drumming his fingers on the kitchen table.

I had just told my parents that I was no longer working for Madame and that I would begin working at the pottery shop that very morning. Not surprisingly, they were suspicious at this turn of events.

"She didn't want an Italian girl working in her fancy shop any longer?" he asked again, taking a sip of his coffee. My mother was standing behind him, leaning on the stove, her arms crossed, watching me with eyebrows raised. It was just the three of us. Fabbia and Vita were already at school, and Frankie had just left to go to the men's bathhouse before work.

"Papa, you aren't listening," I answered, barely able to contain my exasperation. "She did *not* let me go because I'm Italian. She is closing the shop. All of us—the *Irish* gals too—are without jobs because she is moving to New York City. I've told you many times I was very good at my job, Papa. Better than any of the other women in the shop. She never would have fired me for any other reason. But there is no shop anymore. *That's* why I'm going to work at the pottery shop today."

"Yes, this pottery—the Saturday girls club pottery shop—I don't understand," my mother said, clearing the breakfast dishes but still watching me. "How did this job come about so quickly? What will you do there? You can't make hats at a pottery shop. And you don't know how to make pottery."

I had to stifle a groan of frustration. Sometimes I thought my parents believed I didn't even have a brain in my head.

"Concetta—you know, Concetta Leone from Stillman Street?" I said this to them very slowly, even though we were speaking Italian. "She was working in the pottery shop—just taking orders and managing the shop, doing basic chores, not *making* pottery. I found out Saturday that she was leaving because she's going to nursing school. When I told Miss Guerrier and Mrs. Storrow about what happened with Madame's shop, they immediately offered me Concetta's job."

"Well, how much are they going to pay you to

work there?" My father asked. My mother paused in her cleaning and looked at me expectantly.

"Ten dollars a week," I answered, smiling at both of them. It was only a dollar less than I had been making at Madame DuPont's. "I hope to get a job making hats again at some point very soon." *Working for myself,* I silently added. "But it's okay for now, no? I won't miss one week of pay, and it's right here in the North End. I'll be able to help you with the shopping more now."

They looked at each other. My mother gave my father a little shrug signaling she was okay with it, grabbed the broom hidden next to the stove, and started sweeping. My father rubbed his hand over his face, squished up his fuzzy black eyebrows, and said, "Okay, okay. I guess working at this pottery shop is all right then. It's work. It's in our neighborhood. It's decent enough pay. And you don't even have to worry about working in one of those fancy hat shops again, dealing with those uppity Protestants. You can do this work until we find you a nice Sicilian young man, yes?"

I was about to tell him I didn't need him to find me *any* young man. I was about to tell them that I was an adult now and the fact that I needed their approval was ridiculous, when my mother started hollering curses in Italian and beating the broom on the ground.

JRVLS
105 3 ST SE
JAMESTOWN ND 58401

"*Faccia da stronzo*! *Faccia da stronzo*!"

The recipient of her curses was a large cockroach that had met its untimely death on the floor of our kitchen.

"It's okay, Rosina. My sweet—it's okay." My father got up and put his arms around her because he knew the bugs in the tenement made her crazy. This amused him to no end. He accepted the fact that there were bugs in the building's walls and crevices. I didn't think my mother would ever accept it. Looking at the black cockroach smashed and oozing on the floor, I had to side with my mother.

"I'm late. I've got to hurry down to the shop. I'll be back for lunch." My father kissed my mother on the cheek and gave me a quick kiss on the head before hurrying out the door.

"Thank you," I said to my mother, because I knew her opinion mattered more to my father than anyone else's. I got up from the table and put on my hat and coat. "Do you need me to pick up anything on the way home?"

"No, Caprice dear, I've got some *fusilli* for dinner tonight, and I'll pick up some vegetables at the market after I get some stitching done for the shop," she said in Italian, kissing me on the cheek as she continued to sweep under the kitchen table. Dust, dirt, and bugs were no match for Rosina Russo.

I grabbed the satchel that contained my lunch

of black bread and hard cheese, kissed my mother, and headed out to my first day of work at the pottery shop.

I laughed at how quickly I got to Hull House. I opened the front door of the shop with my new key, and the bells inside gave me a little welcome jingle. The basement shop was cool and quiet. I could smell freshly dried paint and the sharp, burnt smell of recently fired pottery.

I took off my coat and hat and stored them in the corner behind the front counter. Smoothing out my black everyday skirt and straightening my shirtwaist, I glanced around and enjoyed this peaceful moment.

There were new dishes, fruit and nut bowls, tea trivets, mugs, and marmalade jars lined up on the shelves along the walls. They were all painted in soft glazes, muted shades of blues and yellows and greens. I ran my hand over the shiny, smooth surface of an ochre-colored cereal bowl.

"So what do you think?" I startled upon hearing Miss Guerrier speak softly from the doorway in the back of the store. She was standing holding strong-smelling coffee in two cream-colored mugs.

"Oh, Miss Guerrier. Good morning," I greeted her as she handed me one of the mugs. I took a long sip. "I think they're wonderful. I am so impressed."

"Yes, me too," she said. She nodded as she surveyed the room, her sparkly deep-blue eyes shining with pride. "Our little business venture has exceeded my expectations. Welcome to your first day here. I'm so sorry Madame closed her shop, Caprice, but I'm thrilled that you're able to help us here—and that we can help you."

"So am I," I answered. "You have no idea how relieved I felt going home on Saturday night."

"I'm sure," said Miss Guerrier with a nod before adding, "Let me give you a quick tour so you have a better understanding of the shop. And then we can go over inventory and start displaying some of the latest wares. How does that sound?"

"Perfect," I answered, but she was already walking back toward the kiln room. After a brief tutorial on how pottery was molded, dried, and fired, she took me upstairs to the workroom, where the pottery decorators sat.

Sun streamed through the enormous windows of the room, and there were fresh-cut red and orange marigolds on each table, their fragrance permeating the air. Fresh-cut flowers—*such* an indulgence. But apparently this was something Mrs. Storrow had insisted upon.

Miss Guerrier and I sat at two work stools on the sunny side of the room as she explained a bit about how they determined the colors and design for each piece, pointing to different pieces in progress as examples. She took a sip of coffee and concluded, "So, Caprice, that's how the pottery shop works!" She put her mug down on the windowsill and smoothed out her gray dress. "We should probably get to that inventory before the decorators start arriving for work, but do you have any questions?"

I shook my head. "No, honestly, I'm sure I will have questions, but at this point I don't. Thank you."

"Of course," she said, a mischievous look in her eyes when she added, "Now . . . do you mind if I ask you something?"

"Um . . . no, what is it?" I answered, a little nervous now, because Miss Guerrier was someone who had no problem asking hard questions.

"Have you thought about when you're going to ask your parents about paying board?" she asked.

"I have thought about it, Miss Guerrier, but it's just finding the right time—and trying to make them understand," I answered. I looked out the huge picture window and thought about my mother, who still wore her clothes from the old country and could barely speak English after all these years in America.

"My mother was married at sixteen, had a baby at eighteen, and was an old woman by the time she was thirty years old," I added with a sigh.

"I'm just not sure if she could ever understand why I want a very different kind of life."

"She might surprise you," said Miss Guerrier. "She is a woman—she influences your household, your father. Talk to her, Caprice; see if you can make her an ally. If you have her on your side, I bet it will be much easier to convince your father."

"Yes," I replied, nodding. "Perhaps I will talk to her first—very soon."

"Not that we aren't overjoyed to have you working here—but I know there are bigger things in your future, Caprice."

"Thank you, Miss Guerrier. Again."

We headed downstairs, and as I was about to start asking her a question about inventory, we were both startled by the sight of a stocky little man standing at the front counter, looking at us. It took me a second before I realized this man with the beady eyes and piggish nose was Mark Toscanini.

"Oh—I hadn't realized we left the front door open," said Miss Guerrier. "Can we help you?"

"Oh, hello," he said, nodding at me in recognition. He looked at Miss Guerrier. "Yes, can you tell me when Maria Santucci is working this week?" he asked. He took off his black hat, revealing his bald head. "I know she volunteers a couple of hours a week here."

"I don't have the schedule in front of me, so

I'm not sure," Miss Guerrier said. She walked over to the counter to stand face-to-face with him. "But if you give me your name, I can tell her you stopped by."

"Well, why don't you just go get the schedule and check for me?" he replied, waving his hand at her. Clearly Mark Toscanini was someone who was used to giving orders.

At this point I walked over and stood next to Miss Guerrier in solidarity. I looked him up and down, not caring that he noticed me do this. He was wearing a dapper three-button cutaway frock coat—again dressed in a manner that was a bit too ostentatious for our neighborhood.

"I'm sorry, sir, but I can't do that for you right now," Miss Guerrier answered in a firm tone, looking right into his eyes, not intimidated in the slightest. I was quite sure she knew the work and volunteer schedule by heart. "You see, the shop is just about to open, and we still have so much to do," Miss Guerrier added. "Now, what did you say your name was?"

"I didn't. But it's Mark Toscanini," he replied, putting on his hat and looking at Miss Guerrier and then at me with annoyance in his eyes. I knew Maria needed to talk to him, but I had already decided that I didn't like him, and I definitely didn't like the way he was treating Miss Guerrier, so I wasn't going to make this easy for him.

"Tell Maria I stopped by to see when she would

be in next," he continued. "And tell her I would have stopped by at the appropriate time, but you ladies were too busy to let me know when she was going to be here. *Arrivederci.*" He turned on his heel and exited the pottery shop, slamming the door behind him.

"Well," said Miss Guerrier, staring at the slammed door with a frown. "I'm not sure he could have been more rude."

"Ugh, such a *gavone*," I said, and Miss Guerrier just laughed.

"Toscanini. Doesn't his father own that chocolate factory in Charlestown?" she asked me. "His father is around your father's age—do they know each other?"

"They know each other, Miss Guerrier, but the Toscaninis are . . . well, an interesting family. My father has never trusted them. As I told Maria the other day, my father thinks the factory is mostly just a front for illegal ventures."

"Why on earth would Maria associate with someone like that?" Miss Guerrier asked, a look of worry on her face.

"I have no idea," I answered. I hated lying to Miss Guerrier, but I had made a promise to Maria.

I considered saying more, but then the bells on the front door jingled and Gemma Ianelli and Sara Galner burst into the room, talking and giggling.

"Caprice!" Gemma exclaimed as she walked in, her black curls bouncing behind her. "I completely forgot you were starting today. Welcome—you're going to love working here. It's so much fun."

Sara, Gemma, and I had started chatting when the bells rang again and Lillie Shapiro and Albina Mangini nearly knocked us over as they came bounding through the door. Soon I was caught up arranging the stock on the shelves, wiping down newly finished wares, and going through the order books. My first day at the pottery shop had officially begun.

CHAPTER 5

*Everyone is kneaded out of the same dough but
not baked in the same oven.*
—Jewish proverb

Saturday, October 17, 1908

Dominic and I walked down the dimly lit street to
get Ada before heading over to where the rest of
the S.E.G. were waiting for the streetcar. People
were sitting on the stoops of their buildings,
enjoying the cool night air. Up above, I could see
the animated silhouettes of women leaning out
their windows, moving their arms as they talked
to each other in Italian or Yiddish.

Tonight the Saturday Evening Girl Players
would perform *The Merchant of Venice* at Mrs.
Isabella Stewart Gardner's home, Fenway Court.
My first three weeks at the pottery shop had
flown by; it was hard to believe it was already
the night of our performance.

"Thanks for walking us tonight, Dominic," I
said as we got closer to Ada's building. "It will
be good for Ada's mother to meet you. She'll feel
more comfortable about your escorting Ada on
Tuesdays and Thursdays."

"It's not a problem, Caprice," Dominic said. "But what time are you going to be back from this Fenway Court? I'm not sure I'll be able to meet you girls later tonight . . ."

"Oh, that's okay," I said. "Our performance is probably going to run rather late, but there'll be a big group of us walking home. We'll be fine."

Dominic and I walked through the building to go upstairs to the Levy family's home. On the first floor, a few women had brought chairs out in the hallway and were talking to each other in Yiddish. We nodded to them as we passed, and they smiled.

We went up the stairs at the end of the hall and knocked on Ada's partially open door, which was directly off the third-floor landing. Ada's mother opened the door wider and greeted us with a warm but guarded smile. She gave me a kiss on both cheeks.

Even though I had known Ada for over seven years, her home still smelled so *foreign* to me. Sauerkraut and herring and pickles—these scents had left a mark on the Levy family apartment over the years, creating a subtle, permanent perfume. Of course, Ada probably thought my family's home had its own odd, lingering odor of things like garlic, coffee, and lentils or some equally strange combination of the things we ate and drank.

Ada's father was sitting at the table with her two brothers, fifteen-year-old twins, Ari and Ben. Her father's nose was in a book, his black yarmulke and frizzy gray hair the only things visible to us. Ari and Ben were also wearing yarmulkes and holding books, although they were staring at each other with their large, identical sets of brown eyes, likely engaged in some silent competition to make the other laugh first.

"Hello, Caprice. Hi, Dominic." Ari and Ben both greeted us with warm smiles and waves before their father gave them a stern look and they pretended to go back to their books.

"Hello," said Ada with a huge dimpled smile as she walked out of her closet-sized bedroom carrying a large bag over her shoulder.

Ada's father grunted what sounded like a greeting before looking back down at his book. I thought I heard him click his tongue. Mrs. Levy hurried to fetch Ada's coat and hat and handed them to her. It was sundown, but after six years of going to S.E.G. meetings, Ada's father still wasn't happy about her leaving at the end of Jewish Sabbath.

"Not too late, Ada?" her mother said in her thick Russian accent as she walked us out onto the landing and quietly closed the door behind her.

"No, Mama, I don't think I'll be too late," said Ada, kissing her on the forehead. Ada's mother was even more petite than she was.

Mrs. Levy looked Dominic up and down with

her dark eyes. Dominic was over six feet tall, but he noticeably shrank at this tiny woman's inspection.

"Caprice, your mother knows I will be talking to her and—uh, was it Domino's?—mother shortly?" Mrs. Levy asked me in a soft whisper, her accent making it a little hard for me to understand.

"It's Dominic, ma'am," Dominic interjected, politely as ever. He took off his cap, revealing his curly dark hair, and stood with his hands behind his back. His shoulders were sloped over, trying to show her respect, but he still took up half the landing.

"Yes, Mrs. Levy, I've told my mother you'll be talking to her and my aunt Cecilia soon," I answered, giving her kisses on both cheeks once again.

"Good," Mrs. Levy said with a nod, although she was still eyeing Dominic with mild distrust. But she nodded and again said, "Good."

We said our good-byes, and the three of us hurried down the stairs into the cool night air.

"Ah, I've been waiting for this night all week," Ada said. She took a deep breath, held her arms wide, and skipped down the cobblestones, her glossy black braids swinging behind her. "I can't believe we're performing *The Merchant of Venice* at Isabella Gardner's mansion. I am so excited."

"Me too," I said. "Fenway Court is apparently stunning."

"Oh, and Dominic," Ada said, touching his elbow. "I can't thank you enough for offering to walk me home from the streetcar on the nights I have class. I know my mother didn't look it tonight, but she's very relieved."

"You're welcome," Dominic said, tipping his cap to her as he grabbed the large bag she was carrying. "I'm happy to do it. Anything to get out of the house at night, you know?"

"Yes, I heard my mother and Aunt Cecilia talking, and they said that they'll ease your mother's worries," I said to Ada, then paused because I had asked this next question more than once before. "But Ada, do you *truly* think you and your mother will be able to continue to keep this all a secret from your father?"

"Caprice, all he cares about is the twins," Ada said, tugging one of her braids. "Though trust me when I say they'll be lucky if they make it through the tenth grade. As long as I keep up with the bookkeeping at our shop, my father won't notice a thing about what I do."

Ada Levy was one of the smartest girls—one of the smartest *people*—I'd ever met. That was why Mrs. Storrow had found her a scholarship to Simmons College. It seemed like everyone in the North End knew how brilliant she was, how well she had done in high school, and how skilled she was at managing the books at her family's dry goods shop. The only one who didn't seem to notice Ada's intelligence was her father.

We could see the rest of the S.E.G. talking and laughing, waiting for the streetcar, as we approached the end of Hanover Street. The car was approaching in the distance.

"Oh, Ada—it's here. We'd better make a run for it," I said, but she had already grabbed her bag from Dominic, and she skipped out in front of me, yelling thank you and good-bye over her shoulder.

"Thank you, cousin," I called to Dominic, and waved as I started picking up speed. "Have fun at the Sicilian Club. I'll see you tomorrow."

"C'est mon plasir"

The inscription was etched above the entryway of the famed Fenway Court, home of Mrs. Isabella Stewart Gardner. "It means 'it is my pleasure' in French," Ada said to me, nodding upward. She not only spoke fluent English and Yiddish and a bit of Italian, but she had also managed to pick up some basic French.

" 'It is my pleasure.' Well, what does she mean by that?" asked Thea, interrupting my thoughts to talk about the inscription. She was walking behind Ada and me with Maria.

"Well, maybe she means it's her pleasure to show her art to the world," I whispered as we walked through the doorway. We started looking everywhere at once, trying to examine the beautiful artwork adorning the walls of the magnificent hallway.

I spotted Miss Guerrier up ahead, holding up her hands to stop the group and quiet us down. Some of the girls in front of us made ooh and aah sounds, so the four of us moved up to see what everyone was looking at.

When we got closer, I gasped at the sight of a palatial courtyard filled with orchids, azaleas, ivy, and tall palms. There were several statues that looked like they were out of Greek mythology and a large stone fountain framed by two sets of staircases going up to a small veranda. My mouth fell open as I looked up and saw that the courtyard was surrounded by four walls, four stories high, with the most exquisite stonework—breathtaking arches and columns. There were nymphs and gargoyles and decorative elements all the way up to the top floor. I had never seen anything like it.

"A little history of Fenway Court before we proceed to the music hall," said Miss Guerrier. There was an older man with graying brown hair, dressed in a black tuxedo standing behind her. I presumed he was the Gardner butler.

"Mrs. Jack Gardner had Fenway Court built so she could display her vast art collection and share it with the world. Her residence is on the fourth floor; the other three floors house her artwork.

Five years ago, she opened the three floors to the public as a museum. The palazzos of Venice, Italy, are what inspired her when she designed it, making it a most appropriate place for our play! Most of the architecture and decorative elements that you see are artifacts that she has collected from ancient Greece and Rome."

We then followed the man down the hallway and ascended a stone staircase. I found myself glancing over my shoulder, back at the magical courtyard.

"*One* person lives here?" whispered Thea, shaking her head in amazement. "This is bigger than our entire building."

I nodded at her in agreement.

We entered a cavernous room with dark wood paneling and enormous beams across the ceiling. The floor was brick-red tile, and there were about seventy-five wooden chairs assembled, facing a stage in front of an oversize stone fireplace with carvings of monkeys. Above the fireplace hung a picture of one of the saints—I wasn't sure which one—in studded armor, holding a spear over Satan.

The walls of the room were covered with enormous tapestries. Maria and I stood together and looked at a series of them entitled "Scenes from the Life of Cyrus the Great." They were silk and wool with brilliant woven illustrations in vibrant reds, golds, greens, and blues.

"It is incredible," said Maria, standing up close so she could examine the tiny details.

"Yes," I answered softly. I had never seen a place with so many beautiful things. "Are you nervous?" I asked her, glancing at the rows of chairs assembled. Maria played Portia, the lead role.

"Not at all," she said, taking her hat off and smoothing her curls. Even if Maria were terrified, she would never let anyone know it.

"Girls! Girls!" I heard a shrill voice from the back of the room and turned around to see a spry elderly woman rush in with Mrs. Storrow in tow. "Please, do not dare touch the tapestries," the woman said, looking around at all of us. "They are *priceless!*"

Maria and I stole a glance at each other and rolled our eyes. As if we would touch the tapestries.

"What does she take us for?" I whispered to Maria. She nodded.

"Ladies, this is Mrs. Jack Gardner," Mrs. Storrow said with a warm smile, placing her hand on the older woman's arm. Mrs. Gardner had lined ivory skin and clear eyes. She had a shapely figure that was highlighted by her simple black silk dress and an exquisite pearl necklace with a large ruby teardrop. Her white hair was pulled up in a tight bun.

"Welcome to Fenway Court," Mrs. Gardner

said, clasping her hands together and looking across the room at all of us. "Please feel free to call me Mrs. Jack. I am so pleased you are here to present *The Merchant of Venice*. Mrs. Storrow tells me that you are magnificent thespians. The guests should be arriving in about an hour, so please take this time to set up. Your costumes and props are in the Little Salon," she said, pointing to a doorway in the back of the room. "You may put your coats and hats in there as well."

We all smiled, murmured our thanks, and quickly started bustling toward the Little Salon to change and get ready.

The guests started arriving an hour later. From "backstage," Thea and I peeked out at all of the ladies of Boston society arriving, and we watched Mrs. Gardner flit across the room with the energy of someone twenty years younger. The women were all dressed beautifully as they kissed hello and appraised each other from head to toe.

"Look at them all, smoking cigarettes!" Thea said. "Can you believe it?" She was dressed as Launcelot Gobbo, with all of her hair tucked up under a hat and a fake moustache drawn on her round face. With her freckled cheeks and long-lashed green eyes, she still looked nothing like a man.

"Yes, and right next to the tapestries," I said in mock dismay. "I notice she's not yelling at *them*."

"Don't you love it? I could get used to that

life." Maria sighed. "Oh! Look at the dresses—how about that rose-colored one in shantung silk. Just *lovely*. I'll have to remember to tell Miss Weld about it. I know a customer who would adore that style. Ada, come over here—aren't you curious?"

Ada was sitting in the corner dressed in costume as Jessica, the daughter of Shylock, but her nose was buried in her biology textbook. She looked up, closed her book—with her thumb still marking the page—and said, "I'm sorry, but it's my very first college exam this week. I can't study at home because of my father, so I've got to take advantage of every spare moment I can."

"Ladies!" Miss Guerrier's loud whisper interrupted us. "Time to take your places for act one, scene one. The guests are starting to take their seats, and Mrs. Gardner will introduce the play in a few minutes."

The actors for the first scene took their places, and there was a nervous stillness in the air.

Mrs. Gardner stood in the middle of the makeshift stage and gave us a surprisingly grand introduction.

"I present to you the Saturday Evening Girls Players," she said, her voice projecting across the great room. "They are from the wonderful little pottery shop in the North End. Please consider doing some Christmas shopping at their store—they have some beautiful and unique hand-painted peasant ware."

"Peasant ware?" I said in a whisper to my friends. I'd never heard it called that before.

"Are we peasants?" Ada whispered back at me, an amused look on her face. "Is that what they think of us?"

"And now, Shakespeare's *The Merchant of Venice*," Mrs. Gardner said. She made a sweeping gesture with her hand and took a seat in the front row.

I took my place behind stage right, where I helped with props and costume adjustments. I was the stage manager, a role I much preferred to being center stage.

Unlike Maria. With a wink at me, she entered act one, scene two as Portia, one of Shakespeare's most beautiful and witty female characters. With her blonde curls pulled up in a chignon that accented her cheekbones and her blue eyes set off by a gorgeous—if cheap—teal-blue costume dress, Maria was stunning. It was as if she were born for the stage. I heard a couple of gasps from the audience as she entered. I felt for the petite, rather large-nosed Danielle Orazio, who was playing the part of Nerissa, Portia's lady-in-waiting. Thea, Ada, and I had all felt like Maria's lady-in-waiting at one point or another.

I was sorting through props for scene three

when Thea whispered, "Hey, who are those men over there?"

They were off to the side, standing, not sitting, dressed in stylish attire that said they belonged here. They looked young, around our age, but in the dark it was hard to tell.

"I have no idea," I answered. "Shhh—this is one of Ada's scenes. Let's watch."

"Do you know she has everyone's lines memorized?" whispered Thea. "She's so smart I think I might be scared of her if she weren't my friend."

Ada closed scene five of act two alone on stage, her huge black eyes staring out at the audience with sadness and irony.

"Farewell, and if my fortune not be crost;
I have a father, you a daughter, lost."

We received wild applause after acts one and two. Partway through act three, scene five, Ada was on stage as Jessica with Thea as Launcelot Gobbo.

In this scene, Launcelot was supposed to tease Jessica about being married to a Christian. Thea stepped into the light, and there were smears of black makeup on both sides of her mouth.

"Oh, no, Maria, look—Thea's mustache is melting down her face!" I said, trying to suppress a giggle.

"Oh, poor Thea, she's nervous enough. I hope she doesn't realize she has a melting mustache," Maria replied, and I stopped laughing because I realized she was right.

Thea danced around Ada—joking and teasing—as they had done a hundred times in rehearsal. But then, Thea said her last line in the scene:

"This making of Christians will all raise the price of hogs: if we grow all to be pork-eaters, we shall not shortly have a rasher on the coals for money."

Except, this time, on the word *rasher*, her shoe caught on Ada's dark-red costume dress, which was far too long for her. Maria and I and the rest of the girls backstage gasped as Thea tried to catch herself but couldn't get her balance and ended up hopping, skipping, and falling off the little stage, literally into the lap of a woman in the front row. The worst part was the woman was about the size of a sparrow, which made poor Thea look the size of an elephant. I felt Maria's fingernails dig into my arm as we watched, helpless to do anything.

The audience's reaction was mixed when it happened; some ladies giggled, others looked absolutely appalled. Thea jumped up as quickly as she could. I heard her stammer an apology to the woman. She then froze, seemingly paralyzed by her mortification, her face scarlet red and streaked with black moustache, which was now all over her chin. I thought she might start crying, when I heard Ada say,

"Oh, dear Lorenzo, you have returned!"

Ada made up this line to cue Lorenzo, played by Katy Abrams, to join her on stage to finish the scene. We all breathed a collective sigh of relief as the scene ended. I scanned the Little Salon to see where Thea had gone, but amid all the chaos of the changing scenes, I couldn't catch a glimpse of her anywhere.

Fortunately the play ended without any additional incidents, and Mrs. Gardner's friends gave us a warm standing ovation.

Backstage, Mrs. Gardner and Mrs. Storrow stood together as we all headed back into the Little Salon to change and get ready to go home.

"Girls, thank you for a beautiful and . . . colorful performance of *The Merchant of Venice*," said Mrs. Gardner. "Please accept these paper fans as a token of my appreciation. Let me also say that you are all so fortunate to have a benefactor like the wonderful Mrs. Storrow. It is such a great thing she is doing, keeping you all from the perils of your neighborhood streets."

We all gave Mrs. Storrow a tepid round of applause.

"Good God," I whispered to Ada. "We're helpless, uncultured peasant girls in her eyes." Ada just nodded and rolled her eyes at me.

Mrs. Gardner exited the Little Salon to join her guests. I was amazed when she didn't say a word to Miss Guerrier.

"Did you see the adorable Saturday Evening Girls bowls that all the society ladies received tonight?" Ada whispered to me.

"You mean the *peasant ware*?" I replied, nodding. "Of course; I helped pack them this week. I can't believe she didn't say a word to Miss Guerrier at the end. Don't you find that a bit rude?"

"Completely," Ada said, shaking her head. "It was like she didn't even exist. Has anyone seen Thea yet?"

We were interrupted when Mrs. Storrow, standing next to Miss Guerrier, called for our attention once more and said, "You girls were absolutely marvelous tonight." I noticed her cheeks were a bit flushed. "I was so proud of *every single one of you*. Miss Guerrier, you have created a first-class theater troupe here. Everyone is to be commended." We all applauded extra loud for our dear Miss Guerrier.

"Thank you, Mrs. Storrow," said Miss Guerrier, addressing all of us with a smile and clasping her hands together as if she were going to give us another round of applause. If Mrs. Gardner's snub had bothered her, she didn't show it. "You ladies were letter-perfect," Miss Guerrier added, before gesturing to our clutter in the Little Salon. "Now let's get ready to go. Your families will be wondering where you are!"

Ada was changing out of her costume and I was packing up props when Maria came over.

"Have any of you seen Thea?" she asked, still in costume and obviously basking in the afterglow of the tremendous round of applause she received. "I wanted to talk to her after she fell into that woman's lap. It was the highlight of the evening."

"Now, Maria, go easy on our Thea," I said, giving Maria a stern look. "I don't think she's up for joking about it."

"I agree," added Ada. "Please don't tease her. Something's going on with her. She seems distracted, like she's got other things on her mind. Maybe it's the new job with that interior decorator."

"You think she seems distracted?" I said. "I don't think it's the new job. She told me on the way over here that it was going really well. She said she might even have a knack for it."

"Oh, no, I promise. I wasn't going to tease her at all," said Maria. "Her fall was terrific. It lightened up the audience a bit. They thought it was part of the show."

"Thought what was part of the show?" asked a

husky male voice behind me. We all turned and saw the two young men who had been standing at the side of the audience. They walked over to our group.

I looked over at Ada, one eyebrow raised, and I almost laughed out loud because she was looking back at me in the exact same way. *What in the world are these two doing backstage?* The young men didn't even notice our expressions because they were gawking at Maria, still radiant in her teal-blue costume dress.

The first thing I noticed was their shoes. They were both wearing fine-looking dark-brown leather shoes. One of the men was a little over six feet tall with sandy-brown hair and light eyes. He had a distinct cleft in his chin. The other one was a couple of inches shorter, with blond hair and freckles; he looked more boyish than the taller one.

"Please, we had to come introduce ourselves to the brilliant Portia," said the shorter one. "I am Henry Osborne, Mrs. Storrow's nephew, and this is one of her 'honorary nephews,' Calvin Spaulding."

"When I was an undergraduate at Harvard, I was in *The Merchant of Venice* myself. I played Bassanio," said Calvin, still not able to take his eyes off Maria. "However, you ladies are far better Shakespearean actors than the troupe I was involved with at Harvard. Portia, you were magnificent. May I ask your real name?"

"Thank you. My name is Maria," she said, giving them a demure smile. "And these are my friends, Ada and Caprice." She gestured to us. We all nodded our hellos, and there was a pregnant pause.

"Calvin and I are in our third year at Harvard Law School," Henry explained. "We're staying at Mrs. Storrow's home this evening and going out to her estate in Lincoln for a party tomorrow."

During this exchange, Calvin stared at Maria, but she completely ignored his attention, listening to Henry talk about the beauty of Mrs. Storrow's country estate.

"Oh, ladies, I see you've met my nephews." Mrs. Storrow came in from the room behind the Little Salon, arm in arm with Thea. Thea's face was tear stained, but she looked happier than she had when she'd exited the stage.

"Aunt Helen!" said Henry, walking over to kiss her on the cheek. Calvin followed suit. "We were just congratulating the players on a job well done."

"Yes, they were wonderful, weren't they?" she said, looking pointedly at the young men. "Gentlemen, my car is waiting downstairs. Will you grab my coat and hat for me, and I'll meet you outside the courtyard in a minute?" she asked. The two of them nodded at her, said their good-byes to us, and exited. Love-struck Calvin looked back at Maria one more time before leaving the salon.

Mrs. Storrow gave Thea a hug and said to us, "I've got to go say my good-byes to everyone. But, Caprice, could you come out in a minute so I can introduce you to a couple of women? They want to meet the gifted trimmer formerly of Madame DuPont's shop."

"They want to meet *me?*" I asked, surprised that any of the women I saw out there would remember the former trimmer at Madame DuPont's. "Are you joking?"

"Now you know I'm not one to joke like that," said Mrs. Storrow. "They were just lamenting the fact that the shop closed and how the trimmer there was the 'best in the city.' When I told them that trimmer was backstage, they wanted to meet you."

"Ooh. The best in the city," said Ada with a smile. "But, of course, we've always known that."

"Go ahead, Caprice—go meet your admirers," Maria said, pride in her voice as she gave me a playful shove.

"Nice to see someone besides Maria having admirers," Ada said, grinning as Maria swatted her on the arm.

"Okay, girls, I'll be back in a minute," I said, following Mrs. Storrow out of the Little Salon into the crowd of ladies. My stomach did a little flip, and I smoothed out my shirtwaist, feeling a little self-conscious around these women who were all dressed to the nines.

"Ladies, I am pleased to introduce you to Caprice Russo, formerly of Madame DuPont's," said Mrs. Storrow, her arm around my shoulder as we approached two women standing in the corner. "Caprice, this is Mrs. Smith and Mrs. Whitman."

Mrs. Smith was short and heavyset, with dark-brown hair heavily streaked with gray that contrasted with her youthful face. She was wearing a gorgeous satin foulard dress in dark burgundy. Mrs. Whitman was wearing an equally beautiful brown silk taffeta dress with a creamy lace yoke. She was of average height with light-blonde hair and a pinched mouth.

We exchanged polite greetings, and Mrs. Storrow said, "Caprice, I have to go meet my nephews now. But I know Mrs. Smith wanted to talk to you briefly about something before you leave."

I nodded, and we said our good-byes to Mrs. Storrow. As soon as she left, Mrs. Smith said, "That Helen Storrow is so wonderful to all of you girls. You're so fortunate to have her."

"Yes, we certainly are," I said with a small forced smile. I was sensing a theme among these women. Mrs. Storrow had *saved* us from the streets. As if we did not have minds of our own to save ourselves. As if we would be running wild, drinking whiskey, and chasing young men down Hanover Street if not for Mrs. Storrow.

"So, Caprice, Mrs. Smith and I just *adored* your work at Madame DuPont's," said Mrs. Whitman, taking a puff of her cigarette and then tapping the ashes right next to the tapestry on the wall behind her. "So unique, such fine quality. I understand you found temporary work at your little club's pottery shop?"

"Well, thank you very much," I said, adding, "and yes, I'm working at the S.E.G. pottery shop at the moment."

"Why, that's darling," Mrs. Smith said. "I know we're not the only ones in this room who lament Madame DuPont's closing—who loved purchasing your hats. But the good news is, I know for a fact that there is an opening for a trimmer at Madame Claudia's shop on Temple Place. You would be *perfect* for the job." Mrs. Smith took another puff of her cigarette. "With your reputation as a trimmer, I'm sure if Mrs. Storrow talked to the owner, Madame Claudia would be open to hiring an Italian—er, open to hiring you."

Mrs. Whitman nodded several times, looking at Mrs. Smith, and added, "Yes, yes. I'm sure she would hire you—if Mrs. Storrow talked to her."

I felt my cheeks start to burn, and I clenched my jaw.

"Thank you. That's very kind of you to think of me, but the truth is, I'm not interested in another millinery job at the moment," I answered. "I plan on working at the pottery shop until I have enough money to open my own shop. My own millinery shop—in the North End."

They looked at me, then glanced at each other with eyebrows raised before Mrs. Whitman frowned and said, "Your own shop? But dear— how in the world will you afford it?"

"I'm going to save up for it," I said, standing as tall as I could, my face flushed red as I tried to control my anger. "I'm going to find a way to have enough money to do it."

"And in the *North End?*" said Mrs. Smith. "But that's not near any of the fashionable shops. It's a . . . well, it's just that it is a highly unusual location for a millinery."

"You both told me you loved my work," I replied. "I hope the location of my shop will not deter you from shopping there. And the women of my neighborhood love fashion as much as the women of your neighborhood. I intend to make hats that are affordable for all women."

"Really, um . . . Clarice . . ." said Mrs. Whitman.

"My name is Caprice," I answered, trying to take a breath to quell my anger.

"Oh, yes, Caprice," she said. Then, speaking very slowly, as if I were five years old, she said,

"Caprice, I think you should think *carefully* about this opportunity, because it's very, very *difficult* to be a business owner. And you need a great deal of *money* to do it."

They looked at each other again, and I wanted to rail at them for their condescending manner. I had had enough of this conversation.

"Yes, I'll think about it." I answered, clasping my hands together tightly and speaking as slowly as Mrs. Whitman. "And after I *think* about it, I'll *open* my shop in the *North End*. It's going to be called Caprice's Millinery. I'll have Mrs. Storrow let you know when it opens. Thank you again for the compliments on my work. I have to go catch up with my friends now. Good night."

I turned on my heel and dashed out of the room.

I found Ada, Maria, and Thea just as they were about to exit the house. I took a deep breath of cool night air, and my anger started to subside a bit.

"Caprice, how was that?" said Ada.

I told them about my conversation, and they reacted with the indignation and fury that only best friends can.

"Those witches!" said Maria.

"But good for you, Caprice," said Ada, and Thea nodded in agreement.

"Thanks, ladies," I said with a sigh. "I'm just glad we're going home. Maria, that Mr. Calvin Spaulding was quite smitten with you."

"Was that the taller one?" asked Thea. "He was very handsome."

"Yes, I suppose he was good looking," said Maria with a shrug. "But, let's be honest ladies, a man like Calvin Spaulding only wants one thing from a poor girl from the North End. The Calvin Spauldings of the world aren't worth my time. I've . . . I've got another young man in mind these days."

"What young man—"

"—who? Who are you talking about, Maria—"

"—tell us his name."

Ada, Thea, and I had started firing questions all at once.

"Well, I'm not ready to tell you his name," Maria said, clearly loving that she was keeping us in suspense.

All the way back to the streetcar, Ada and Thea tried to get the name of the mystery man out of her, and Maria refused to confess. But I had a sinking feeling that I knew who she had in mind.

Mark Toscanini. I felt slightly ill. I hoped she really wasn't thinking that Toscanini was worth an ounce of her time. But I couldn't ask her in front of Ada and Thea; I made a note to talk to her about it as soon as we had a moment alone.

When we finally got off the streetcar at North Station, I put my arm around Thea and said, "Now, dear Thea, you must admit, the look on that tiny woman's face when you fell on her was very funny."

I was hoping it made her feel better, but all three of us held our breath until Thea started laughing and said, "*Oy vey*! I felt like such a *schlemiel*. Did you *see* that woman? She couldn't have weighed more than seventy pounds! I was so afraid I was going to crush her or she was going to faint or something."

"Well, if she had fainted, we could have all revived her with our enormous paper fans!" said Ada, her voice laced with sarcasm.

The four of us walked the rest of the way home through the North End's moonlit cobblestone streets, laughing and talking about the night's events, happy to be back in our own crowded, crusty neighborhood.

CHAPTER 6

A good mother is worth a hundred teachers.
—Italian proverb

Thanksgiving
Thursday, November 26, 1908

Thanksgiving morning was brisk, with the whisper of winter in the air. The cobblestone streets of our neighborhood were shrouded in fog, and the briny scent of Boston Harbor permeated everything.

By the end of October, the awkward feeling of being the new employee at the pottery shop had disappeared, and I had gotten caught up in the comfortable rhythm of the workday. It was so pleasant working side by side with Miss Guerrier and joining the pottery decorators at lunchtime—to work with people whom I considered friends. Because I was so busy, the weeks had flown by.

Fabbia, Vita, and I were walking down to Hanover Street to buy some of the food for the Thanksgiving celebration we would have with our family that evening.

"Caprice, I don't want to go into Mr. Caroli's pasta shop. He smells funny," said Vita, holding her nose with one hand with her threadbare rag doll, Bambina, dangling in the other. She was twelve years old, and yet she still dragged Bambina with her everywhere. Fabbia and I tried not to tease her about it too much.

"Vita! That's not a very nice thing to say," I answered, raising my voice as we nearly bumped into the old street performer playing his fiddle. "But you don't have to go in; Fabbia can go get the pasta for tonight."

"Me?" said Fabbia, tossing her long brown braid behind her back. "Why me? Oh, see—he *does* smell funny, Caprice. Why else would you make me go into the shop?"

I smiled at them as we turned the corner and walked into the bustling crowds and loud voices of Hanover Street. "Okay, maybe he does smell a little odd, but he still has the best pasta for the best price. Fabbia, if you go in today, I'll go the next time."

"Oh, okay," she said, letting out a dramatic sigh.

"Thanks," I answered, handing her some money. "If you want to pick up the coffee and sugar at Mr. Patkin's too, Vita and I will meet you outside of Valenti's Butcher Shop, okay?"

"All right, I'll meet you in ten minutes," yelled Fabbia over her shoulder as she headed into the crowds toward Caroli's shop.

"Vita, isn't that the Santosuosso boy you go to

school with?" I asked, pointing to a dark-haired boy about ten feet ahead of us, holding a large sack and kicking a piece of coal down the street. "He's quite handsome."

"Ugh, Caprice, he picks his nose and eats it in class," Vita said, making a sour face. "He's a horrible boy!"

"Does he smell like Mr. Caroli too?" I asked, teasing her some more.

She bumped me with her hip and started giggling, flipping her rag doll around with both hands.

"Nunzio Caruse is a *very* handsome young man," she said. I frowned at her. I didn't know who in God's name she was talking about.

"Nunzio—who is Nunzio?" I asked. "The name sounds familiar . . . do you go to school with him too?"

Vita looked up at me, her brown eyes grew wide, and she started stammering. "Oh, um . . . just . . . um . . ."

"Vita, who is Nunzio?" I stopped and pulled her to the side of the street. We were just a few doors down from Sal Valenti's shop. "Tell me who you're talking about. *Now.*"

"Nunzio Caruse is coming over for dessert tonight," said Vita, her cheeks turning pink. "To meet you. Papa invited him."

"Are you joking? Papa didn't even *tell* me!" I said, loud enough for a couple of women walking by to look over at us. "I can't believe he didn't even tell me this time."

"Well," said Vita, pausing to choose her words carefully. "I think after that last young man—the shoemaker's son—he knew you might not be happy about another man coming over. So he didn't mention it to you. But this one, Nunzio, is quite handsome—Fabbia pointed him out to me the other day. Trust me, Caprice, he's way better looking than that skinny singing Enrico."

"Fabbia knows too!" I answered, getting more aggravated by the minute. "Am I the only one in our family who doesn't know that Papa is bringing someone over for me to meet tonight?"

"Well, I'm not sure if Papa's told Frankie," Vita said, looking at me with sympathy in her eyes. I sighed and started walking toward Sal Valenti's shop. She started running to keep pace with me.

"Caprice, you never know," she answered, hugging her doll to her chest as she hurried beside me. "You may marry this one."

"Oh, Vita," I said, laughing out loud. "Just because Papa invited him over for dessert does not mean I am going to marry him. I don't even *know* him."

"Yes, but Mama's and Papa's parents arranged their marriage. And some of the girls in your club have had arranged marriages," said Vita, and I could tell she had been discussing this with Fabbia.

"Yes, but, well . . . that's not what *I* want."

"Why?" asked Vita, looking up at me with curiosity in her eyes.

"Look, you know how Papa is always saying something is *la vecchia maniera siciliana*—the old way?" I asked her.

She looked at me and nodded.

"Having your parents arrange your marriage is the old Italian way," I said. "I'm a young American woman. I want to choose how I live my life. I want to *choose* whom I marry."

"Well, who do you want to marry, Caprice? Is it someone we know?"

"No, Vita," I answered, rolling my eyes. "I haven't met anyone I want to marry yet. Enough questions; we're here."

Sal's shop was so tiny that two men and one woman were waiting in line outside. We got behind them and waited. I adjusted my hat and rubbed my hands together, thinking of the hot coffee waiting for me at home. I knew it would be crowded and stuffy in our home today, but at least it would be warm.

I cupped my chilly hands and peered through the window of the shop to see Sal working behind the counter. He immediately caught my eye and gave me a wink and a smile as he rang up the order of an elderly woman with a hunched back. She patted his hand and squeezed it before leaving with her order.

"How nice, two of the Russo girls have come to see me Thanksgiving morning," he said, spreading his arms out wide when we finally entered the shop. "What did I do to deserve such an honor?"

"Happy Thanksgiving, Mr. Valenti!" Vita said, giggling at his flirtation. She sat down on the small shelf next to the window and placed her doll down next to her.

"You know you can call me Sal, Vita," he said to her. "And of course you know you can too, Caprice," he added, giving me another one of his annoying winks. "Let me go get your order."

"Good idea," I snapped back at him—perhaps a bit too sharply.

In less than a minute he brought us our chicken wrapped in brown paper. As he was ringing it up, I looked behind me at the line out the door and said, "It looks like business is good."

"Yes, thank God," he said with a proud smile. His upper lip was a bit larger than his lower lip, and he had a dimple on one side of his face that I had never noticed before. He was even better looking when he smiled.

I was about to ask him more about running his own business when he looked beyond me, saw the line, and said, "As you can see, the shop is too small for all of my customers these days! And I have to get to my other orders. Happy

Thanksgiving, Russo girls! Please come back and visit me again soon!"

Vita jumped up from the shelf, said good-bye, and headed out the door. It bothered me that he was rushing us out. *He's got quite the reputation as a Lothario.* I reminded myself of Maria's words and tried not to feel bothered.

"Happy Thanksgiving, Mr. . . . um . . . Sal," I said, and followed Vita out to meet Fabbia. As I walked past the window, I looked back at him one more time. He had moved on to his next customer. But he was smiling at me.

Vita and Fabbia were in the sitting room chopping vegetables on a little card table. Father and Frankie were at the men's bathhouse with Uncle Arthur and Dominic. As I worked in the kitchen with my mother, it occurred to me that this might be the perfect time to finally have the conversation I had been putting off forever. I took a deep breath and thought carefully about my words.

"Caprice, the eggplant caponata is simmering, but you can start the lentil sauce for the pasta," my mother said in Italian as she wiped her hands on her apron. "The chicken is in the oven. I'm going to start making the white bean bruschetta." This was one of the only days of the year that my mother was not quite as frugal with our food budget.

"Okay, Mama," I said, and we both got to work on our respective dishes. We worked in silence for a short while, me at the stove, my mother at the kitchen table. I was enjoying this quiet camaraderie, but I knew I would have to disrupt it now or I never would.

"So, Mama," I said, pausing for a moment. My mother looked up from the bruschetta she was assembling. I didn't quite know how to say it, so I just blurted it out.

"I've been thinking it's time for me to start paying board. Like Frankie," I said, taking another deep breath. "I want to start saving my own money so I can go back to millinery work someday. I want to make hats again. In my own shop. Here, in the North End. I want to . . . I want to open my own shop."

She put the piece of bruschetta down on the plate and studied my face for a few seconds. My stomach churned, and I held the wooden spoon I had been using to stir the sauce so tightly it might have snapped.

"You want to pay board, Caprice?" she asked, in Italian of course.

"Yes, Mama," I answered. "I think it's time."

She nodded slowly, thinking it over.

"But you want to . . . to what?" she said, furrowing her brows. "Open your own shop? Here? Are you serious about this?"

"Yes, I'm very serious."

"But what about getting married, Caprice?" she said. "What about starting a family?"

"I want those things too . . . at some point," I answered. "But I want to have my own shop. I'm a very talented milliner. And I want to work for myself and not someone else."

She shook her head and didn't say anything for a moment.

"You girls today, you think you know every-thing, but you don't," she said. "You think the old ways, the Italian ways, are so old fashioned. You think you should go to college, have big jobs. Now even have your own *shops*. Why—do you think that will bring you happiness? More than *marriage?* More than *children?*" She threw up her hands and continued talking. "And then—and then of course you all think you should marry for love. For *romance*. Don't you realize that could lead to a lifetime of heartache?"

"Mama, I'm not even *thinking* about marriage right now," I said, trying to contain my exas-peration. "God knows I don't have any romance in my life. I don't know who I want to marry . . . or . . . or when. I just want to pay board—to save some money of my own. To try to open my own shop someday. Maybe Vita and Fabbia could even work there."

"What?" said Fabbia from the next room. "Work where?" I realized they were probably straining their necks to hear every word.

"Nowhere, Fabbia; keep chopping!" I answered. "Mama—*please*." I sat down across from her at the kitchen table. I was tempted to get down on my knees and beg her.

She grabbed my hands across the table and looked at me intently. Again seconds passed that felt like an eternity.

"Caprice, we will talk to your father. And . . . and he will agree to have you pay board," she said, and I nearly fell off my chair from shock. "You will give us half of your pay envelope as board, and you can keep the rest yourself. *But*— you must agree to help with Vita and Fabbia's expenses when we need you to."

"Yes, Mama, of course. Clothing, books, shoes—anything," I said, smiling. I wanted to dance the tarantella down Charter Street I was so happy.

"But this shop idea—I don't know, Caprice," she said. "Don't mention that to your father yet. I need to think about it." She gave my hands a tight squeeze before pulling away. "I just *worry* about you, Caprice. I know where my place is in life. But these choices you want to make. Do you know where your place is going to be? *Do you?*" She looked at me, searching my face.

"What if this shop idea does not work? What if it fails? Then you are left with no shop, no job, no marriage, and I shall be the one living with a broken heart—over my oldest daughter's misfortunes."

"Mama, I won't fail," I said to her, frustrated and moved by her words. "I promise you. And if I don't do this—open my shop—then I will be living a life that feels like no life at all. A life always regretting, always wondering *what if . . .*"

"Well, I still don't know," she said with a sigh as she got up from the table. She put the bruschetta in the tiny cupboard to keep for dinner. "I need to think about it. Please do not mention the shop idea to your father yet."

I came up behind her and gave her a hug because I knew she was torn about this decision. But being torn about supporting me was better than not supporting me at all. "Thank you."

She turned and hugged me tightly, then stood back to look at me once more. "Okay," she said, nodding and touching my cheek lightly with her fingers. "Enough talk; we need to finish cooking. Everyone will be here soon."

CHAPTER 7

At the table, one does not grow old.
—Italian proverb

Thanksgiving dinner was delicious, rambunctious, loud, hot, crowded—and *wonderful*. Aunt Cecilia, Uncle Arthur, Dominic, Frankie, Vita, Fabbia, my parents, and I were sitting around the makeshift extended dining room table in our sitting room. On the walls were new brightly colored pictures my mother had found in a calendar—pictures of the countryside, of a meadow or a forest—things that reminded her of Sicily. My parents' marriage certificate and their one wedding picture hung on the wall as well.

Dinner was over, and my Aunt Cecilia had just brought out a parade of desserts—cannoli, ricotta pie, and several kinds of cookies. My face was flushed from the heat of the crowded room and the glass of red wine I had drunk with dinner. But I was happy. My conversation with my mother had gone as well as I could have expected, and hopefully by this time next week, I would be paying board and saving my own money.

My mother went out into the kitchen to get more coffee, and I heard her say in her heavily accented English, "Ada. Thea. Come in, come in—we're just having dessert. How nice of you to stop by."

She gave my friends kisses and hugs as they walked through the door before ushering them into the sitting room. I was so glad they had accepted my invitation to come for Thanksgiving dessert.

"Ada, Thea, please sit," said Dominic, touching Ada's elbow to lead them over to the seats my uncle had pulled up to the table.

"Here, Thea, take my seat," said Fabbia, getting up from her chair. "Vita and I were going to finish our game of checkers in the bedroom."

"Where is Maria?" I asked, looking at Ada and Thea. "I thought she'd be with you too."

"Um, I think she's having dessert at the Toscaninis'," said Thea, giving me a questioning look.

"Toscanini?" said my aunt Cecilia, her eyebrows raised as she walked out of the kitchen with glasses of red wine for my friends. "Not of Toscanini Chocolates—that family?"

"Um, yes, Mrs. Russo," Ada replied for Thea. "I believe Mark Toscanini Junior invited her over for dessert."

"The son they call the chocolate prince?" my father said, putting down his cannoli to chime in. There was a trail of powdered sugar down the front of his shirt. "What is our beautiful Maria doing hanging around with that old bald *gavone*?"

"Caprice, does her mother know she's over there for dessert?" my mother asked me.

"I honestly don't know," I answered. "I am going to talk to her about him though. I just haven't had a moment alone with her in weeks."

"She should not be spending time with that man or that family, Caprice," my father warned. "There is a reason that family has such a bad reputation. They are no good. She should—"

My father was interrupted by a loud knock at the tenement door.

"Bambina! Bambina!" I heard Vita yell. "I've been looking for her all day. Thank you, Mr. Valenti. Thank you, thank you."

Vita came running into the sitting room clutching her rag doll. "Mr. Valenti from the butcher shop brought my little Bambina to me," she squealed. "I thought I had lost her."

Sal Valenti walked in after her, practically ducking to enter the sitting room. He was wearing a bowler hat and a black overcoat, looking odd without his white butcher apron. My father and mother had just gotten up to make introductions when another handsome young man walked into the sitting room. He was just a couple of inches shorter than Sal, with light-brown hair and somewhat angular features. Fabbia followed after, looking up at him with big moon eyes.

There was an awkward pause as my friends,

105

my aunt and uncle, and I looked at these men, wondering what was going on.

"Sal, how nice of you to bring Vita her doll," my mother said, greeting Sal with a kiss on the cheek. She turned to introduce Sal to my father, but my father was already greeting the young man who I had never seen before.

"Oh, Nunzio, welcome, welcome to our home," my father said, shaking his hand. *Oh, Jesus, Mary, and Joseph.* I had been having such a good evening, I had completely forgotten about my father's surprise guest. Nunzio looked at my friends and me, as if he was trying to figure out which one of us was Giuseppe Russo's daughter.

I glanced over at Ada and Thea, who were trying to hide their amusement at the whole situation. But they were failing miserably. They weren't facing the doorway, so the two of them tried to get me to laugh by making faces at me. I kicked Thea's foot under the chair because she was the one I could reach, and she stifled a giggle.

Dominic had pulled his chair over next to Ada. He was eating a piece of ricotta pie, looking at Frankie across the table, who was trying to whisper something to him.

"Mrs. Russo, this is for you from my mother." Nunzio handed my mother a jar of homemade preserves as my father introduced her.

"Thank you, Nunzio. It's nice to meet you," my

mother said to him. "Giuseppe, Nunzio, this is Sal Valenti, the young butcher who has the new shop on Stillman Street."

"Oh, Valenti—your family is from Avellino, yes?" my father asked, shaking Sal's hand and looking him up and down.

Oh, dear God. For some reason, there was animosity in the North End between the Italians from Sicily and the Italians from Avellino. It was just absurd.

"Uh, yes, sir, my family is from Avellino," said Sal, and he looked at me like he was thinking the same thing.

My father just grunted and sized him up again. How rude. I attempted to give Sal an apologetic smile.

Nunzio was still standing next to the table, hands at his sides, looking a little uncomfortable. Maybe it was because my sister Fabbia wouldn't stop staring at him like she was his puppy. I was grateful that Vita noticed this and pushed her back into the bedroom.

"Well," my father said, rubbing his hands together like he was not sure what to do next. "Let me make the introductions. Here, sit— Frankie, grab those extra chairs that Uncle Arthur brought down. They're in the corner of the girls' bedroom." Frankie was glaring at Nunzio as he walked into the bedroom. Now what was *his* problem?

My father made the introductions around the table for Sal and Nunzio. Thea and Ada gave both men warm greetings. Thea started smoothing out her shirtwaist, which was a little tight on her stomach. She did this when meeting people, like she wanted to rub some of the fullness off her belly. Ada was sucking her cheeks to keep from laughing, and I thanked God she didn't.

My father left me for last.

"Caprice, you know Sal the butcher," my father said, waving Sal to sit, dismissing him. Sal just smiled and winked at me. He was as amused by the situation as my girlfriends were. "But this is Nunzio Caruse. I know his father well. We grew up in Sicily together. Isn't that nice?"

"Very nice, Papa," I replied, wondering if he could be more obvious. "It's a pleasure to meet you, Nunzio," I shook his hand and gave him as sympathetic a smile as I could muster.

"It's a pleasure to meet you, Caprice," he said, giving me what looked like a forced grimace.

Sal began talking to my brother and Dominic about different friends from the neighborhood. Frankie was still eyeing Nunzio with distaste. I was relieved when Ada and Thea started talking to Nunzio and things began to feel less awkward.

I knew my father was satisfied with the way things were going because he started talking to my uncle about their tailoring business again.

Twenty minutes passed, and I was thinking the evening wasn't so bad. But then all of a sudden, my uncle Arthur took a bite of cannoli and—with his mouth still full of ricotta filling—said, "Caprice, do you have a fella? It's about time—you should be married by now." He nodded his head up and down really fast as if to emphasize the point, and powdered sugar sprinkled from his lips to his chin.

This time, Thea kicked *me* under the table, and Ada nearly spit out her drink.

My uncle Arthur was not a subtle man, particularly after a few glasses of wine.

Warmth flooded my cheeks. I sighed and looked up at the ceiling, only to notice a tiny black bug crawl into a crack in the yellowish-white plaster. I wished I could follow it.

Sal cleared his throat, and Nunzio took a huge gulp of wine from the glass my mother had put in front of him.

"Quiet, Arthur. Caprice is an American girl," my aunt Cecilia said as she grabbed the bottle of red wine on the table and refilled my wine glass. "She doesn't need to be married so young like we were. Imagine—sixteen years old. Such babies we were."

"Such babies," said my mother, nodding, bringing yet another plate of treats from the kitchen and putting them on the table. She shrugged and added, "But everyone did it."

"We're not married either, Mr. Russo. Right, Thea?" said Ada, looking at Thea.

"Um, yeah, right. That's true. No husbands for us yet. No husbands at all. We're not engaged or anything," said Thea as her face turned crimson. Ada raised her eyebrows at her.

"Um . . . Nunzio, haven't I seen you at the tavern on the waterfront? O'Shea's?" said Frankie, looking at him with a blank face. I was surprised. Normally Frankie would have loved to continue the conversation about young men and marriage just to mortify me even more. I was thankful that he had decided to be charitable tonight and change the subject.

"Uh . . . yeah . . . yeah . . . you might have seen me there," said Nunzio, his eyes widening slightly.

"Yeah, I thought so," Frankie replied, frowning. "And aren't you going with Mr. O'Shea's daughter, Fiona? I know I've seen you there with her at least once or twice. Aren't you promised to her or something?"

I covered my mouth with my hand and swallowed a laugh as I looked over at my father. Now he was the one whose face had turned red, and he was staring at Nunzio.

"Um . . . you know, well . . ." Nunzio swallowed hard. "It's like this, see . . . my parents don't want me to marry an Irish gal, and well . . . I don't know . . . I promised . . . I should just . . . I think

. . . I think I have to go." Poor Nunzio pushed his seat out and stood up.

I felt a little sorry for him because my brother and Dominic looked like they might take him outside and pummel him. I glanced at Sal and noticed that he was studying my face, so I quickly looked away.

"Caprice, it was very nice meeting you," Nunzio said, backing away from the table. "Nice meeting all of you. Mr. and Mrs. Russo, thank you for dessert. I can see my way out!" And with that, Nunzio Caruse literally ran out of my life.

"I cannot believe it! *Un bastardo*! His father didn't say he was seeing an Irish gal! Do you think his father knows?" my father asked no one in particular.

"Uncle Giuseppe, practically the whole North End knows," Dominic said with a laugh.

"Yes, I had heard that too," said Sal, looking right into my eyes. His mouth turned up in a small, amused smile that made my stomach do a flip.

Frankie ran his fingers through his thick black hair and shook his head. "Papa, the next time you're thinking of someone for Caprice, at least tell me his name first, okay?"

"Thanks, big brother," I said, standing up to plant a kiss on Frankie's cheek. "And, Papa, if you're going to invite someone over, *please* at least tell me?" I asked. I kissed him on top of his

111

head even though I really felt like squashing a piece of ricotta pie on it.

The rest of the evening was much more relaxed after Nunzio's hasty departure. Sal, Dominic, and my brother told funny stories and tried to outdo each other. My father got over his anger after some more wine and cookies. He and my uncle Arthur started telling stories about all the trouble they had gotten into together as boys in the old country.

At the end of the night, we cleared away plates and started saying our good-byes.

"Ada, Thea, I'll walk you home, okay?" Dominic said.

"Okay," they both answered, and I noticed the small smile Ada gave him in return as their eyes locked for a moment.

"Dom, meet Sal and me for a drink after you walk the girls home," Frankie said, and then with a laugh added, "Maybe we'll go to O'Shea's."

"Thank you for a wonderful evening, Mr. and Mrs. Russo," said Sal, giving my mother a kiss on the cheek. Ada and Thea did the same.

I walked everyone out into the hall.

"Ladies, thank you for making my evening so much better," I said.

"Of course," said Thea. "Please, it was way more fun than being at my house with my obnoxious brother-in-law and condescending sister."

"Things are always interesting at the Russo home," said Ada, her cheeks flushed.

Just as everyone was heading toward the staircase, Sal turned and walked a few steps back to me. He touched my elbow, leaned down so that his face was very close to mine, and said, "I will see you soon, yes?"

His light-brown eyes were sparkling. My stomach had done another little flip when he touched my elbow. What a nerve he had, flirting like this with me. I stepped back from him, anxious that my father might be listening and annoyed that Sal was trying to charm me as he'd charmed so many other young women in the North End.

"Um . . . yes, yes. I'll see you at your shop. Happy Thanksgiving, Sal," I answered.

"Happy Thanksgiving, Caprice," he answered with a wink and an amused look I didn't quite understand. I turned on my heel and hurried in to help clean up.

As I finished cleaning the kitchen, my father came in and sat down at the table with a glass of wine and a local Italian newspaper. My mother came in from cleaning the sitting room and joined him, sewing buttons on a shirt under the tiny kerosene lamp.

It was well past eleven o'clock, and I was exhausted and ready to join Fabbia and Vita in our bed when my mother said, "So, Giuseppe,

Caprice is going to start paying board next week."

She didn't even look up from her sewing when she said this. My father put the paper down, looked at her, and blinked a few times. I was frozen in the doorway of the sitting room; I couldn't even speak.

"What?" he asked her.

"Caprice is going to start to pay board," she said, looking up at him. Her eyes looked tired and red. "She'll help with Vita and Fabbia's expenses, though. Okay?"

I looked at him, barely able to breathe. *Please say yes. Please say yes.*

My father rubbed his hand over his face a couple of times and ran his fingers through his hair. He looked at her, looked at me, and then back at her again. I wasn't sure if he was too tired to argue or too mellow from red wine or what it was, but he just looked again at me and her, shrugged, and said, "Okay, as long as she helps with expenses."

I kissed them both good night and fell into bed next to my snoring sisters, exhausted but exhilarated. I was going to start paying board. I would finally be able to start saving for my shop—to take the first important step toward opening my own business.

After my mind calmed down, I finally fell asleep and dreamed of standing with pride in front of a little whitewashed storefront with my name in red letters across the top. In my dream, I saw a very tall young man with olive skin and light-brown eyes standing across the street, looking over. And I couldn't tell if he was admiring my shiny new store . . . or if he was admiring me.

CHAPTER 8

A bad beginning makes a bad ending.
—Italian proverb

Saturday, December 12, 1908

The night of the annual Saturday Evening Girls holiday party was always the second weekend in December. As was tradition, we had invited female family members to attend, so it would be an enormous crowd with sisters, mothers, aunts, and grandmothers joining us to dance and socialize and eat delicious desserts. This year I had volunteered to stay after work to decorate and set up the assembly room for the soiree.

It was an hour before the party, and I was in the pottery shop arranging pumpkin-colored bowls on the shelves when I heard the click of Miss Guerrier's shoes behind me.

"Oh, Caprice, you're here," she said, looking relieved.

"Yes, I'm still here," I said. "Ada, Thea, and Maria are coming to help decorate for the party soon. I'm not even going home for dinner. Is everything okay? You look a bit worried."

"Everything's wonderful. Thank you for all of your hard work this week," she said, smiling.

"But I wanted to talk to you—I have a bit of an unusual request. Mrs. Storrow and I are concerned about getting all of these pottery orders delivered in time for Christmas. She has graciously offered her car and driver to help us finish them. Would you and your friends mind leaving the party a little early this evening to make some of the deliveries?"

"Would I mind?" I asked with a laugh. "*Of course* I wouldn't mind. I'm sure Ada, Thea, and Maria won't either. It's not every evening we have a car and driver."

Miss Guerrier clasped her hands together, her eyes glistening. "Wonderful. I thought that would be your answer, but I just wanted to make sure you wouldn't be upset about missing some of the festivities. I've got to go upstairs and get the pitchers of lemonade in my apartment. I'll meet you in the assembly room in a few minutes."

The sound of Miss Guerrier walking upstairs was interrupted by the jingle of the front door. Maria walked in, escorted by none other than the red-faced chocolate prince, Mark Toscanini.

"Hi, Caprice," Maria said, giving me a dazzling smile. "Caprice, you remember Mark."

"Um, yes," I answered, trying for Maria's sake to control my response and sound cordial. "Nice to see you again, Mark."

"Yes, Caprice, nice to see you again." He looked at me with a thin smile on his lips, though his eyes remained dead looking. "*Thank you* for being so very helpful when I was in here last time."

"Oh, you're quite welcome, Mark," I answered, grimacing at him so hard my cheeks felt tight. "Um, shall we go get ready for the party?" I said to Maria, eager to get away from this man.

"Yes, here," Maria said, taking two white paper bags from Mark and handing them to me. I noticed that she was at least two inches taller than him. She was Snow White and he was one of the dwarfs.

"Mark has generously donated *five pounds* of chocolates from his factory for our party," Maria said to me. I knew she sensed the animosity in the room. Maria was no fool. So I didn't know why in God's name she was spending time with this man, who clearly *was* one.

"Oh, thank you, Mark," I answered.

"Of course, Caprice," he answered, giving me that dead stare again. "Anything for Maria and her friends." Then he turned to Maria and said, "I will see you at church tomorrow."

It was an order, not a request.

"Yes, nine-thirty Mass?" Maria said.

"Yes, I'll see you in the morning," he answered. I noticed that his eyes weren't dead when he looked at her. He looked at Maria with a kind of desperate longing. Like she was a piece of meat in the butcher shop window, and he was starving.

He tipped his hat at me and said, "Have a wonderful evening, ladies."

I muttered a good-bye, and Maria and I started up the staircase to the assembly room.

"So, what do you think of Mark?" Maria asked. She took off her coat to reveal her gorgeous, deep-rose-colored dress with the lace-trimmed cuffs. She had made it herself with material she had bought for pennies off some of the pushcarts that sold fabric remnants, but it looked like something you'd see in the windows in Back Bay.

"Maria, what in the world are you doing?" I asked, stopping in front of the door to the assembly room. "What do I think?" I continued. "Frankly, I think you're far too good for him. Why are you even spending time with him? Does this have to do with the money your father owes his father? Is this how you're paying him back? You've heard all the rumors about his family . . . you know the gambling one to be true . . ."

"No! This is *not* how I'm paying him back. What do you take me for?" Maria said this a little too forcefully. "Mark and I figured out a way for my father to pay off his debts over time; that's not at all why I'm spending time with him. Look, Mark is clearly crazy about me. I'm just enjoying the attention at the moment."

"I don't know why you would want attention from him at all," I said. "Maria, you are way too good for the likes of him and his family."

"I'm too good for *him?"* she said, anger flashing in her eyes. "Caprice, he's a young man on the make. He's very successful—he *owns* a tenement building and a chocolate factory, for heaven's sake."

"His father owns them," I replied.

"Caprice, his *family* owns them, so *he* owns them," she said, cracking one of her knuckles, an unladylike habit she revealed when she was annoyed. "And his father is far from the only businessman in the North End to be involved in a little gambling . . . and most of those other rumors have been spread by his father's adversaries, businessmen jealous of the family's success. His family's business, the factory, all the rest of it, are completely on the level."

"I don't know about that, Maria. I think you're hearing only what you want to hear," I said. "I don't think the rumors about the family's . . . well, other illegal activities are unfounded. And I'm not the only one in the North End who feels that way. Please think about what I've said—and please be careful."

"I'm always careful, Caprice," she answered angrily, turning her regal nose up in the air a fraction of an inch, a defiant confidence in her voice. "I know exactly what I'm doing."

I started to open my mouth to reply but thought better of it. The two of us silently headed into

121

the assembly room and started setting up for the party.

Ada and Thea arrived ten minutes later as Maria and I were moving all of the chairs to make room for dancing. Ada helped me set up a table in the front of the room, next to the fireplace, for all the desserts and refreshments that people were bringing. Thea set up the Victrola in the corner of the room on the other side of the fireplace.

I told Ada about Mark and my conversation with Maria. But I kept my promise and did not tell her about Maria's father's gambling debts.

"Well, just keep talking to her," Ada said. "I will too. The more I hear about him, the more I think she should stay far away from him."

"I agree," I said with a sigh.

We were smoothing out the tablecloth when I heard a booming voice coming up the stairs.

"Hello? Anybody here? I have a delivery for Miss Guerrier." I whirled around to see Sal Valenti carrying a large cake box. His frame filled the doorway of the assembly room, and he smiled wide when he saw me.

"Ah! Caprice Russo, the redhead!" he said with a laugh, and Maria let out a snort behind me. "I haven't seen you at my shop since Thanksgiving—why is that? Only your sisters have come to visit me." He gave me an exaggerated pout as he walked over and placed the cake box on the table, then took off his hat.

122

"What are you doing delivering cake?" I blurted out, annoyed that he had brought up my red hair—*again*. I started smoothing it out despite myself. Maybe I shouldn't have worn my green dress tonight. It only seemed to accent my hair color. "Are you a butcher and a baker now?"

"And a candlestick maker," he said with a laugh. "My uncle owns Fabrizio's Bakery on North Square. I stopped by to see him after work, and he asked me to deliver this chocolate cake to Miss Guerrier at the pottery shop for the Saturday Evening Girls party. I told him—deliver a cake for a party of ladies? I would be happy to!" He grinned again. Out of the corner of my eye I saw Thea and Ada smiling as they watched this exchange.

I blushed and found myself not sure what to say next. "Do you need to be paid?" I asked.

"No, no," he said with a wave of his hand. "But can I stay for the party? It looks like fun."

"Sorry, Sal," Ada answered as she walked up behind him carrying a plate of rugelach. "But it's ladies only tonight."

I gave him a small smile and a shrug and felt warmth creeping up my cheeks.

"Ada, Thea, good to see you again," he said, nodding. Maria was now standing on a stool, hanging ribbons at the other end of the hall, ignoring the conversation.

123

"Oh, and over there is Maria—" I said, but he interrupted me.

"Maria Santucci, yes, I know who she is," he said with a nod.

Of course he did. What young man in the North End didn't? But why did it bother me?

"Well, if this is a 'girls only' party, I should be going before Miss Guerrier gets here," he said, putting his hat back on. "I remember her from the library—she's a tiny woman, but she can be frightening when she wants to be."

"Uh, yes, yes, you probably should," I answered. He looked at me for just a moment, right into my eyes, and I felt my stomach getting jittery. But this was a type of stomachache that felt different—butterflies, not bee stings.

"Caprice, please come by and visit again soon," he said. "Regards to your family. *Buon Natale!*" He turned to my friends. "Girls, *Buon Natale!*" He gave them all a big wave and exited the hall.

"*Buon Natale!*" Maria yelled, not even looking up from her ribbons.

"Happy Hanukkah!" said Ada, and we all started laughing.

I heard the distant jingle of the front doorbell as he left the building, and I found myself wishing that he had stayed, if only for a little bit longer. Ugh, *why* was I feeling this way about an overly flirtatious butcher from Avellino?

"Caprice," called Maria, stepping down from

her stool to move it to another part of the hall to hang ribbons. "Was that Sal Valenti showing up to see you *again?*"

"Maria, you missed it. He was the young man that Caprice's father *didn't* invite on Thanksgiving evening," said Ada, walking across the room with more ribbons.

"Oh, yes. Thea, you told me about that," said Maria. "Caprice, I thought it was very interesting that he came by on Thanksgiving night just to drop off Vita's doll."

"Oh . . . but it's Vita's favorite doll . . . her *only* doll . . . and well . . ." I started stuttering a bit and felt my face grow warm again. "But as you said yourself, Maria, he's got quite the reputation. And what a braggart—girls, you should have heard him when he told me his shop was the first of *many* butcher shops he will own," I answered, rolling my eyes.

"Oh, you know, now that you mention it, I have heard that about him," Ada said with a nod. "Who was that girl who worked at the factory with you, Thea? Didn't she have a crush on him?"

"Oh my goodness, yes!" said Thea, biting her nail. "Now what was her name . . . ?"

"Was it Louisa Covello? Maria already told me about her," I said.

"No, it was Francesca Parma," Thea said. "Oh, she was completely in love with him, and he would walk her home from work now and then.

But then she came in one day in tears—she had seen him with that Louisa girl."

"He certainly does get around," Ada said, eyebrows raised.

"I told her that," Maria said smugly. I could tell she was still angry about our conversation on the stairs.

"Still, he seemed nice at your home that night, Caprice," said Ada. "And you liked him too, right, Thea? Thea?"

Thea was staring off toward the fireplace, so Ada nudged her and repeated the question.

"Oh, yes, sorry," said Thea, nodding slowly. "I did like him. I thought he was much better than that Nunzio, who was secretly promised to the Irish gal."

"Ladies, trust me, there's no way I'm getting involved—or whatever you want to call it—with a young man who goes from girl to girl like that, no matter how nice he seems . . ." I was stammering because thinking about Sal made me feel a little strange, almost lightheaded, and I wished it didn't. I started pulling decorations out of the boxes on the floor. "Anyway, I *can't* be interested in a young man right now. I don't have the time. I have to focus on trying to save money, making plans for my shop . . . and, besides his reputation, which is bad enough, he's from Avellino, and you saw my father's reaction to *that.*

"Anyway, enough about Sal. Thea, I haven't even asked how your new job with the interior decorator is going. Do you like it? Are you happy?" I was eager to change the subject to something other than Sal Valenti.

"You know, I was really nervous at first, but my boss, Miss Thatcher, is nicer than I ever expected," said Thea. Her cheeks were flushed. "She told me the other day that I'm a much faster learner than her last girl, and she's going to start bringing me to appointments with clients more. It's a dream compared to the factory. I'll never be able to thank Mrs. Storrow enough, frankly."

Ada started to ask Thea something when Miss Guerrier walked into the hall holding pitchers of lemonade.

"It looks wonderful in here, ladies," said Miss Guerrier, looking around the room. Ada and I took the lemonade from her, and Miss Guerrier hurried over to the Victrola to make sure it was working properly. I started setting up cups and napkins on the table.

"Hey, Ada! Caprice!" Thea yelled to us from across the room, where she was now standing on chairs with Maria. They were hanging the last of the red and green ribbons and bows, strings of popcorn, and cranberries that Miss Guerrier and some of the club members had made earlier in the week. "Could you two please come over and help us finish this? I just heard the door open downstairs; people are starting to arrive."

As we hurried over to help them finish up, Ada said to me in whisper, "Oh, Caprice—I've been meaning to tell you . . . Thea's behaving awfully strange lately. Really nervous—anxious, even more so than usual. It doesn't appear to be because of her new job. On the way here I asked her if everything was okay, and she said yes, but I don't believe her. Just watch her tonight; see what you think."

"Do you think it's because her mother and her sister, Bessie, are coming tonight?" I asked, whispering back. "That Bessie can be just awful."

Ada shrugged. "No, I don't think so. I don't know what's going on with her. But she's not acting like herself. She's been acting a bit strange since the night of *The Merchant of Venice*."

Just then, Martha and Anna Epstein came in with their mother and grandmother. Gemma Ianelli arrived with her mother and sisters. Katy Abrams brought her aunt, mother, and younger sister. Danielle Orazio, Naomi Goodman—all the S.E.G. girls started flowing into the room accompanied by family members. Thea's mother and sour-faced Bessie entered the room. Bessie was holding her son, David, in her arms. He was red faced and looked like he was going to start wailing any minute.

Ada and I picked up all the empty decoration

boxes and brought them downstairs so they were out of the way.

We ran back upstairs to help with last minute preparations as guests continued to arrive. I was arranging the table of desserts when I spotted my mother walking in with Fabbia, Vita, and my aunt Cecilia.

I was always surprised when I saw my mother out in public. She looked smaller to me, dressed in her modest black dress with buttons down the front. I could tell Fabbia and Vita had helped her put up her hair in a more modern look than her usual style at home. She was carrying a tray of my favorite chocolate spice cookies.

I walked across the room to greet them. Fabbia and Vita looked adorable in their matching navy-blue-and-white Sunday dresses. Their hair was plaited with navy-blue satin ribbons.

"Mama, Aunt Cecilia. I'm so glad you all came to the party," I said as I leaned in to give them kisses on both cheeks.

"Is Ruthie here?" Fabbia asked, eyeing the table of candies and desserts.

"Is Antonetta here?" asked Vita.

"Yes, yes," I said, laughing at their urgency. "All of your friends are here or on their way. I believe I saw some of them sitting in the meeting room downstairs, sampling sweets." With that the two of them hooked arms and walked away.

"We're going to go find some seats, Caprice,"

my mother said. "Come on, Cecilia, I see some chairs over in the corner with a nice view of everything."

"But Mama, Auntie—remember, you have to dance, at least once," I said as they started walking away.

"Oh, we'll see if we can get your mother up and dancing, Caprice," said my aunt with a laugh. "We'll see . . ."

The assembly room was crowded now, the smells of fresh challah bread and *torrone* candy mingled with other sweets. I spotted Mrs. Storrow as she walked to the center of the assembly room.

I saw Thea over at the refreshment table and went to join her and get some lemonade. Thea, who was always at her most comfortable and happy here, at the S.E.G. among friends, did seem a bit preoccupied. She was staring off into the room again. I nudged her and whispered, "Where are your mother and Bessie? I saw them when they arrived."

"Oh," she said, her lips pursed, "they already left while you were bringing all the decoration boxes downstairs. David started having a crying fit, so they decided they better just leave. Just as well—Mama's not in a terribly good mood tonight anyway, and Bessie was . . . well, you know Bessie." Thea shrugged and looked off into the crowd, adding, "Ruthie stayed here with me of course. She's off with Fabbia and Vita eating treats."

I nodded at her, although she was too lost in her own thoughts again to notice me.

"Ladies! Ladies!" Mrs. Storrow said, smiling and looking across the crowded room. She was beautifully turned out as always in an amethyst-colored silk shantung dress. "Welcome to the annual Saturday Evening Girls holiday party! Thank you to all the friends and family who have joined us tonight. Merry Christmas and happy Hanukkah to you all!" Everyone gave a round of applause.

"By now most of you in the room know of my love of folk dancing, and I can't wait another minute to get started," she said. "If everyone could please clear out of the center of the room, I'd like to start this evening's dancing with the tarantella. Perhaps later I can convince some of you to try the new English folk dances I've recently learned. If some of the S.E.G. ladies could please join me, we can begin."

Miss Guerrier was at the Victrola, waiting to start the music for the tarantella. I ran over to my mother and aunt, grabbed both of them by the hand, and pulled them to the center of the floor too. My mother was shy and didn't want to go, but Aunt Cecilia gave her a gentle push and jokingly refused to let her sit back in her seat. Maria, always the first to seek the spotlight, was already standing in the middle of the room, flanked by her sister and mine.

The gay music for the tarantella began, and my mother started dancing, becoming less and less inhibited as the music continued. Her face became flushed, and she was laughing with Aunt Cecilia as she missed a few steps.

"Look at Mama," I said in a loud whisper to Vita, who was dancing next to me. "She looks twenty years younger." Vita bent her neck to look over at her and smiled.

Later in the evening, I was sitting with my family enjoying Christmas cookies and lemonade when Mrs. Storrow walked up behind my chair and touched my shoulder.

"Caprice, the car is here, if you could please gather up your friends and get ready to go. Oh, hello, Mrs. Russo. I'm sorry, I didn't even see you—are you enjoying yourself?"

My mother gave a small nod and could barely look at Mrs. Storrow. She was so strong and confident at home. It was always a bit disconcerting to see how shy she was outside of it.

"I'm so glad," said Mrs. Storrow, giving my mother a warm smile before adding, "You know, we are so lucky to have Caprice at the pottery shop. She's invaluable. But her reputation as a milliner is such that I don't think she'll be working here too long. Did you know how highly regarded she is as a hat maker? Many ladies of

Boston society are just distraught that she no longer works at Madame DuPont's."

"No," my mother said, her accent thick. "I did not know that, Mrs. Storrow."

My aunt Cecilia patted me on the shoulder and gave me a proud smile.

"Oh, yes, Caprice is a *most gifted* hat maker," Mrs. Storrow said. "She really needs to work on that plan of hers, of opening her own shop here in the North End. Don't you think that is a wonderful idea?"

I was a bit overcome by Mrs. Storrow's directness with my mother. My stomach lurched as I looked at my mother and she looked back at me, a combination of pride and nervousness in her eyes. I could almost see the thoughts running through her head: *what about marriage, what about babies, what about the old ways . . .*

"Yes, Mrs. Storrow," my mother said, nodding slowly and saying in tentative English, "I think . . . I think it maybe . . . it *may* be a good idea."

"Mrs. Storrow, I'm going to go find my friends and get ready to go," I said. "Thank you for the use of your car to do this—thank you . . ." I wanted to say more. She grabbed my hand.

"You're welcome, my dear," she said, smiling and nodding that she understood. "Now go— have *fun* doing the deliveries."

I kissed Mama and Aunt Cecilia good-bye and went to find my friends.

CHAPTER 9

The heart sees farther than the head.
—Italian proverb

Ada, Thea, Maria, and I tromped out of Hull House together, each of us weighed down by several packages of pottery to be delivered. It was a chilly night, with no stars in the sky. The cold, crisp air smelled like snowflakes. There was a sleek black touring car that I recognized as Mrs. Storrow's parked outside. A man in a navy-blue driving coat was standing in front of it.

"Ladies!" the man said, smiling and tipping his driver's hat to reveal a shiny pink bald head. "Are you my charges for the evening?" He hurried around and opened the car's door.

"Yes, you must be Edward," I said, placing my load of parcels into the car and reaching out to shake his hand. I introduced my friends as they handed their packages to him.

I had seen Mrs. Storrow's car before but had never gotten a close look at her driver until now. Edward had very large apple-red cheeks and big fleshy lips. His blue eyes almost disappeared when he smiled. I imagined that if he had a long white beard he might look a little bit like Santa Claus.

Edward helped us when we went back inside, grabbing the remaining packages and loading them into the front seat with him.

"Edward, Mrs. Storrow told me to tell you we have a total of fifteen stops to make," I said, pulling the list of names and addresses out of my coat pocket. "She wants us to try to get them all done before ten."

Edward nodded and opened the car door for us. I climbed in first and sank into a well-cushioned backseat upholstered in black leather.

"I could get used to this," said Maria with a smile, her eyes taking in the car's interior. "We could fit five more people in here."

"This is the life!" said Ada, taking off her hat.

"Here are some flasks filled with hot chocolate and some bags of fudge and peppermint candies that Mrs. Storrow left for you," Edward said, handing them back to us.

"How sweet!" said Thea, popping a peppermint into her mouth.

"Caprice, we'll start with the addresses on Commonwealth Avenue first, okay?" Edward asked from the driver's seat.

"Yes, please, Edward," I answered. "I'm sure you know the streets of Boston in a car much better than I do."

"So, Ada, how did your final exams go?" Maria asked. "I'm so glad we're doing this. I feel like I've barely talked to any of you for weeks."

"I got two As," said Ada with a smile. "My mother, as you know, has been unsure about these classes—but she was so happy when I told her. She kept saying, '*My* daughter, in *college*. Getting *As* in *college*.' I've already signed up for two more classes for next semester—organic chemistry and an anatomy and physiology course."

"And has Dominic been promptly escorting you from the streetcar?" I asked.

"Oh, yes," Ada said with a nod. "Dominic's escorted me every time except once when he had to work late. He said he's going to do it next semester too—you know, so my mother won't have to worry. He said most of the time it doesn't interfere with his work schedule at all. He makes me laugh; he's so funny, Caprice. I had forgotten how funny he was . . ."

She stopped midsentence and looked around at us, catching herself before she said anything more. Ada was not one to gush about anything.

Jesus, Mary, and Joseph. My cousin. Ada was gushing about my Italian, Catholic cousin. I opened my mouth to question this when she continued talking.

"Thea, tonight my mother told me your family is celebrating the first night of Hanukkah with the Robinowitz family." Ada leaned over the seat to look across at Thea, deftly changing the subject. "Why on earth would you be celebrating with them? Your family barely knows them."

"Who are they?" I asked, making a note to ask Ada about Dominic. But I was curious as to why Thea's face now looked deep scarlet even in the dim light of the backseat. "I've never heard you mention them before."

"Um . . . yes, we're celebrating with the Robinowitz family," said Thea, looking out the window before turning back to all of us. "Of course, my mother *would* mention that to you, Ada. We've been spending some time with them lately. They have all boys, older than us. The youngest boy is twenty-three, and he is . . . uh . . . he is . . . well, he's . . . he's my new fiancé."

There was a moment of stunned silence as Maria, Ada, and I all took in this monumental news.

"Thea!" Maria yelled, breaking the hush. She wrapped her arms around Thea. "We didn't even know you were going with anyone. And what's his first name for goodness sake?"

"What a surprise! I can't believe it—this is such big news. Wow, congratulations, Thea!" I said, leaning in from across the car to kiss her on the cheek. "That's so exciting—please, tell us the whole story."

"Well, it was finalized last night," said Thea, clearly relieved at our reaction. I turned to look at Ada. She had offered no congratulations and just stared out the window, pulling at one of her braids.

"It's a *shidduch*, an arranged marriage," Thea continued, biting her nail as she glanced at Ada. "I went to a *shadchanit* . . . with my parents. The *shadchanit* arranged the match, and the families agreed on it this week. I've only met him a few times . . . the fourth time was last night. His name is Joshua."

"Mrs. Joshua Robinowitz," I said, grabbing Thea's hand. "Thea, you're going to be someone's *wife*."

"The wife of somebody she doesn't even *know*," said Ada in an exasperated tone, looking at Maria and I like we were crazy to be congratulating Thea. "Someone she has barely talked to *ever!*"

"Ada . . . ," said Thea in a quiet voice. "I just . . . well, I'm not surprised that you're upset."

"First stop on Commonwealth Avenue, Caprice. The Louis residence," Edward announced, interrupting the tense moment.

"Ada, will you help me with this order?" I asked, frowning at her. The two of us got out of the backseat into the flurry of snowflakes that had started to fall.

"What's wrong with you?" I said to her in a whisper as I closed the car door. "This should be a night for *celebrating*. Thea just got engaged— the first one of us. I can't believe you would react like this."

We walked up to the front door of a four-story brownstone. There was an enormous Christmas tree in the bowed front window on the first floor. The snowflakes stuck to my eyelashes, and I wanted to pull my wool turban hat down, but I was afraid I would drop the packages in the process.

"Caprice, I just don't understand it," said Ada, squinting to keep the snow from getting into her eyes. "She finally has a new job that Mrs. Storrow helped her find. She loves working at the interior designer's—she even has a *talent* for it—and she's no longer sitting at that horrible factory. Why in the world would she agree to marry a stranger? It's so . . . so foolish and old fashioned. Using a *shadchanit*—we might as well be back in Russia."

"Ada, it's not fair to judge her too harshly," I said. "Of course, I'm surprised too, and no, it wouldn't be my choice, but it's done. And just because she's getting married doesn't mean she's going to give up her new job. Listen, we're in this beautiful car driving through the streets of Boston. Let's just enjoy being together and try to be happy for her."

Ada's dark eyes were glistening in the light of the front entrance, and I wasn't sure if it was snow or tears. "I just want more for her in life than this," she said with a sigh. "I want *her* to want more for herself."

A butler answered the door of the brownstone, gave us a polite greeting, and took the packages.

As we walked back down to the car, I grabbed Ada by the arm and said, "Ada, just because you or I wouldn't choose it for ourselves doesn't mean we should judge her for it. Now please, *please,* don't ruin this night for Thea. Don't ruin this night for us either. The four of us have so few precious times together like this."

Ada stuffed her hands in her coat pockets, pausing before we got into the car.

"Okay, okay," she said, "now you're making me feel bad. Let me talk to her before we go to the next house. I will try to be more charitable about this—but it's hard for me to accept."

"Thank you," I said, giving her a hug as Edward opened the car door for us. I climbed in, but Ada lingered back.

"Thea, could you please come out here for a moment?" Ada asked.

Thea stepped out of the car. I climbed in with Maria, telling Edward that they just needed a minute to talk. He just nodded, a glimmer of amusement on his face.

"Did you say something to Ada?" Maria asked me before taking a bite of fudge.

"Yes, I think she's calmed down a bit," I answered.

"I understand how Ada feels," Maria said. "But I understand Thea's decision too. Now I wouldn't agree to something like an arranged marriage in a million years. But Thea is . . . well, she's Thea.

I think she feels like she doesn't have many choices."

"Maria, she has as many choices as any of us!" I said. "She just doesn't have the confidence in herself to see that."

"Caprice, I *agree* with you," Maria said. "That's why I said she *feels* like she doesn't have many choices."

"Oh, sorry, I misunderstood," I answered, taking off my hat to shake off some of the dampness. There was still tension between the two of us after our conversation about Mark.

"It's okay," she answered. "So what kind of hat are you working on right now? At work the other day, I was looking at some dress designs in a stylebook from New York City. Some of the new hats are really smart looking."

"You know, I have many hats that I want to work on right now—that I've been dreaming about. I just haven't had any time at all with the pottery shop," I said, thinking about the many nights I'd stayed up planning for my hat shop. "All I've been doing lately is scribbling down designs on scraps of paper and keeping them in a little tin box beneath my bed. And I've barely saved a penny yet." It hurt my pride to admit that. There had been too many expenses to help my family with, despite paying board and having some money that was supposed to be my own.

Ada and Thea opened the door and climbed

in, looking much more relaxed than they had minutes earlier.

"Okay, ladies, two more stops on Commonwealth Avenue, and then we'll head over to Boylston Street," Edward announced from the front seat.

"Thank you, Edward," I answered.

"Everybody grab a flask," Maria said, passing out the remaining hot chocolate. "I want to propose a toast."

We all raised our flasks.

"Congratulations to our beautiful, freckle-faced Thea on her engagement." Maria smiled at Thea and, with her usual dramatic flourish, added, "Just think, the first of us to become a married woman. We love you dearly. *Per cent'anni*! May you have love and happiness for a hundred years."

"Per cent'anni!" we all said in return, taking sips of hot chocolate.

"Mazel tov," added Ada with a small smile. Her eyes were tinged with a bit of sadness, but she toasted anyway.

"Mazel tov!" Maria and I said in unison.

"Thank you all so much," Thea said. "I know you may not understand my decision," she said, looking pointedly at Ada. "I know it's old fashioned, but I can't explain it; it feels like the right thing for me to do."

She took a sip of hot cocoa, as if for courage.

"And you have to understand, it's a way to get out of the house. My father—do you know what he says in his morning prayers? He says, *'Thank you, God, that I'm not a woman.'* I hear that every single morning of my life. What is so terribly wrong with being a woman?" Thea shook her head. "And my mother—my *mother,*" she said, throwing up her free hand. "She's either complaining to me or insulting me." Thea frowned and imitated her mother's thick Russian accent, " *'Theodosia, you don't help me clean the house enough. Theodosia, you did not fold this laundry properly. Theodosia, why are you so fat?'* She would never agree to let me take college classes like your mother, Ada. My mother would never defend me against my father—for *anything.*"

Thea looked out the window at the night sky before continuing.

"And as I told Ada outside, I'm still going to keep this new interior decorating job. I love it so far, and besides, there's no way I'm just staying home, having babies right away and being miserable like Bessie. But . . . I need to get out of my house," she said in a soft voice, biting her thumbnail again. "And this is a way I can do it. And Joshua Robinowitz is a decent, hardworking young man from a good family. Now, I don't love him . . . of course I don't. You're right, Ada— I still barely know him. But I need to do this for myself. I see it as the only way I can escape."

"Oh, Thea, trust me when I say I completely understand," said Maria, patting her hand. "Frankly, if I had a way out of my house, I would take it. I hate my father."

Ada, Thea, and I stopped sipping and eating and looked at her, silent.

"There. I said it. I. *Hate.* My. Father," Maria said, a resigned expression on her face as she looked around at all of us. "I must say it feels good to finally admit that. He's horrid, although I know you're all aware of that. He spends most of his money on booze and . . . Lord knows what else, instead of his family. He comes home almost every night so drunk he can hardly stand. If he *can* stand, he's usually screaming at us or the wall . . . or no one. Or vomiting on our floor. Or finally passing out under the kitchen table.

"I can't tell you how many times I've comforted Antonetta in the middle of the night. How many times Richie has had to carry him to his bed. And my mother just puts up with it. So I don't blame you, Thea. Someday I will find a way out of my house, a way to escape my father for good."

She pursed her lips and took another swig of hot cocoa, and her hand was shaking. But then she took a deep breath and added, "But, Thea—I apologize. This is about celebrating your good news." Maria's eyes were shiny with tears. "I don't know what came over me. Just being with

145

all of you, and Thea, everything you were saying . . . I'm so sorry. I don't want to ruin this night for you."

"Don't be silly; you haven't ruined anything," said Thea, hugging Maria. "It's good for you to talk about it. It's a relief to hear you talk about it. We all know the strain your father puts on you at times." Ada and I nodded in agreement.

"Well, thank you all for listening, but for the rest of the night, let's just try to enjoy ourselves, okay?" Maria said, and we all agreed and finished eating our delicious sweets.

The next hour of deliveries went quickly, and the four of us took turns getting out of the car and carrying the packages to the doors. And what doors, to the most gorgeous homes. Ornate wooden doors with shiny brass knockers, covered with enormous Christmas wreaths with red velvet and satin bows. From the front hallways I saw the oriental rugs on the shining hardwood floors and the enormous crystal chandeliers. The imposing staircases with Christmas garland wrapped all the way up their banisters. It was a glimpse into another world, one that I didn't give much thought to in my day-to-day life on the streets of *my* Boston.

Thea and I climbed back into the car after the last delivery on Beacon Street, and Maria started leading all of us—even Thea and Ada—in singing "God Rest Ye Merry, Gentlemen" at the top of our lungs. Edward glanced back at us, shaking his head and smiling at us with those big red Santa Claus cheeks.

"*Oy vey*!" said Ada, giggling. "Thea, if our fathers heard us right now!"

"Last delivery stop, ladies!" Edward said from the front seat. "I'm bringing you home after this one."

"Come on," I said, grabbing Maria by the arm. "Let's all deliver these last few packages together."

We all ran out into the snowy night, like the children we were when we first met so many years ago. And just for a moment I felt like we were that young again as we giggled and slipped up the walkway to the last brownstone, trying to catch the snowflakes on our tongues.

But the reality was that one of us was getting married. It was a turning point—a change in the order of things—that made me uncomfortable and a little bit sad. I suddenly realized that was the other reason Ada was so upset tonight. Thea—*our Thea*—was going to be married. And she wouldn't ever be our Thea in quite the same way again. Thea's revelation tonight was a reminder that any semblance of our childhood was melting away, as quickly as the snowflakes hitting the cobblestones.

CHAPTER 10

People make plans and God laughs.
—Jewish proverb

Saturday, January 2, 1909

I barely saw Ada, Thea, and Maria in the
weeks following our night of deliveries in Mrs.
Storrow's car. The pottery shop was, thankfully,
bustling with holiday shoppers, and I had ended
up working until six or seven o'clock most
nights. Christmas Day was a brief but welcome
respite from work. Christmas morning we went
to Mass at St. Leonard's and had dinner later that
day at Aunt Cecilia and Uncle Arthur's tenement,
crowded into their little apartment. Even
Dominic's brothers and their wives were there.
The following day it was back to work, taking
orders and doing inventory at the pottery shop
and trying to catch up with all the little chores
that I had fallen behind on during the holiday
rush.

Miss Guerrier had been kind enough to give
everyone at the pottery shop New Year's Day and
the day after off, saying we had earned it after
a tough holiday season. And the S.E.G. meeting
was also canceled because so many of us wanted

to go to the New Year's dance down at the church hall on Saturday night. It was always held the first Saturday of the new year.

"Caprice, do you want any of this *torrone*? Vita is about to eat what's left of it!" Fabbia yelled to me from the kitchen. I was in our room trying to finish putting up my hair in a chignon, but it was not cooperating. I settled for a braid and walked into the kitchen.

"No thank you," I said. Fabbia and Vita were sitting at the kitchen table eating candy. They were both in their nightgowns, freshly scrubbed from their weekly baths in the metal tub we always set up in the sitting room.

"Oh, you look so pretty, Caprice," Vita mumbled through a cheek full of *torrone*. She swallowed before adding, "I wish we could go to the New Year's dance with you." Her long brown hair was tucked behind her ears and hanging down her back, making her appear even younger than her twelve years.

"In a few years, Vita; *pazienza*. Be patient," I said, giving her a kiss on the head before grabbing my coat near the door. "Are you two going to be okay until Mama and Papa get back from visiting their friends?"

Fabbia nodded and rolled her eyes at me. "Of course we are. I'm not *that* much younger than you, you know."

"I know, I know," I answered, giving her

a kiss on the head too. "Good night, my sweet sisters. I've got to hurry; I'm sure my friends are downstairs waiting for me."

They both called good night to me as I headed out the door and down the stairs. I nodded and exchanged greetings with various neighbors sitting in the hallways, gossiping with each other and enjoying leftover New Year's treats of candy or cookies.

I rushed out the door, and Ada, Thea, and Maria were there waiting for me on the steps, standing close together for warmth and chatting and laughing.

"*Felice Anno Nuovo*," said Maria when she saw me, her breath showing under the streetlamp. "Just so you know, I told my mother Frankie was escorting us to the dance tonight."

"I told my parents the same, but he already left with Dominic," I answered. "And happy New Year to all of you," I said, giving them each a kiss on the cheek. "I've missed you."

We started walking quickly down Charter Street, and I noticed that Thea had taken off one of her gloves and was chewing on her nails.

"Thea, I nearly forgot tonight is the night we meet Joshua Robinowitz," I said. "I can't wait."

We turned the corner onto Hanover Street, and I could already hear the music coming from the hall at St. Leonard's Church.

"Do you think Joshua's here already?" Maria

asked, pinching her cheeks, as if they weren't already perfectly rosy.

"Yes, he should be," Thea said, nodding and finally taking her fingers out of her mouth. "He was going with a couple of friends. He may not talk much; he's a bit shy until you get to know him. He's a watchmaker, so you know, they're sort of the quiet type. He's very nice to me though—and he's very polite."

"He's a really nice young man," added Ada, knowing that Thea was trying to make excuses for him. "My whole family adores him already." Thea gave Ada a grateful smile.

"Mark is going to be here too," said Maria. "He has a couple of friends who are quite handsome, Caprice."

I ignored this comment as we walked up the steps to the hall. I wasn't interested in meeting any friend of Mark. I wished Maria would stop feeling like she owed him and get bored of him already.

We walked through the doors of St. Leonard's hall to the sounds of the band playing a rather clumsy version of "Peacherine Rag." I was blinded for a minute as my eyes made the adjustment from dark streets to the bright lights and colors of the dance hall. We were late, so it was already packed. The air inside was warm and humid, and it smelled like sweat and peppermint candy and too much cheap perfume.

We gave our tickets to a dark-haired boy sitting on a stool just inside the door and went down a narrow corridor to check our coats and hats. As we entered the main hall, Thea was holding her hands together tightly in a desperate attempt not to chew her nails. Maria had already taken on a bored and unaffected look, as if she were above these silly neighborhood dances.

Ada was standing on her tiptoes, scanning the crowd, I assumed, for Joshua and his friends.

"Do you see him?" I yelled directly into Ada's ear so she could hear me above the music. She looked radiant tonight, like a little porcelain doll. A red satin ribbon tied two small braids together at the back of her head while the rest of her silky black hair cascaded down her back. She was wearing a stylish new dress her mother had just made her for Sabbath. It was a black-and-white satin print with a lace yoke. A crushed girdle of material that accented her tiny waist joined the bodice and skirt.

"No, I can't find him," she answered back in my ear, still looking around the hall distractedly. "He said he was coming with Frankie and some of the other guys."

"What?" I asked, giving her a quizzical look until I realized who she was talking about. "Oh, oh God. You're looking for Dominic, aren't you? Ada, what's going on?"

Ada looked at me, and her face turned a deep

crimson. She was about to answer when Thea grabbed my arm.

"I see him," she said, her face flushed with nervous excitement. "He's over there in the corner." She took a deep breath and added, "Come on, ladies. Time to meet my soon-to-be husband."

She pulled me along, and Ada and Maria followed behind us. As we headed toward the far corner of the dance hall, I spotted three young men sipping punch and laughing with each other. One of them was short with thick, curly brown hair and a rather large pointy nose. The other two were average height, but one was a little bit heavyset and had straight black hair and glasses while the other had reddish-blond hair and a long face. I tried to guess which one was Joshua Robinowitz.

The heavyset young man with the dark hair and glasses spotted us first, and his face lit up. He smiled and waved.

"Hello," he greeted Thea, leaning down to give her an awkward kiss on the cheek that ended up on her ear. "Glad you made it."

"Yes, me too," said Thea, a little breathless as she nodded her head up and down about ten times. "Let me introduce you to two of my friends you haven't met yet, Joshua. This is Caprice Russo and Maria Santucci."

"So nice to meet you both," Joshua said,

smiling warmly and shaking both our hands before turning to Ada. "And Ada—good to see you, as always. Ladies, this is David and Marc, two friends I've known since elementary school."

We shook hands with the young men. David, the shorter one with the big nose, could not take his eyes off of Ada. Ada didn't notice because she was still distracted, stealing glances around the dance hall for my very Italian, very Catholic cousin. *Jesus, Mary, and Joseph.*

The four of us talked with Joshua and his friends for a while. Joshua was very attentive, not just to Thea but to all of us. Ada was right. He was very nice.

"Caprice, there's Frankie and Dominic with some other guys. Do you want to go say hi?" Ada asked.

"Yes, I think I'd better," I answered, giving her a pointed look. "They're supposed to walk us home."

Ada and I excused ourselves from the group, but not before David could say something about hoping to see Ada at Shabbat next week. She didn't even hear him.

"Okay, Ada," I said, grabbing her elbow as we walked across the dance floor. I tried to speak above the band's mediocre rendition of another ragtime song. "What is going on with you and my cousin?"

"I don't know, Caprice," she answered. She

was walking faster than I was and seemed giddy. "For the first time in my life, I don't know what the heck I'm doing!"

I wanted to say more, but we were only a few feet away from the guys. Dominic looked up and spotted Ada. The smoldering look in his eyes as he saw her told me all I needed to know. I looked down at Ada, and she couldn't take her eyes off of him either. It was like no one else in the room mattered to either of them. And neither of them could even pretend to hide it.

Frankie was standing next to Dominic, and he looked at me with raised eyebrows as we watched the two of them quietly walk away to a corner of the room so they could talk alone. The other guys were too busy trying to flirt with some girls across the dance floor to notice what had just happened.

"Frankie, what in God's name is going on?" I asked.

"Caprice, you aren't really surprised, are you?" he said with a snort, lighting a cigarette and shaking his head. "Ever since he started walking her from the streetcar so she can go to her fancy college classes, he hasn't stopped talking about her."

He took a drag of his cigarette and continued, " *'Ada is the smartest girl I've ever met. Ada is so little and so beautiful! She has the most gorgeous hair and big black eyes . . .'* Ada, Ada, Ada! He's crazy about her, Caprice. Absolutely crazy about her."

"But, Frankie—this is impossible," I said, exasperated at the thought of what might happen. "Her parents would never, ever allow it! Oh, God, think of what her father would do! And Uncle Arthur and Aunt Cecilia—well, it's a disaster! What do you think is going to happen? What should we do?"

Frankie just shrugged and took another pull of his cigarette, running his fingers through his thick hair and scanning the room.

"Caprice," he said, "I don't know what's going to happen, but it's too late for us to do anything anyway. I think they're both off their rockers. But now that you finally understand what's going on—I wouldn't breathe a word of it to anyone, especially to Fabbia or Vita. They have big mouths, and we don't want the family finding out. I think we should just stay out of it."

He dropped his cigarette and stubbed it out with his foot. "Now, I'm going over there to ask that pretty girl in the red plaid dress to dance before I lose my chance. I'll meet you out front later to walk home."

A slow song came on, and I saw Joshua and Thea walk onto the dance floor. They seemed surprisingly at ease with each other. Thea's eyes were shining, and her cheeks were flushed. She looked . . . happy.

I spotted Maria in the corner talking to none other than Mark and a couple of his *compaesani*. Mark was standing next to Maria, looking at her like she was a shiny trophy. I knew I should go over, but I just couldn't stomach listening to that *cafone* right now.

I saw Ada and Dominic dancing in the corner of the room. Dominic had taken extra care with his appearance. His curly hair had an extra shine to it, and he was wearing the crisp white shirt and black wool pants he wears to Sunday Mass. He towered over little Ada, gently putting his hand on her small waist and whispering something in her ear that made her laugh. I wanted to be happy for them, I *wished* I could be happy for them, but instead I felt ill thinking about what would happen if our families discovered their romance.

"Good evening," a deep voice said into my ear. I nearly jumped, and whirled around to see Sal Valenti standing there, grinning broadly.

"Oh!" I said, looking up at his face a foot above mine. "You startled me. Hi . . . I . . . um, I didn't know you were here."

"May I have this dance, Miss Russo?" He did a little bow and held out his hand, and I had to laugh at his formality.

"Yes, Mr. Valenti, you may," I answered in a tone every bit as overly dramatic as his. I reached out and put my hand in his, and he led me out to the dance floor, putting one arm around my waist and holding my hand with the other.

As we started dancing, I noticed how nice Sal smelled, not like the sawdust from his shop floor. Tonight he smelled like sea salt and pinecones. I felt a warmth in my chest that rose up to my cheeks. We danced in comfortable silence for a while.

I kept trying to remind myself about all the stories. About Louisa and Francesca and God knew what other girls. But I didn't want to. I just wanted to enjoy dancing in his arms for the moment.

I saw Maria walk onto the dance floor with Mark. They faced each other, and he put one of his little sausage hands on the small of her back. She was smiling at him, but not in the way Ada smiled at Dominic. More the way Maria smiled when she was on stage acting a part.

"Your friend Maria . . . she's been spending some time with Mark Toscanini," Sal said quietly in my ear, and I knew I must have had a look of distaste on my face as I watched them.

"Yes," I said with a sigh. "She has."

"You don't like him," Sal noted.

"How do you know I don't like him?" I answered, giving him a sly grin.

"Oh, Caprice Russo, you're not very good at hiding how you feel," he said with a quiet laugh.

"No, I suppose you're right about that. I just . . .

well, I know what my father has said about the family . . . the other things I've heard. I just don't trust him."

"Your father is right. You shouldn't trust him. And neither should Maria," Sal said with some urgency in his voice.

"What have you heard, Sal? What do you know?" I asked, looking up at him with a frown. I felt his arm pull me a little tighter, and it made me catch my breath.

"Probably what you've already heard. That it's a well-known secret that their factory is just a cover for businesses that are not so sweet. A cover for the *Cosa Nostra*, for their *other* ventures—prostitution, gambling . . . worse than that even."

"Worse than that?" I said, feeling my stomach turn while looking at Maria, who was laughing at something Mark was whispering into her ear. "I've heard about the gambling, the rumors about other . . . er, activities. You've confirmed my worst fears."

"I know he has money—his family does—but he's no good. The family is no good," Sal said. "You need to talk to her. She deserves better."

"She really does. Thank you; yes, I will talk to her. I've been trying to talk to her," I answered, thinking about my last conversation with her about Mark and how it had ended. I sighed. "But it's not easy. Maria can be stubborn. She doesn't like to be told what to do."

We danced quietly for a few minutes longer, both of us seemingly lost in thought.

"You know, you haven't come by my shop lately." He said this directly into my ear so I could hear him above the music. I felt his warm breath on my cheek, and it made me feel a bit lightheaded. He continued. "Are things very busy at the pottery shop? So busy you have to send your sisters to see me instead?"

"Yes, we really have been very busy," I answered with a nod. I couldn't help but feel flattered that he had been looking for me. "And I'm trying to work extra hours when I can, because I'm trying to save up some money. When I work past seven o'clock in the evening for more than two nights, Miss Guerrier tacks on another dollar to my pay at the end of the week."

"Save up for what?" he asked, looking down at me with curiosity. "Some more of those pretty hats that you like to wear?"

I paused, wondering if I should tell him. Why not? He was a business owner; he would probably understand why I would want a shop of my own.

"Well . . ." I took a deep breath before looking up at him and said, "I want to open my own millinery—my own hat shop—here, in the North End. I worked for years at Madame DuPont's Millinery, and I'm quite skilled. I understand the business very well. I could go back and work for someone else, but . . . as you can probably understand, I want to work for myself. I'm working at the pottery shop until I can save up enough money to open my own shop."

Sal pulled his head back and looked at me intently. "Is this something you're sure you want to do?" he asked. "A woman owning a business—it's very difficult, you know. Wouldn't it be easier to go work for another Madame Duponi or whatever her name is? On Temple Place or Washington Street—you know, where all those fashionable shops are?"

"No, no, it wouldn't," I said, trying to control my voice. "Madame DuPont's was not a pleasant place to work. The other shop girls, Madame DuPont herself—I dreaded going to work there every day. I want to be my own boss. I want my sisters to work for me—I want to make my own way."

"Yes, but it's really hard work, having your own business—trust me, I know," he answered, frustration in his voice. "You don't want to be one of those spinster shop owners, do you? Don't you want to be married someday? Have a family?"

Echoes of conversations with my father and my uncle. How could I ever expect any man to understand? I immediately regretted telling him anything. Why was I even dancing with Sal Valenti anyway? What was the point? I didn't want to be his next "conquest."

"I am *not* going to be a spinster shop owner!"

162

I said, my voice growing loud enough that the couple dancing next to us glanced over. "Just because I have ambition does not mean I don't want to be married and have a family. This is America! It is *not* Sicily. It is *not* Avellino. I want to have a shop *and* a family—why should I have to choose one or the other?"

Sal opened his mouth and started to say something but immediately closed it. We danced in awkward silence for the rest of the song. I didn't have anything more to say to him. I felt ridiculous for thinking he would ever understand me.

Just before the music ended, he pulled me closer to him for a few brief seconds. I breathed in his scent, and despite my anger, I found myself wanting to stay in his embrace for a moment longer. Instead I pulled away and dropped my arms to my sides.

"Thank you for the dance. I have to go find my friends now. *Felice Anno Nuovo*," I said, my voice quiet again. I didn't even look up at him before I turned on my heel to go. I scanned the room, but the only one I saw was Maria, who was unfortunately still with Mark and one of his friends. Not seeing any other options, I walked over to them. Mark was very animated, telling a story, his beady eyes bright with laughter. I heard what he was saying as I got closer.

"So I had to completely Jew the guy down,"

he said with a guffaw. "He thought he could pull one over on me, but I Jewed him down ten dollars on the price of the rug. Those Yids are so cheap it's unbelievable. They think they can sell you anything for twice the—oh, hello, Caprice," Mark said, the first to notice me walk over.

"Uh . . . hi, Mark, how are you?" I said, burning with anger that he was disparaging Jews. This man was an ignorant pig.

"Oh, Caprice, I didn't even see you," said Maria. She crossed her arms, and her face turned red. I looked right into her eyes and tried to communicate that I had heard every word Mark had just said. She pressed on. "Uh . . . I saw you dancing with Sal. How is he?"

"He's fine, he's just fine," I said, hoping the disappointment in my voice was not too obvious.

"Caprice, we were just talking about how cheap some of these Jewish store owners are around here. Don't you find that?" asked Mark, amusement curling his lips. I looked back at him with a loathing that I couldn't hide. Maybe I should have been intimidated by what he was, by the type of associates he had, but I wasn't. All I could think about was his nasty words about Jews and how I could best get Maria as far away from him as possible.

"No, Mark, I've never noticed that in my entire life. How could you even say such an ignorant thing?" I answered. "I find them to be very fair.

Maria and I have a couple of Jewish friends whose fathers are store owners, and we've always found them fair, haven't we, *Maria?*" I looked at her pointedly, trying to control my anger but feeling my jaw get tighter.

Maria nodded vigorously, her rosy cheeks growing pinker. "Yes, Mark. Really, I haven't found that either. Maybe that rug merchant was just having a bad day?"

"Nah, everyone knows the Jews are so cheap, you gotta Jew them down for everything," said the burly, dark-haired young man standing next to Mark. I'd seen him with Mark before, but this was the first time I'd ever heard him speak.

"Oh, Caprice—this is Rocco, a *collega* of mine," Mark said. "He works at the chocolate factory with me."

"Nice to meet ya, Caprice," said Rocco with a nod. I noticed he had an angry scar above his right eye. He didn't even reach out to shake my hand, and I didn't offer mine. "Maria's told me a lot about you. She's right; you do have very pretty red hair," he said, looking me up and down like I was a piece of meat. I noticed his eyes settled on my chest for a few seconds longer than they should.

"It's auburn. And I've had enough of this conversation. Two of our best friends are Jewish, and it disgusts me to listen to this nonsense," I answered. "Maria, they're your best friends too!

I'm surprised you can listen to this and not be as offended as I am. I'm going to find Frankie. I'll meet you out in front of the hall at the end of the dance, okay?"

"Caprice—I—wait . . . ," she said, pleading with her eyes for me to stay. But I had heard enough, and just being in such close proximity to Mark was making me feel sick.

"Always a pleasure, *Mark,*" I said, trying to control the sarcasm in my voice.

I knew it hadn't been lost on him when he answered, "Oh, yes, *always* so nice to see you, Caprice."

The dance hall was packed with people now, and I didn't see Thea and her beau or Ada and Dominic anywhere. So I spent the rest of the evening trying not to think about what I was going to say to Maria or when I was going to see Sal again or what was going to happen with Dominic and Ada. I sat in the corner, laughing and joking with Albina Mangini, Katy Abrams, and some of the other gals from the S.E.G. A few times, despite myself, I searched the room to see if Sal was still at the dance. But there was no sign of him anywhere.

At the end of the night I waited on the steps out front for Maria as the crowds flowed out of the hall.

"Hey." She snuck up behind me and tapped me on the shoulder.

"Ready to go?" I answered, my voice flat. "Frankie is still talking to that girl in the red plaid dress, so I told him we'd be fine without him."

"Yes, I'm ready," she said as we started walking toward Charter Street. "Mark and Rocco could've walked us, but they had some business to attend to tonight at the factory."

I frowned at her. "Oh, too bad, I really wanted to hear them insult Jewish people some more."

"Caprice . . . I—" Maria started, but I held up my hand to stop her.

"Maria, what is wrong with you? Normally you would never put up with any kind of talk like that from anyone. Why would you put up with it from them? What if Ada or Thea had heard that?"

"Caprice, you're right. I should have said something, but . . . I just didn't. That's the first time he's ever said something like that, I swear. I would have been horrified if they had heard," she said, looking genuinely ashamed.

"Of course you would have been!" I said. "And don't you find it strange that they have business at the factory tonight? Is there a chocolate emergency?"

"No, no emergency; don't be silly. Just work, a meeting." She waved her hand. "I don't know."

"You don't know, Maria, or you don't *want* to know?" I said, the icy-cold air making my breath glow white under the streetlamps as we walked.

"What do you mean, Caprice?" She stopped walking and looked at me.

"Maria, you know about the gambling, but you can't tell me you haven't heard all the other rumors about the Toscanini family," I answered, knowing full well that she had. "About where all their money comes from. Not just the gambling, but other criminal activities. About the prostitutes—the *prostitutes,* Maria!"

"Caprice, yes, they are involved a little bit in gambling, obviously, like many others in the North End," she said. "But that's it. Those other rumors, about prostitutes and whatever else you've heard, that's just nonsense. Those rumors come from people in this neighborhood, in this city, who are jealous of the Toscanini family's success. They're not true," she answered, crossing her arms in front of her chest, daring me to dispute it.

"Oh, really, Maria?" I answered. "I'm not so sure about that, and I bet you're not really so sure either. I think you need to maybe pay attention to what people—what most of the North End—is saying about the Toscaninis. Really, I have to ask you again, are you spending time with him to pay back the debt your father owes?"

"No, no, I'm not!" she said. "That gambling debt, we have almost paid it off, little by little. My stupid father got in over his head with Mark's father, and now my mother and I are helping to bail him out, like we can afford to. Mark is doing us an enormous favor by letting us pay it back over time. And look, he obviously worships and adores me, so I'm spending some time with him. He's not all bad; he's been very generous."

"He's not *all bad?*" I asked, not believing what I was hearing. "Maria, will you listen to what you're saying? Even if the other rumors aren't true, isn't the gambling and the . . . the *bigotry* bad enough? What are you doing? When are you going to see him for what he really is and stay far away from him?"

"Caprice! How dare you?" she lashed back at me. Anger was flashing in her eyes. "You don't even really *know* him! He's actually very good to me. Plus he's successful, ambitious, and smart."

"Maria, he parades you around like you're on display, like he *owns* you. Is that how you want to be treated? Really?" I started walking quickly because it was very cold and I was so frustrated at her. She caught my elbow, and we stopped at the bottom of Charter Street.

"Look, Caprice, I know that this," she said, pointing a finger to her beautiful face under the streetlamp, "*this* is my one card to play. Look at my mother—her beauty was wasted. I'm *not* going to make the same mistake. My mother fell head over heels in love with my father, a handsome man with big foolish dreams. Now he's a ditch digger and a drunk who spends too much of his paycheck on liquor and gambling instead of food for his family. I want the security my own family has *never* had. Don't judge me for this. I know your father makes you crazy sometimes, but your family is normal. You have no idea what—" Her voice started to choke with tears, but she kept talking.

"My mother stays up half the night working to make up the extra money with sewing that she takes in—and then every morning she's out in the cold with that awful pushcart," she continued. "She's aged a hundred years since she married him. That is not going to be me, Caprice. I am not going to end up like her!"

"It's not going to be you, Maria," I said, hooking arms with her so we could keep walking, because at that point I could feel the cold in my bones. Maria wiped some of the dampness off her cheeks as we walked.

"Of course it's not going to be you—you have to know that," I repeated, wondering how I was going to get through to her if this was how she really felt. "You *are* so beautiful, but that's far from your only card to play. You're smart, you have business savvy, you're an extremely gifted dressmaker—that's why you don't ever have to end up with someone like Mark Tosc—"

"Caprice, listen . . ." She paused, and I waited for her to finish, but instead she stopped walking and said, "Why are there so many people in front of our building?"

I could make out a crowd of people standing on the steps and around the doorway to our home. People leaned out windows on both sides of the street to try to see what was going on below.

The door of our building was wide open, and I saw two men, dressed in what looked like police uniforms, carrying a stretcher. Whoever was on the gurney was wrapped in white. Whoever was on the gurney wasn't alive.

"Oh, dear God, who is it?" I said, my voice shaking. *Please, no one in my family. Please. Please. Please.*

Maria and I broke into a run until we reached the edge of the gathering. Gasping for air, I frantically searched for my family and spotted my father. I grabbed Maria's hand and pulled her over to him.

"Papa, what happened? Who is it?" I said, jumping up and wrapping my arms around him, hugging him tighter than I had in a long time. He pulled back, and when he saw Maria, he put his arm around her.

"Maria," my father began, and the sorrow in his voice was all she needed to hear. She looked up at him, and her face blanched as she quickly turned and broke away from us. She shoved through anyone in her way, running up the front steps and through the door in a blur of motion.

CHAPTER 11

*Sympathy is a little medicine to soothe the
ache in another's heart.*
—Jewish proverb

Tuesday, January 5, 1909

The morning of Joseph Santucci's funeral was
an appropriately murky, overcast winter day. The
wind off the harbor was so bitter and icy it felt
like it was piercing my face. It was mourning
weather.

They said it was his heart, but the whole
neighborhood knew it was the whiskey that had
killed Maria's father. It was the most dreadful
way to start 1909. In the two days prior to the
funeral, Maria had been catatonic. She had not
done much more than hug Antonetta and drink
coffee. We hadn't been able to get her to eat.
Or talk. She had not even cried. While Maria's
mother and her father's sisters had been keening
for Joseph Santucci in the way only Italian
women could, Maria had remained emotionless.

My father and my uncle Arthur had taken up a
collection in the neighborhood to help Maria's
family with the funeral expenses. Before dawn on
Monday, someone had dropped off a substantial

donation at the Sicilian Club that had covered everything from the priest's fee for the Mass to the burial plot. The donor had wished to remain anonymous, but the description of the black touring car and bald driver who had dropped it off was very familiar to my friends and me.

As soon as the burial at the cemetery ended, Thea, Ada, and I hurried down the hill to the Sicilian Club to set up for the postfuneral reception.

"So do you think we'll finally be able to get her to talk? To let us help her somehow?" Ada asked.

"God, I hope so," I replied, shaking my head. "She's barely said two words since it happened."

"And I'm worried she's going to get sick; she isn't eating," said Thea, pulling on her brown mittens. "She is looking skinnier already."

"Maybe when we get there, we can put together a plate of her favorite things to eat," Ada said.

"Maybe," I said, pulling my wool coat tighter around me.

We all got quiet again, thinking about Maria and watching our steps on the cobblestones, trying to avoid the ones glazed with black ice.

"Caprice,"—Ada looked up and over at me—"I spotted Sal at the church. Did you see him?"

I nodded. I had seen him. And I didn't know what to say about it, so I just said, "Yes, *Dominic* was there too." I still needed to talk to her about what was going on with her and my cousin.

But before Ada could comment, Thea blurted out, "Well, I counted. Everyone came. All forty of the Saturday Evening Girls. And Miss Guerrier and Mrs. Storrow."

"Well, of course," said Ada. "Are you surprised?"

Thea shrugged. "I wasn't sure, it being a workday. But don't you feel proud to be a part of such a wonderful group of women? I felt quite proud seeing everyone there."

I had not counted, but I was sure Thea was right. I'd seen so many of the club members exiting the church. Fanny Goldstein, Gemma Ianelli, Naomi Goodman, Isolina Grasso, Katy Abrams—so many wonderful friends from the S.E.G. coming to support Maria. My eyes started to water, and I gulped the icy air.

"I felt the same way, Thea. Very proud," I said. "I saw your fiancé there too. It was very thoughtful of him."

Thea nodded. "Yes, it was. He's really very sweet."

"Of course that awful Mark was there," said Ada. "But I noticed he didn't sit anywhere near Maria's family in the church or stand with them at the cemetery. And it's strange—I thought he'd be at their home day and night, but he's been there, what, once?"

"Yes, and he only stayed for a few minutes," I said. "The best thing to come of this would be for

Maria to see Mark for what he is and stay away from him from now on."

"Yes, I think so too," said Ada. "But why *was* Maria spending any time with him at all? She has to have heard some of the rumors; everyone else has."

"Well, yes, she's well aware of them," I answered. I felt chills as I recalled my discussion with Maria just before we had seen her father being carried out of our building. "She's aware of them, but she chooses to ignore them. She's so terrified of ending up like her mother, maybe even more so now. Mark has money and property and stability—all the things her family doesn't have."

I repeated my conversation with Maria after the dance before adding, "I have no idea what she's thinking or feeling now, but I hope to God she gets rid of him."

"I don't know, Caprice," said Thea. "Maria can be so completely stubborn when she wants to be."

"Isn't that the truth," added Ada, just as we reached the entrance to the Sicilian Club.

We hurried through the doors to finally escape the cold and breathed a collective sigh at the warmth and coziness of the place. We were in a narrow entryway that opened to a hall about the size of the S.E.G. assembly room, with several lamps, but no natural light. There was a long wooden bar with half a dozen stools on one end and three doors leading to a kitchen and two smaller meeting rooms on the other. It had a musty smell, with hints of stale cigarette smoke and red wine. Above the bar hung two posters: one displayed the club's red-and-green fraternal symbol, and the other was an enormous map of Sicily.

"So *this* is what the Sicilian Club is like inside," I said.

"Ladies!" Miss Guerrier called to us as we walked into the main hall. "Leave your coats and hats over in the corner behind the bar. The coffee is almost ready. I'm sure you could all use some after standing in the freezing cold at that cemetery."

Miss Guerrier was in the process of putting cream-colored oilcloths on two long tables in the back of the room. She was dressed in the simple, well-worn pale-gray dress she nearly always wore, her reading glasses on a silver chain around her neck. It was comforting to have her here on such a sad occasion.

"Miss Guerrier, we didn't expect you here," I said to her after I had put my things aside. I gave her a long hug to show my appreciation. "Where do you think we should start?"

"Well, people have been dropping off every kind of food—breads and cheeses, pasta, desserts," she replied. "Mr. Buonopane, who let me in, has been putting them all in the kitchen. Ada, why don't you start getting them ready to serve? I already put the oven on in case you need to warm them up. Caprice, why don't you and Thea help me here, getting the small tables and chairs ready and setting out the refreshments and utensils for the buffet?"

Thea and I had grabbed a few of the folding chairs that were leaning up against the wall when I heard her whisper in my ear, "Caprice, I've been dying to ask you—has Ada said much to you about her and Dominic? What's going on?"

"Thea, I'm afraid to say this, but I think they're . . . well, I think they're really in *love,*" I whispered back. "I haven't had a chance to talk to either of them about it given all that's happened the past few days. It's crazy. Ada should know better. If her parents found out—"

"If her parents found out, it would be a *disaster,*" Thea interrupted me, still keeping her voice low as we arranged chairs around one of the small tables. "Her father . . . he doesn't even know she's taking classes. If he wouldn't approve of that, just imagine how he would feel about her going with an Italian guy. Not to offend Dominic—you know I love him—but he's not Jewish. Ada's father would lose his mind if he found out. Do you know how important it is that she marry a Jewish man?"

"Oh, trust me, Thea, I understand," I answered. "My aunt Cecilia and uncle Arthur feel the same way about Dominic marrying a Sicilian girl—not even just an *Italian* girl; it has to be a girl from *Sicily*. And Catholic, of course. They would be out of their minds if they found out."

Thea and I grabbed some of the black-and-white checkered oilcloths off the bar. She shook her head as I handed her one. "I don't understand it, really, Caprice. I don't know . . . I've never been in love. Do you think love just makes you insane and . . . *stupid?* Ada's so smart, but it's like something's gone wrong in her brain."

I started to laugh because Thea looked so perplexed as she chewed on one of her nails and arranged the tablecloth with the other hand. For a minute she looked like the freckle-faced little girl I had met seven years ago. It was hard to believe she would be a married woman soon. A married woman who had never been in love.

"I've never been in love either, Thea. But it does seem to make people act like complete fools sometimes."

"Well, shouldn't we do something?" said Thea. "This thing with the two of them is not going to end well."

Out of the corner of my eye, I saw a couple of people walking through the doors to the hall. "I'm not sure. I don't know if there's anything we can do. But I'll talk to her as soon as I can."

179

We finished setting up just as the rest of the funeral attendees began to arrive. Through the crowd I spotted Maria with her mother, Richie, and Antonetta, and I hurried over to them.

"Maria." I wrapped my arms around her in the tightest hug. I wished I could squeeze some of the grief right out of her. Maria gave me a weak smile as I helped her take off her coat. Thea was right; she looked like she had already lost weight, which was emphasized by a borrowed black silk dress that was at least a size too big. Her eyes were bloodshot and tired looking. Her beautiful blonde curls were pulled into a severe-looking bun that only highlighted how pale she was.

Her mother, Agnes, looked even worse than she did. Wearing an old black dress with frayed sleeves, her graying blonde hair stuck out under a black lace mantilla that had been used one too many times. With the deep lines etched in her face and the dark purplish rings under her eyes, Maria's mother could have been mistaken for her grandmother.

"Ada is putting together plates of food for you, of all of your favorite things. Are you hungry?" I asked, hoping they would say yes.

All I could see was the top of Antonetta's long brown braids as she stared at the ground. She had not looked up once. Maria's mother shook her head no. Only Richie, the new man of their house, offered up a small nod and said, "Thank you, Caprice. That would be nice."

I brought them over to the table and Ada took over, getting them refreshments as I went to put their coats away behind the bar.

"Caprice." My aunt Cecilia tapped me on the shoulder and gave me a kiss hello. "There's a delivery at the front door for you."

"For me?" I answered, frowning. "Are you sure?"

"Yes, they said it was for you; go get it." She dropped her voice to a whisper and nudged me toward the front entrance. "Before your father sees," she said, then continued in a normal tone. "I'm going to go sit with the Santuccis and try to get them to eat."

She walked away before I could ask why my father would care. I spotted my papa at the far end of the bar, talking with some of his *compaesani*, friends from the same village in Sicily.

When I walked into the front entry hall, I saw Sal carrying an enormous white cake box and two sacks. He nearly had to duck to keep his head from touching the ceiling of the tiny hallway. I felt my heart flutter and nearly cursed out loud. *Why did he do this to me?* I smelled sugar in the air around him.

"Let me guess, a delivery from your uncle, the baker?"

He nodded and smiled. "Yes, Miss Russo. Two

bags of almond cookies and biscotti and the biggest *cassata* you've ever seen."

"A *cassata*?" I asked. "But that's a Sicilian cake. Isn't your uncle from Avellino too?"

"Well, yes, of course," he said with that smile that made him look like an overgrown boy. "But we are from the same country, you know."

I gave him a small smile back, nodded, and took the sacks of cookies from him.

The doors to the main hall were now shut, so it was quiet by the entry. And we just stood there and looked at each other for a couple of seconds. I noticed again his light-brown eyes and long eyelashes, his enormous hands.

"Thank you for coming to the funeral," I said, looking down at my black shoes, my voice quiet. "That was very kind of you."

"Well, I know she's a good friend of yours," he said. He paused again for a couple of seconds before he said, "Caprice, can I say something about our conversation the other night? At the dance?"

I looked up into his eyes and caught my breath, not sure what he was going to say. Not sure I wanted to know. I thought about his reputation. I thought about my shop ambitions. I tried not to think about how much I wanted his hands to be holding mine right now.

"Are you going to give me some more reasons I should be looking for a husband instead of saving money for a hat shop?" The words came out bitterly, and I immediately wished I hadn't said them when I saw his hurt expression.

"No," he said, his tone bruised, his eyes cautious. "I was just going to say—" He paused, frowning, his cheeks rosy. "I was just going to say that, of course I think you can open your own shop. You can do anything you want to in life because . . . well, frankly, Caprice, you're unlike any girl . . . any *woman* I've ever met."

"Oh . . . well . . . ," I stuttered back, feeling redness creep up my face. "I'm sorry, I didn't mean to be rude when I said that before."

I wasn't sure how to respond to the other comment. *Unlike any woman I've ever met . . .* No one had ever said that to me. No one had ever said anything even close to that. But was this something he said to all the girls? To make them feel the way I felt right now?

He put the cake down, took the sacks of cookies from me, and set them aside. He then took my small hands in his and squeezed them. Was he reading my thoughts?

Sal started pulling me toward him, and I was so close I could smell the coffee on his breath. I could hardly believe he might kiss me. I couldn't believe I might let him. I caught my breath when all of a sudden the doors of the hall flew open and Maria ran past us sobbing and went out the front door of the club into the icy air. I then saw black braids flying as Ada hurried by us, followed by Thea.

"It's like it's all finally hit her, Caprice," Thea said as she ran past. "She just started sobbing and saying, 'Papa, Papa,' over and over, and then she ran out."

"Oh, God," I said to Sal, already moving toward the door myself. "Could you please bring the food in? I have to follow them."

"Yes, of course, go, go," he replied, a hint of disappointment in his voice. He reached out and touched my face, his eyes looking into mine in a way that made me want nothing more than to stay with him a bit longer, but I kept moving because I had to. And because I took it as a possible sign, a warning that my instincts about this young man were dead wrong and everything I had heard about him was right.

Just as I was about to leave, Mark busted into the entryway and was about to follow me out when I raised my hand up to stop him.

"No," I said to him, a little too forcefully. "No, Mark, she needs her friends right now, not you." She did need us. Who was he except someone who paraded her around like a trophy?

Mark's eyes were filled with rage, and he stepped forward almost as close to my face as Sal had been only seconds before. Except he looked like he wanted to slap me instead of kiss me.

"I just want to help her too, Caprice," said

Mark, his voice seething. "I just want to see if she's okay."

"Come in with me, Mark," Sal said, putting his hand on Mark's shoulder. "Caprice will go get Maria. I'll get you a drink." It sounded more like an order than a request, and I was surprised to see Mark's face change as he seemed to calm down. Perhaps he realized that if he screamed at me in the middle of a funeral reception, it would not be good for even his reputation.

"Okay, Valenti, I'll take you up on that offer," Mark said. "Bring her in right away, Caprice. It's cold out there."

I rolled my eyes when he turned his back.

"I will see you soon," Sal said as I walked backward out the door.

I gave him a grateful smile and mouthed, "Thank you."

I heard Maria crying and followed the sound to the alleyway next to the Sicilian Club. She was kneeling in the dirt, and her body was racked with sobs. Thea and Ada were crouched around her. Thea was rubbing her back. It was disgustingly filthy back here; the smells of urine and rancid garbage made me put my hand over my mouth.

"Maria, sweetheart, please, *please* get up," Ada said as I walked up to them. "You're going to get sick from the cold, and God knows what is on the ground back here."

"I don't care! I don't even care," sobbed Maria,

smearing her hand across her face to wipe away some of the tears, creating a brown streak of mud down her cheek. "Oh, God, it's like I wished this. All those things I said to you in Mrs. Storrow's car that night. It's like I wished for this to happen, and I *swear* I didn't!"

"Of course you didn't," said Thea, handing Maria a handkerchief. "We know you didn't."

"I know I said I hated him," she said, her voice shaky. "But I just hated him when he drank . . . I loved him . . . I *did* love him . . . he . . . Jesus Christ, I still can't believe this is real. I can't believe he's gone. It's like a never-ending nightmare. And my mother . . . and poor Richie and Antonetta . . . my God . . ."

She let out a long wail that was so forlorn, so heartbroken, my eyes welled up. If sadness had a sound, it would be Maria weeping for her dead father in the dirty alleyway. I glanced over to see tears streaming down Thea's cheeks already. Ada was blinking fast, her dark eyes cloudy like mine.

"Oh, Maria, I'm sorry. I'm so, so sorry," I said as I reached down to lock elbows with her. I motioned for the girls to help me pull her up. "But know that we all love you so much. We're here for you, to help you through this. Whatever you need."

"That's right, Maria," Ada added. "We'll *always* be here for you. Always."

We pulled Maria up, her slight frame still

shaking with small sobs she couldn't control. Ada and I were on one side of her and Thea was on the other as we started walking out of the alley, arms hooked around each other. We walked close together, trying to protect ourselves, and especially Maria, from the cold, but also trying to somehow protect her from the pain and sadness engulfing her. If only we could.

CHAPTER 12

It is better to live one day as a lion than a thousand years as a lamb.
—Italian proverb

Saturday, February 6, 1909

Holy Mary, mother of God, please bless my family.

Please bless Maria and her family during this time of grieving. And please help her see Mark Toscanini the way . . . the way the world sees him.

Please bless Ada and Dominic, so that they end their secret romance before their families—and the entire North End—find out.

Please bless Thea tonight, the night of her engagement party, as she prepares to marry a young man she barely knows.

And please, Holy Mother, please give me the strength and perseverance I need to open my own hat shop. Even though I'm a woman and an immigrant, I feel being a business owner is what I'm meant to do in life.

And, if you can, please help me understand my feelings for Sal . . .

Thank you for—

"Caprice, it's—what in the world are you doing on the floor on your knees? Oh, are you *praying?*" Fabbia had her hands on her hips, her head was tilted, and she was looking at me like I had lost my mind. I didn't blame her. I couldn't remember the last time I had prayed at our bedside. But in the past few weeks, life had become complicated. A couple of prayers to the Virgin Mary certainly couldn't hurt.

"Why are you praying right now?" Fabbia demanded as I got up off the floor. "What's the matter with you?"

"Nothing's the matter," I said, brushing off the front of my dress and quickly making the sign of the cross. "I just have a lot on my mind right now, Fabbia. I felt like praying about it. What were you going to say?" I asked, eager to change the subject.

"Papa's home; it's time for dinner," Fabbia said, and then, dropping her voice to a whisper, added, "You should see the gift he brought home for Mama. It's so . . . well, you just have to see it."

"Giuseppe, please!" I heard my mother say as we walked through the sitting room. "The oilcloth we had was perfectly adequate. We didn't need a new oilcloth. It's too . . . it's . . . it's too extravagant."

"But I bought it from a pushcart vendor at

Haymarket," said my father. "It was a great price."

I walked into our stuffy little kitchen. My father was standing with his back toward me.

I saw that our old red-and-white checked oilcloth, the one that matched the kitchen curtains my mother had made, was gone. In its place was a new oilcloth with an enormous picture of Christopher Columbus standing on a rock. Columbus had one hand on his hip, his hair was blowing, the ocean was behind him, and the sun was setting. It was the most ridiculous oilcloth I had ever seen.

"Caprice." My father turned around and held his hand out, motioning toward the new oilcloth. "Look at the gift I got your mother. She says I'm being extravagant, but I thought she deserved a special surprise."

I gave my mother an amused look as I kissed my father on the cheek. She glared back at me, warning me with her eyes.

"Yes, what a nice surprise, Papa! It's so, um . . . special," I said in Italian. I couldn't even look at him because it was an outright lie. No wonder he had gotten it for a bargain. Who else would buy an oilcloth of Christopher Columbus for their kitchen table but Giuseppe Russo?

"A portrait of one of the greatest Italians of all time," said my father. "You'll see, Caprice. Someday America will finally recognize him with a national holiday. Today, we will start with an oilcloth." And with that, he patted Christopher Columbus's shoe.

"And while I appreciate your papa getting it for me, I think we need the money more than we need a rather . . . uh . . . such a gift," my mother said. "For instance, Vita needs new shoes. Fabbia's old ones no longer fit her. They're really hurting her, aren't they, Vita?"

Vita nodded as she set the table, knowing my mother needed some support to get rid of the ugly oilcloth. "Yes, Papa, they're squeezing my toes."

"Well, Caprice can buy her new ones with her money," my father replied. "Caprice, be sure to get Vita some new shoes this month."

"Okay, Papa," I answered, letting out a sigh. There went the money I was going to save that week. And next week. It seemed like there was always some new expense I needed to help out with. If things kept going the way they had been, I'd be worse off than when I was handing over my entire pay. I was going to be eighty years old before I saved up enough money.

"Still, Giuseppe, we don't need a new oilcloth. It's . . . it's *too much*," my mother said. And I knew by the tone of her voice that she didn't mean it was too much money. My father just gave her a smile, shrugged, and sat down to eat, so we all did the same.

"Why are we starting without Frankie?" I asked after we had said grace.

"Still down at the docks, working late again," said Mama as she started filling our bowls.

"What time does Thea's engagement party start, Caprice?" Fabbia asked as my mother handed her a bowl.

"After sundown. Six o'clock. Same time as the regular S.E.G. meeting starts."

"Thea is going to be a *married* woman," my mother said, shaking her head in disbelief. "It's wonderful."

"Thea's being a good daughter, honoring her parents," my father said, ripping off a piece of black bread and pointing it at me before stuffing it in his mouth. "Marrying someone they chose *for her*," he continued, the piece of bread now puffing out his unshaven cheek. "Someone whose parents are from the same village in Russia as her family. Now see, Caprice, I always knew that Thea was smarter than she looked."

I knew this was coming. I wasn't even sure what he meant by *smarter than she looked*. But he was not finished.

"I think this is the year," he said, nodding to himself. "You'll be twenty-one years old in July. This is the year we find you a husband."

I gritted my teeth. He made me so furious, telling me *this is the year*. As if it were completely up to him to decide my entire future. As if I were still a child without a mind of my own. I took a deep breath. I was so tired of pretending, of not telling him what I really wanted. And of putting up with this talk of an arranged marriage that I would never, *ever* agree to.

My mother was looking at me, warning me again with her eyes.

"Papa—this is *not* going to be the year," I said, raising my voice, trying but failing to stay calm. I felt my cheeks start to burn. "I am *not* going to get married this year. I am *not* going to let you find me a husband. I keep trying to tell you this in different ways, but it's like you never really hear what I'm saying!

"I don't want *la vecchia maniera siciliana*—I don't want the old Sicilian way. I want to get married on my terms, to someone I love— someone *I* choose. Or I don't want to get married at all. Ever."

My father was looking at me, shocked into speechlessness. Vita had her spoon halfway to her mouth, and my mother and Fabbia were looking at my father to see what was going to happen next.

"I'll tell you what *is* going to happen this year," I said, looking around the table. "This is the year I'm going to open my own hat shop, here in the North End. I am. I'm not sure exactly how I'm going to do it—I'm still saving the money for it. But I am going to own my own hat shop in 1909.

I don't care how hard I have to work. And 1909 is definitely *not* the year I'm going to get married."

"Open your own—your own *what?*" My father burst out laughing. He thought it was a joke, which made me livid. "What in God's name are you talking about, Caprice? Open your own hat shop—a *woman* in the North End opening a hat shop! Ha! With what money? And where in heaven's name is this all coming from, Caprice?"

"Giuseppe, please, lower your voice—Caprice . . . let's talk calmly," my mother said, trying to intervene.

I got up from the table and went to grab my coat and hat. I was so angry my hands were shaking. I needed air. I needed to get out of there.

"It's coming from the past two years of meeting young men who, like me, want *no part* of an arranged marriage! It's coming from a dream I have—to have my own shop. This is America, Papa; a woman can have her own shop here and succeed at it! Look at Madame DuPont. I am *just* as smart and ambitious and talented as her. Maybe more so. I know I can do it, and I'm going to!"

"How dare you talk to me this way!" he yelled. "How dare you—it's like I don't even know my own daughter! Who are you? Who are you to talk so disrespectfully to me? You are going to do *nothing* without my consent! You are still my daughter. You still live under *my* roof!"

"I know I still live under your roof," I answered, talking through my clenched teeth. "I know it every time I give money for board. I know it every time I climb into bed with my sisters at night. I wish I didn't have to live here, but I am a woman, so I don't have many choices. If I could, I would move into Hull House with Miss Guerrier."

"Maybe you should!" my father hollered, so loud I was sure everyone in our building had heard him. His face was tomato red as he stood across the table from me. I thought I could see steam coming out of his ears.

I didn't even say good-bye. I just stormed out the door. I heard my mother call for me to wait, but I couldn't go back. I needed to calm down. *He needs to know. He needs to finally understand what I really want in life. I am not a little girl. I am a young woman—a young American woman.* I said this over and over in my mind, but it did nothing to help me calm down.

I walked downstairs to Maria's apartment on the second floor, putting my coat and hat on as I went. I rubbed my hands together to try to stop them from shaking and wiped the smudge of a tear out of the corner of my eye.

I was relieved when I saw Maria in the hallway, drinking tea and talking to her neighbors, Mrs. Orzo and Mrs. Petrelli. It was drafty in the halls on this cold February night, so Maria was already wearing her wool coat and hat. Antonetta was on the floor with blankets wrapped around her, playing dice with Mrs. Petrelli's daughter. I gave them all a warm greeting, trying to hide my anger.

"Caprice—I didn't expect you this early," said Maria, and with one glance at my face, added, "Oh—sweetheart, we . . . we heard someone yelling. Is everything all right? What happened?"

"Um, do you mind if we go for a little walk before heading over to Hull House?" I asked. "We should probably get there early to help set up." I didn't want to talk about anything in front of Maria's neighbors, particularly Mrs. Orzo, or everyone in the building would know every detail of my fight with my father.

"Of course," said Maria, getting up. "Let me just put my teacup inside. Mrs. Petrelli—are you sure you're okay watching my sister?"

"Yes, Maria, go, have fun. Antonetta will be fine," said Mrs. Petrelli with a smile and a wave. "We'll have fun, girls, won't we?"

"Yes!" the girls said in unison.

Maria kissed her sister good-bye and ducked into her apartment to put her teacup away, and we headed down the hall to the stairs.

"Maria, where's your mother?" I asked as we walked downstairs.

"My mother is sick again. The poor thing. She's in bed," said Maria, and for the first time

I noticed the dark circles under her eyes. "She's still grieving, of course. We all are. I hear her crying at night. When she's not working, she's sleeping. I've tried coaxing her out to at least eat dinner with us, but so far I haven't had much luck."

We left the tenement and started moving in the general direction of Hull House. We walked arm-in-arm to keep warm.

"So what the heck happened to you?" Maria asked. "It feels like you're still shaking."

I told her about the fight with my father, getting upset all over again.

"Caprice, honestly, I think this is good," said Maria. "You're a woman. You're *not* a little girl anymore, and it's about time he realized this. It's also about time you stood up to him. It had to happen."

"I don't think I've ever seen him that angry," I said, thinking of my father's red face. "I don't know. I'm so tired of him not listening to a word I say. But now he knows about my wanting to open the shop, and he's totally against the idea. He looked at me like I was completely out of my mind when I told him."

"So what are you going to do now?" Maria said. "Are you going to try to talk to him about it tomorrow?"

I shook my head. "No, no, definitely not. I'm not even sure I want to go *home* tonight. I'm just so furious and . . . frustrated. I need a little bit of time to think."

"And I think giving *him* some time to think about everything you've said tonight is good," she said. "Maybe he'll start to come around to the idea after he cools down."

We walked quietly for a block, listening to the sound of Italian music coming from one of the men's clubs.

"You mentioned your mother wasn't doing well. How are *you* doing?" I asked Maria, glancing at her sideways.

Maria let out a dramatic sigh.

"I'm doing . . . okay. Some days I go along feeling fine, and then I see something that reminds me of my father and burst into tears. Other days, I'm so busy working at the dress shop and taking care of Antonetta that I don't have time to think much. Miss Weld has increased my responsibilities, and I have to say it's been helpful to be so busy there."

"Well, you know I'm here if you need me, even if it's just to go for a walk like this," I said. I paused for a moment, then asked, "Have you seen much of Mark?"

Maria shrugged, looked ahead, and said softly, "I see him once in a while."

She was a good actress, so it was hard to tell if she was lying.

"Now look at where we just 'happened' to walk

by," said Maria, teasing, and I realized I had led us down Hanover and back up to Salem Street. We were standing right in front of Sal's butcher shop. I saw him through the glass, mopping the floor, and I felt . . . hopeful.

Despite his reputation, I had been having a hard time not thinking about him. I had thought a lot about that day in the hallway of the Sicilian Club. Had he really left a trail of brokenhearted young women throughout the North End? I was starting to hope that his reputation had been greatly exaggerated.

"Oh, um . . . shall we go in and say a quick hello?" I asked, ignoring the amused look on Maria's face when she nodded back.

The door jingled as we entered. Sal looked up, and his face instantly brightened when he saw us.

"Ah, it's the two most beautiful girls in the North End," he said with a huge grin. "To what do I owe this pleasure?" His eyes did not leave my face.

"We're heading to Thea's engagement party at Hull House, and we're a little early so we thought we'd take a walk, go the long way," I answered. I heard myself add, "And I wanted to stop in to say hello."

"Well, can I get you a hot cup of coffee or tea or something?" Sal asked. "It's freezing out there."

"No, thank you, Sal. Caprice, we actually should get over there soon to help out," said

200

Maria. I could tell by her tone that she was still not convinced his reputation was exaggerated. This annoyed me, given the male company *she* had been keeping lately.

"That's true," I said with a slow nod. "We don't really have time for a coffee tonight unfortunately."

"Oh, okay," said Sal. Disappointment crossed his face, and he looked into my eyes and said, "You look beautiful tonight . . . I mean . . . um . . . both of you. Just beautiful."

"Well, thank you," I said, adjusting my hat. Warmth crept up my cheeks, but for the first time that evening it was not out of anger.

"Thank you. Have a good evening, Sal," said Maria.

"Well, I'll be in on Sunday," I said as I started to follow Maria out. "I'll see you then."

I had turned to go when Sal said, "Oh, Caprice, would you mind if I stopped over at your home on Sunday afternoon, maybe after dinner?"

I looked at him, surprised he would try to invite himself over for dessert, but I thought of my father and answered, "I'm sorry, Sal, I don't think it's a good idea. You see, I'm not on good terms with my father, and he—"

"It's okay," said Sal, holding up his hand and giving me a wink. "Another night maybe, yes?"

"Yes . . . um, maybe," I answered. "I better go. Good night, Sal."

"*Buonanotte, tesoro*," I heard him say as I went out the door. *Buonanotte, tesoro.* Good night, sweetheart—had he really just said that?

"So has he tried to kiss you again?" Maria asked, linking arms with me.

"Oh, I'm not even sure he was going to kiss me, Maria," I said, regretting I had said anything to her about it. "I mean . . . maybe he was, but who knows. Anyway, we're just friends. And I know he's known as a cad. And I've got enough to worry about right now. I have no interest in complicating my life further with Sal Valenti."

"Uh-huh," said Maria with a huge grin.

"What?" I said, elbowing her. "I'm serious."

"Caprice," she said, eyebrows raised as she looked sideways at me, "I don't know how to tell you this, my friend, but your life is already complicated by Sal Valenti. It's written all over your face. And *his* too. So you can try to tell yourself you're not going to get caught up in it because of his reputation or because he's from Avellino—which is ridiculous—or because of your shop ambitions, but it's too late. You're *already* involved."

"No, I am not," I said defensively. But I knew she was right.

"Yes. You. Are. Come on, Caprice. You know you are," she said, laughing. "Your feet definitely know that you are. Tonight they walked us right up to his shop door."

I let out a groan. "Okay, maybe you're right," I answered. "Maybe I have feelings for Sal. Even though I shouldn't. I don't know what I'm doing, frankly."

"Well, just be careful," Maria replied, her tone a bit condescending. Not that I could say anything—I had acted the same way with her about Mark. Although I had much better reasons for warning her to stay away from him.

"I will be careful," I answered, feeling myself tense up. "Nothing's *really* going to happen with me and Sal anyway."

"We'll see." Maria laughed, clearly unconvinced. She pulled my arm toward Hull House. "Come on; let's hurry. We've got to set up for the party."

CHAPTER 13

It is easier to guard a sack full of fleas
than a girl in love.
—Jewish proverb

"And now, before some dancing and feasting on delicious-looking desserts, we have the presentation of the gifts," Miss Guerrier said. She was standing at the front of the assembly room with Mrs. Storrow and Thea.

Thea looked so pretty in a new champagne-colored dress that flattered her green eyes. But something was a bit odd about her tonight. Maybe it was because she was the guest of honor. She was holding her hands together, pulling at her fingers. Her neck was covered in red splotches, and her usually rosy cheeks were drained of color.

Maria, Ada, and I walked to the front of the room holding the boxes that contained Thea's wedding gifts from the S.E.G., but she didn't even look at us. We placed the boxes on the small wooden table next to her. Mrs. Storrow put her arm around Thea and, facing her toward the group, started to speak.

"As all of you are aware, it is our new tradition to give every Saturday Evening Girl bride a set of dishes, handmade and painted by the pottery shop," said Mrs. Storrow. "Thea, here are the dishes that were made here, for you, with love from all of your friends."

Mrs. Storrow opened one of the boxes on the table and lifted up a glazed butter-colored serving platter with tulips painted around its border. Everyone started clapping, and I saw that Thea's eyes were glassy with tears. Turning over the plate, Mrs. Storrow showed Thea where all forty of us had signed our initials on the back of the platter, with the letters *S.E.G.* etched in the center.

"Thea, dear, we wish you love and happiness in your upcoming marriage," Miss Guerrier said, giving Thea a hug. Now tears were flowing down Thea's cheeks.

"Thank you," said Thea, her voice shaky when the applause subsided. The splotches on her neck appeared to be getting worse. "Thank you all so very, very much. Most of you know I'm not particularly good at being the center of attention. But I just want to say that this club . . . well, when I joined seven years ago, I had no idea what this group would come to mean to me. It's . . . it's *everything*. It adds sweetness and fun to my life. And as I prepare to marry . . . well, I . . ." Thea's voice cracked, and more tears started to well in her eyes. "Just thank you all, Miss Guerrier, Mrs. Storrow—all of you."

We all broke into applause again, and Maria, Ada, and I embraced Thea before the rest of the girls started coming over to offer their congratulations.

"Okay, I'm going to start the music now, and please, everyone help themselves to desserts and lemonade," Miss Guerrier said loudly above all the talk and laughter.

Thea was swept up in a crowd of well-wishers, so the three of us made our way over to the refreshments.

"We have to talk," I said in Ada's ear after we had been socializing for a while. Maria was in an animated debate with Naomi Goodman about the next theater production for the S.E.G.

"Let's go sit down in the corner," I added. Ada looked at me and nodded. She was wearing her black-and-white dress, the same one she had worn the night of the New Year's dance, when I knew for sure that she was in love with my cousin.

"Ada, I know you've been avoiding me. Dominic has too. I haven't had a moment alone with either of you since the dance. You're one of my closest friends in the world, and yet you haven't talked to me at all about what's going on between you and my cousin. Why?" I asked.

"Caprice, I'm sorry. I'm truly sorry for not talking to you more about it," Ada said, and the look of remorse in her eyes told me she meant it. "It's just that, well, I know what you're going to say. And I know you think we've both lost our minds, and, I agree, we probably have. But frankly, I haven't wanted to hear it from you. From anyone. I've just wanted to enjoy this feeling for a while, enjoy being . . . being in love with Dominic. Having to talk about it, to think about the consequences—I just didn't want to spoil it for now."

"Well, Ada, for God's sake, you have to talk to someone about it at some point," I said, though she was spot on regarding my opinion. "Have you *really* thought about what would happen if your parents or my aunt or uncle found out? Doesn't that concern you at all?"

"Of course it concerns me. How could it not?" Ada said, speaking right into my ear so no one would hear us. "But . . . Caprice, we . . . we fell in *love*. I had never thought much about Dominic at all. But then he started walking me from the streetcar after classes. And we would talk and talk. And soon I realized I was counting the hours until I would see him again. It was at Thanksgiving—having dessert at your house that night—when I realized he felt the same way.

"And we're truly in love. I had no idea what it was to be in love until Dominic. I thought I knew everything. I thought I was so smart. I feel like I knew *nothing* about life until now."

"Ada, I understand that you two are in

love. Trust me, it's obvious. But the religious differences . . . it's just too much. Your families would disown you. You have to break it off; you know that, don't you? You have to *end it,* because sooner or later one of your families is going to find out. This neighborhood is too small. There's nowhere to hide."

"I know that, Caprice," Ada said in a loud whisper, nodding and looking around furtively. "And that's why . . . that's why we're considering eloping." Ada whispered this last part very softly into my ear.

"You are *not!*" I said back to her, then lowered my voice because some of the girls in the crowd had turned to look at us. I felt the heat rise up my face and gave them a tight smile and wave like Ada and I were just joking.

"Ada, please, you don't really want to do that. You *can't* do that. Think of your families. Think of your friends." I felt queasy at the thought of my best friend and my cousin disappearing from my life, never to be seen again.

"I know it sounds crazy to you, but right now the thought of life without Dominic seems unbearable to me," she said. "I don't want to live a life without him. All I think about is being with him. I want to marry him, Caprice. I really do." Her voice was thick with emotion as she looked at me, trying to make me understand this madness.

"And what about Simmons? What about finishing college?" I asked. "I thought that was the most important thing to you. We've both talked about these ambitions we've had forever. I just don't understand—how can you throw it all away?"

She shook her head. "I know, I know," she answered. "I'm not throwing . . . I . . . we haven't decided what to do yet. And Simmons . . . well, it's still my dream to finish and get my diploma. To become a teacher. Maybe more. But sometimes things change."

"Listen, Ada, just promise me you won't do anything rash," I said, taking her hand. "Think things through with that brilliant mind of yours, okay? And please, please, talk to me . . . *tell me* before you go anywhere, promise?"

"I promise," she said as she reached out to give me a hug. "I know you think I'm crazy. For goodness sake, *I* think I'm crazy. But you don't know what it's like to be in love. I can't explain it. It's turned my world upside down."

I felt myself bristle at this comment. I felt like I'd been harassed enough after my argument with my father. I didn't really need Maria and Ada commenting on my love life, or lack of one.

"Caprice, Ada—how are you both?" Miss Guerrier came up to us and, seeing our expressions, frowned. "Oh—is everything okay?"

"Yes, yes, Miss Guerrier, everything's fine

for the moment," I said. "Actually, that's a lie. Everything is *not* fine with me. I need to talk to both of you." I told them about what had happened with my father earlier in the evening, becoming incensed all over again.

"Oh, Caprice, I'm sorry," Miss Guerrier said, patting my shoulder. "But I've lived in this neighborhood long enough to know that many Italian fathers have a hard time seeing things their daughters' way, even when they're adults."

"Jewish fathers too," Ada added.

"Yes, Jewish fathers too." Miss Guerrier said. "Now, do you want to stay over here tonight at Hull House? The accommodations won't be much, but if you think it would help to clear the air between you and your father, you're welcome to."

"Thank you, Miss Guerrier. I appreciate the offer," I said, relieved at the thought of not going home but knowing that staying at Hull House might only make things worse. "Oh, and I saw that Mrs. Storrow had to leave," I said. "Is she going to be at the S.E.G. meeting next week?"

"Yes, yes, I believe she is," Miss Guerrier said, taking a sip of lemonade.

"Good. I want to talk to her after the meeting if that's possible," I said.

"What are you going to ask her?" Ada said, and I was about to explain when Maria came running over to us.

"Excuse me, Miss Guerrier," she said, a bit out of breath. "Ada, Caprice, you have to come with me. We have a bit of a . . . a *situation* with the bride. She's downstairs in the pottery kiln room."

"Oh no—can I help?" Miss Guerrier said, concerned.

"I'll let you know, Miss Guerrier," said Maria. "I'm hoping the girls and I can calm her down."

"Yes, please do," Miss Guerrier said, frowning. "Poor Thea did not seem herself tonight."

Ada and I followed Maria as she hurried through the crowd, poured a glass of lemonade, grabbed a sweet roll, and flew down the stairs.

"What the heck happened, Maria?" I asked, nearly out of breath when we reached the kiln room door.

"I really don't know, but Thea is an absolute mess."

We walked in to see Thea sitting in a heap on the floor next to the pottery kilns. The splotches I had spotted earlier on her neck had spread to her face as well, and her cheeks were stained with tears.

"Thea, what's going on, sweetheart?" I asked. "Why are you so upset?"

"Oh, girls, I don't know if I've done the right thing," Thea said, throwing her hands up. "This whole marriage—maybe you were right, Ada. I'm not sure what I'm going to do . . ." She put her head in her hands and buried her face in the skirt of her dress. Maria, Ada, and I looked at each other in disbelief.

"Thea, Joshua is a really nice young man. What happened? Why are you saying this now?" asked Ada in a gentle voice. She took a handkerchief out of her sleeve and tried to blot Thea's face. After a few seconds Thea lifted her head up, took a deep breath, and started to talk really fast.

"I stopped by my sister Bessie's a few hours ago, to see if maybe she wanted to come to my engagement party with me. Of course, she didn't," Thea said, rolling her eyes. "But as I was leaving, she said to me, *'Thea, I don't think you know what marriage is really like.'* And I answered, *'Well, what is there to know? I know that you sleep together in the same bed.'* And then she said, *'No, the man has a pe-... pe-...* penis, *and it gets real big.'* And I asked, *'Gets very big? What do you mean? What does it do after it gets real big?'* But she just gave me a sly smile and wouldn't tell me. And then I started really thinking about it and, well, I've just been a miserable wreck ever since."

Ada, Maria, and I were kneeling on the floor around Thea in silence. Thea put her head down again for a second, and Maria looked above her at Ada and me, her eyes enormous and her hand over her mouth.

"So where does it go, ladies?" Thea said, looking up again at all of us. "I ... I think I might know . . . but you have to tell me for certain, since my own sister wouldn't."

"Thea, dear, I thought Bessie would have told you long before this," I said, taking her hand. "Or your mother . . ."

"So I'm the only one who doesn't know where it goes?" Thea asked, looking around. "How do you all know? *How?*"

"Well, I overheard my mother and aunt talking years ago," I said.

"I read about it in a book," added Ada.

"I actually heard my parents one night and figured it out myself," said Maria, making a sour face.

"Well," Thea said, curiosity and fear both in her eyes, "who's going to tell me? Where does it *go?*"

Maria, Ada, and I just stared at each other, none of us really wanting to be the one to answer her.

"Ada—you're the one who wants to be a science teacher," said Maria, eyebrows raised as she pointed to her. "You tell her."

"I second that," I said.

"Oh, for goodness sake, someone please *tell me!*" yelled Thea.

"Okay, Thea, I'll tell you since these two are too scared," said Ada, giving us both a scowl. She leaned across the floor, cupped her hands, and whispered in Thea's ear. I looked across at Maria, who was biting her lip.

As Ada whispered, Thea's eyes grew as large as salami slices. She pulled away and looked at Ada for confirmation of what she had just heard, and Ada nodded. Then she looked at Maria and I, and we both silently nodded too.

She paused for a second and looked away, her face going from white to crimson. She then put her face in her hands and buried herself in the skirt of her dress again. Her body started shaking. I thought she was sobbing, but when she looked up I realized she was laughing, a deep belly laugh so hard she could barely breathe.

"I . . . that . . . that is by far the most ridiculous and, quite frankly, shocking thing I have ever heard in my life!" She kept laughing, tears flowing down her cheeks. "I can't believe I didn't know that! Is that *really* what happens? That is big—well, no . . . you know, I mean that is big *news* . . . that is . . . it's just . . . so . . . funny!"

Thea kept laughing, holding her stomach, leaning up against the wall, and wiping the tears streaming down her cheeks. Ada was the first to lose her composure, collapsing in a fit of squeaky giggles right along with Thea. Then Maria broke down, laughing so hard she actually started snorting. Maria's snorts made me start howling so hard I was blinded from the tears clouding my eyes. All four of us just sat there on the floor of the pottery shop, unable to speak because we were laughing so much.

"Holy Mary, mother of God! I just cannot believe it. To find out now—*two months* before your wedding. Thea, you poor thing," said Maria, wiping her eyes and taking a deep breath when we finally calmed down a bit.

"That Bessie is just such a *witch*. I can't believe she didn't tell me before this. I can't believe I didn't think to *ask* before this either, though. Really—what was I thinking? I'm so naive," said Thea, shaking her head. "And Joshua . . . oh no . . . I'm really, really not ready yet. The wedding's only two months away. I can't . . . girls, what am I going to do? I don't want him to see me . . . with no *clothes*. To see my body." She started smoothing down the front of her dress, sucking in her stomach, a look of horror on her face.

"Thea, as Ada said, Joshua is a sweet man. I think it's going to be fine," I said, hoping I was right. "I don't think he'll force you to do anything you don't want to do."

"I agree," said Maria. "He's a gentleman, and I think if you talk to him about things, it's going to be okay."

"I want to believe you're right," said Thea, "I *think* you're right . . . but . . . I still can't believe that's how babies are made. I can't believe I didn't know. I feel so stupid. As I said, it's a bit of a shock."

Maria and I nodded, but Ada had a huge smile on her face and started giggling. "I'm sorry," she said as she waved a hand in front of her face in an attempt to stop the giggles. "I'm sorry, it . . . the . . . I don't know . . . it's all so . . ."

Ada was overcome with squeaky giggles again, and for the second time, we all just started laughing so hard that we were practically rolling on the floor.

"You know, in all seriousness, Thea, it could actually be really . . . quite lovely," Ada said, her face still red from laughing.

"Quite lovely, huh?" Maria said playfully. "Why, Ada, do you have some experience in this area that we don't know about?"

"Maria!" Ada said, swatting Maria on the arm. "What do you take me for? Of course I don't. But, if we're being completely honest . . . for the first time in my life, the thought of it does not seem so strange." Ada's face was even more flushed now. "Not that I ever would before marriage, of course."

"So what about you, Maria—have you ever? With Mark?" I said. I couldn't resist asking after she'd asked Ada.

"Oh, please, Caprice, you must be joking," said Maria. "I'm Catholic, and I know that's one thing a woman does not give away before marriage. I've been spending time with Mark. But in a million years, I would not spend time with him doing *that*." She made a face and wrapped her arms around her waist.

"Ladies, I wish we could stay down here and talk more, but Thea, I think we need to get you back to your engagement party," Ada said. "Everyone is here to celebrate with you."

"Yes, you're right," Thea said with a nod, smoothing her hair with her hands. "I'm feeling a little calmer now, thank you."

The three of us helped pick Thea up off the floor. I started smoothing out her rumpled dress. Maria took a powder compact out of her pocket and started blotting the tear stains on Thea's cheeks. Ada smoothed out Thea's hair and pinned back some of the honey-colored pieces that had fallen out of her chignon.

"Well, Maria, I can't tell you how great it feels to hear you really laugh again. It's been a while," said Thea, putting her arm around Maria. "That might—*might*—make it all worth it."

"Amen to that," I said. "Now let's go dance. Ada, you and Thea promised to teach us some of the Jewish wedding dances."

We grabbed hands and hurried upstairs to bring Thea back to her engagement party.

CHAPTER 14

*You can't force anyone to love you or
lend you money.*
—Jewish proverb

Saturday, February 13, 1909

I did not end up sleeping at Hull House after
Thea's engagement party, although a part of me
really wanted to. It was guilt about my mother
that made me go home. I hadn't been able to stop
thinking about her, lying in bed, her eyes wide
open, staring at the shadows on her bedroom
ceiling, waiting to hear the door squeak open
when I finally arrived home.

So I stayed out very late talking with my friends
and finally went home sometime after midnight.
When I tiptoed inside and heard my father's
familiar snore, I made up my mind to keep my
distance from him for a while.

In a tiny two-bedroom home, you might have
thought it impossible to avoid seeing or talking
to someone. But my father and I both did a fairly
good job of it. We barely acknowledged each
other the morning after Thea's party. At nine-
thirty Mass, we sat on opposite sides of the
pew with Frankie, Fabbia, Vita, and my mother

in between. And at Sunday dinner we had Aunt Cecilia, Uncle Arthur, Dominic, and my siblings and mother all squeezed around the dinner table, making it easy not to talk to one another directly.

For the rest of the week, I left early in the morning for the pottery shop before anyone else in the house was awake. At night I came home after my father had gone to bed. I made excuses for missing dinner, saying that there was an enormous amount of work to do at the pottery shop—several orders to fill for weddings and parties and such. My mother looked at me with her tired eyes and nodded. I knew she knew I was lying, but she shrugged her shoulders and let it pass. She hadn't even asked if anyone had walked me home in the evening. Perhaps she realized that both my father and I needed some time and space before we resolved the issues between us.

I said a prayer of forgiveness to the Virgin Mary and promised to go to confession for lying to my mother and not completely honoring my father. But I still did not regret saying all the things I said to him the night of Thea's engagement party.

In truth, there *was* a great deal of work to do at the pottery shop, but that wasn't the only thing I had been working on that made my days so long.

I had finally started laying out the plans for my hat shop in a coherent way, and I planned to present it to Mrs. Storrow after the S.E.G.

meeting tonight in the hopes that she might have some advice, or even help me find an investor or two. I had taken the cigar box from under my bed, brought it to the shop with me, and laid out all the scraps of paper I had stored in there for over a year. On them were designs for hats—hats with chiffon taffeta crowns, wide-brim children's straw hats with silk fringe, sailor-shaped hats in rough satin straw, a couple of extremely dressy hats with wild roses made from pink silk satin—for every season and occasion. The hats would be low to moderately priced—nothing too expensive. I could use lower-cost materials and ready-to-wear and ready-to-trim hats, so I could sell hats for both the ladies of my neighborhood as well as the ladies of Back Bay.

On other scraps of paper, I had written ideas on what the interior and exterior of the shop would look like. Thea had given me some great suggestions; she really did have a knack for interior decorating. The inside would be painted a soothing pastel green with pale cream-and-gold accents. On one piece of paper, I had even sketched out what the lettering on the outside of the shop—*Caprice's Millinery*—would look like.

I had put all of these thoughts and musings in one document, neatly organized. At the end I had included a budget for start-up costs: used furniture for workstations, mirrors, and shelving;

a glass case for trimmings; sashes and curtains; and shop rent. I had also included a part-time salary for Fabbia, whom I would train as a maker. When she was old enough, Vita could become an apprentice too.

Looking over my completed business plan for Caprice's Millinery after closing up the shop late Saturday afternoon, I felt like I was finally ready to make my business proposition to Mrs. Storrow. It was time to take a risk and ask her; it was time to take responsibility for my future instead of just waiting for it to happen. Asking Mrs. Storrow for help felt like my best option—perhaps my only one. Saving money was taking too long, and no bank would give a loan to a young, poor Italian woman.

"Caprice, are you staying right up until meeting time, or are you going home for dinner first?" The sound of Miss Guerrier's voice made me jump. I hadn't even heard her walk into the shop from the back stairway.

"Oh, hello," I answered with a smile. "No, I'm staying right up until the meeting, if that's okay with you."

"Of course it is," she answered. "I'm making some soup, and I have bread from the bakery. I'll bring both down and we can have dinner together. The soup should be ready in about thirty minutes. I can't promise it will be as good as your family recipes, but it's not bad."

"That sounds wonderful, Miss Guerrier, thank you. I'll clear off the counter; we can eat right here if you like."

"Perfect. I'll be back in a bit."

As I was cleaning off the counter, the bells at the front jingled. I whirled around and was surprised to see Sal standing there, his enormous frame dwarfing the door. I hadn't seen him since the night of Thea's party.

"Good evening," Sal said, taking off his hat. "I've been meaning to stop by, but my own shop's been so busy. I thought I might walk you home. Are you going home for dinner before your meeting?"

"Oh . . . uh, thank you," I answered, and I could feel myself blush and my stomach start to flutter. "Tonight I'm actually going to stay and have dinner with Miss Guerrier. She's coming down soon."

"Oh, okay, that's too bad," he answered with a smile, though there was disappointment in his eyes. "I was going to take you the long way home. Maybe past somewhere we could get an espresso or . . . or something."

"Well, maybe we could another night?" I answered. Did I really want to, though? Did I really want to go down this path with Sal Valenti? But right at this moment, I thought maybe Maria was right—maybe I was already too far gone. Despite his reputation and all the other real and

223

imagined reasons in my head, I had already made a decision with my heart.

"Yes, Caprice. Another night," he answered, his deep voice soft as he walked over to the counter where I was standing. He traced the dark wood of the countertop before he looked up and said, "Another night very soon. You and I have things to discuss. We've waited long enough." And then, without hesitation, he put one of his hands on my cheek. It was warm, and it smelled like soap. I tried to pull away because I knew I should, but he and I had been doing this dance for months, and it felt like I physically couldn't avoid it any longer. Instead I put my hand on his hand and closed my eyes for a second. A moment later I felt his breath on my face, and then his lips were on mine. A kiss—*my first real kiss*. A soft, gentle kiss that was over almost as soon as it began. I put my own hand on the counter because I felt a bit dizzy. I looked up at him, and his eyes were still very close, looking right into mine.

"I've been wanting to do that for a very long time," he said.

I was speechless. I felt like I had been wanting him to do that my entire life. I just smiled back at him.

"I will see you soon, okay, Caprice?" he said.

"Um . . . yes, that would be nice." I said. *Oh, God, what was I doing?* I should have told him that this shouldn't be happening. There was still that little voice of apprehension in the back of my head, but I was tired of listening to it.

He took my hand off the counter, kissed the back of it, and winked at me. "I'd better leave before Miss Guerrier sees me. *Buonanotte*, Caprice," he whispered.

"*Buonanotte*, Sal."

With a wave he ducked and headed out as the bells jingled his exit.

I stood there for a few moments before nervous energy took over. I finished clearing the counters and swept out the entire shop. My head was spinning, and I had to stop and steady myself. I burst out laughing and held my hand in front of my mouth, only to notice that it was trembling. Sal Valenti had just kissed me at the pottery shop counter. I tried to replay the way it had felt in my mind—his lips on my lips, his warm hand on my face. The smell of his breath.

I heard footsteps on the stairs, and Miss Guerrier came in with bowls of fragrant vegetable soup and a loaf of brown bread, spoons and napkins under her arm. I didn't even have an appetite now. I looked down and shook my head, trying to calm the giddiness I felt, and I hurried over to help her set up dinner on the counter. The same counter that Sal had kissed me at just minutes earlier.

Miss Guerrier and I sat across from each other, and I said grace. And then I just sat staring into my soup bowl, my face still warm from the afterglow of Sal's visit. It was hard to think about eating. It was hard to think about anything other than what had just happened in this very spot.

After a couple of bites, Miss Guerrier was the first to start talking.

"Is it too hot in here from the kiln, Caprice? Your face is as red as your hair."

I whispered, "No," and suppressed a laugh, not even bristling at the hair comment. I wished I could tell her, but I couldn't. I was quite sure Miss Guerrier would not approve.

"I've been so busy this week, running back and forth between the shop and the library," she said, breaking off a piece of bread. "I feel like we've barely had a chance to say a few words to each other."

I nodded after taking a sip of soup. *Concentrate, Caprice; stop thinking about Sal and concentrate.*

"I agree. Thank God the shop has been so busy, though," I answered. "Orders have continued to be steady since the holidays. You can tell Mrs. Storrow has really been talking about us in her social circles. We're getting a lot of customers coming in from Back Bay."

"Yes, Mrs. Storrow has been great spreading the word about our little pottery," said Miss Guerrier. "Which reminds me—you were planning on talking to her tonight, yes?"

My stomach did a flip, because I realized I'd

be having my conversation with Mrs. Storrow in just a short time. I needed to clear my head of Sal. There were too many other things to think about tonight.

"Yes." I nodded. "I'd like to talk to her for a few minutes after the meeting if she has the time."

"She does," Miss Guerrier answered. "I already mentioned to her that you'd like a word. Do you mind if I ask what you're going to discuss? Does it have to do with the long hours you've been keeping here?"

I nodded, knowing that this question was coming. I hadn't been sure that Miss Guerrier even knew I was coming and going so early and late. But I should've realized that nothing escaped her notice.

"Yes, Miss Guerrier," I answered, taking a deep breath. I told her all about my business plan and about asking Mrs. Storrow for business advice and thoughts about potential investors.

Miss Guerrier sat back on her stool for a moment and looked at me, a bemused expression on her face.

"Caprice . . . well, I'm impressed." Her look turned into a huge smile. "That's wonderful. I'm really thrilled you're taking the initiative. Was it the argument with your father that compelled you to do this?"

I felt my stomach relax, relieved at her

reaction. I was afraid she was going to say I was overstepping my bounds.

"Of course it's my father," I answered. "But to be honest, Miss Guerrier, I think it's a combination of things. It's finally paying board, only to not save any money because I have to help my family. It's my father constantly talking about getting me married to a Sicilian-born stranger." I paused and took another sip of soup.

"It's Maria's father's death. It's Thea's engagement," I said with a sigh. "It's like life is moving forward so fast, and I want to move forward too. I'm tired of thinking about my hat shop but not actually *doing* anything about it. I suddenly feel an urgency to open it that I never did before. I need to . . . I need to choose a life that is *mine*. And if my parents aren't happy about it, I'll suffer the consequences."

I had realized when I'd had that argument with my father last week, that I couldn't keep my dreams quiet anymore. I couldn't keep living a life on my family's terms, pretending that I didn't want something . . . something *more*. I would die if I had to live like that any longer.

"Oh, but please, Miss Guerrier—I hope I don't sound ungrateful for my job here. I love working at the pottery shop. It's so much fun. It's just . . ."

"No need to explain, Caprice," she said. "I understand, trust me. We love having you here, but I knew this was temporary. This is not getting you where you want to go. It's not . . . well, it's not Caprice's Millinery."

"No," I said with a smile. "It's not Caprice's Millinery."

"Good luck with Mrs. Storrow tonight," said Miss Guerrier. "I honestly don't know if she'll be able to help you at all, but I'll keep my fingers crossed. I've always believed that what we become in this world, even as women, no— *especially* as women—is the direct result of our personal desires. I've never doubted you; I know you can do this. And I'm glad that now you no longer doubt yourself."

I reached across the table to hug her, knowing that she was right.

"Thank you, Miss Guerrier," I said. "For everything."

CHAPTER 15

A half truth is a whole lie.
—Jewish proverb

I was lining up rows of chairs in the assembly room when Ada, Maria, and Thea walked in.

"Hi, girls, I already set up our usual seats in the back," I said, still feeling scattered from Sal's visit. "I'll join you in a minute. I have so much to tell you. I've got my business plan together to show Mrs. Storrow—I'm nervous, but excited. And you'll never believe what happened tonight. Sal came by and . . . wait . . . what?"

When I'd mentioned Sal, they all looked at each other, but none of them would look directly at me.

"What's the matter? Why are you acting strange?" I asked.

"Caprice, let's go sit," Ada said, taking off the blue hat composed of silk braid and chiffon that I had made her for her birthday. "Maria just told me and Thea something on our way over here. You need to hear it."

My stomach lurched as we walked to our chairs. I wasn't sure I agreed with her.

"So?" I asked after they had finally gotten their coats and hats off and we were all settled.

"Caprice, it's about Sal," said Maria quietly, looking down at her hands.

"What about Sal?" I asked, bracing myself.

Maria looked at me, took a deep breath, and started talking very fast. "You see, I was talking to Mrs. Orzo, and she was asking me who among our friends has a fella. I think she wanted me to talk about Mark. But I didn't want to give her any information, so I told her that you might be seeing a young man, Caprice. I said it was Sal Valenti, that nice young butcher. And she said, not Sal Valenti whose parents are Rose and Nino Valenti? And I said, yes, I think those are his parents; how many Sal Valentis can there be in the North End?"

"Maria, what is the point of this?" I asked, annoyed that she had gossiped about me to divert attention from her own secretive love life. "And why in God's name would you tell the biggest gossip in the North End about me and Sal when there's nothing going on?"

"Let me finish, Caprice," Maria said, holding up her hand, completely ignoring my question. "Years ago, before she became a skilled seamstress for the Leopold Morse clothing store, Mrs. Orzo worked in a button factory. She worked with Sal's mother, Rose. And they became work friends, close friends. Anyway, Mrs. Orzo sees her from time to time for coffee—"

"Maria, please." I interrupted her because the

meeting was about to start any minute. "Just *tell me*. What do I need to know about Sal?" My stomach was sinking farther every second.

"Caprice." Maria took a deep breath and blurted it out. "There is actually a reason behind Sal's reputation as a cad. There's a reason that he's spent time with a few different girls, only to stop pursuing them at a certain point. Sal is *engaged*. To a girl from the old country. A girl named Pupetta Falcone. She apparently has very bad skin but is a wonderful cook. She's still there, but she's coming over in July. They're going to be *married* in July."

The hairs on my neck stood up, and I felt a little lightheaded. *No. This can't be true. Not after he came to see me tonight. Not after we kissed.*

"Pupe—*what!* Maria . . . what are you talking about?" I asked. "That . . . that just can't be true. I would have heard about this by now. Someone else would have told me. Sal would have told me."

Maria put her hand on mine.

"Caprice, I'm so sorry to be the one to tell you, but I'm afraid it's true," she said. "My neighbor heard it from Sal's mother—if she had heard it from anyone else, but it was Sal's *mother*. And it really does explain his reputation, his behavior toward that Louisa girl and that other girl, what was her name . . . ?"

"And *me!* Oh, God . . . just as I was starting to

233

trust . . . to believe his feelings toward me were real," I said, staring up at the ceiling. "Engaged—getting married! That *stronzo*! That bastard! I can't believe I was so stupid! And I can't believe he *kissed* me tonight!"

"What?!" the girls said in unison.

"What do you mean, he kissed you tonight?" Thea asked. "Like a kiss on your hand?"

"Oh, no, like a real kiss," I said, eyebrows raised. "In the pottery shop when I was closing up. Oh, Jesus, my father was right. I can't believe he would do this to me! I thought he was what he seemed . . . I thought he, well, I thought he might be falling for me. And I feel physically ill, because . . . because I . . . I *was* definitely falling for him. It hurts so much to even admit that. He was so sweet just now; it's hard to believe he'd do that and be engaged to some . . . someone else. Was he really just pretending with me? I can't believe he would deceive me this way!"

"We're all shocked," Ada said. "I like Sal. And I also really thought he was falling for you."

"Me too, Caprice. I guess he's a hell of an actor. But better to find out now," said Maria, holding my hand. "Better than being surprised when you see him walking out of St. Leonard's some Saturday in July with a bride with bad skin."

I wanted to tell Maria I could throw the same statement back at her. *Better to find out now.* But she was still being purposefully blind to all of it.

234

And if she was avoiding talking to her neighbor about Mark, that meant there was still something to talk about.

"I didn't expect to feel this way. God, I finally decide to open myself to the possibility . . . of love—what was I *thinking?*" I said, looking at all of them, knowing they wouldn't be able to answer me. "I will never make that mistake again, ladies. And thank you for telling me. I'm glad I know, even though I'm completely crushed right now. And I feel bad for this future wife of his—Pupupa, or whatever her name is." I tried to bury what I felt when I pictured Sal with a bride on his arm that wasn't me.

"Ladies! Ladies, I think we're ready to get started," Miss Guerrier said. She was standing at the front of the room holding up her hand. A tall elderly man with a salt-and-pepper beard was standing next to her.

The room went quiet, and Miss Guerrier cleared her throat and said, "Today we're privileged to have a special guest speaker. Doctor Edmund von Mach, a professor at Harvard, is here to discuss 'the German perspective.' "

I didn't hear a word of Dr. von Mach's discussion. I didn't hear Fanny Goldstein's announcements or much of Miss Guerrier's news about her new book delivery service via an old banana cart. I was completely lost in my thoughts for the next hour. I tried to push Sal's kiss out of my mind, but it was impossible. I wished I could just keep on reliving it, the deliciousness of the way my stomach had fluttered, and the way I had felt warm all over when he put his hand on my cheek. But instead I felt sick. Maria's revelations about his fiancée had ruined the afterglow. I felt like Thea at her engagement party. How could I have been so naive?

"Caprice! Caprice, hello, do you hear me? Mrs. Storrow is coming over here," Ada whispered in my ear. She elbowed me in the ribs, jolting me back to reality.

"Hi, Mrs. Storrow," Maria and Thea said together. They had already stood up and were greeting our patroness with kisses on her cheek. Ada grabbed my arm and yanked me up with her so we could greet her too.

The four of us chatted with Mrs. Storrow for a couple of minutes about Dr. von Mach's talk.

"And Ada, how are your classes going this semester?" Mrs. Storrow asked.

"Terrific, Mrs. Storrow, thank you," said Ada. "I'm taking an organic chemistry course and a biology course. I'm really enjoying both of them."

"And who is walking you from the streetcar after class?" asked Mrs. Storrow, eyebrows furrowed, giving Ada a look I couldn't quite decipher. "Is it Caprice's brother?"

"Uh . . . it's her cousin, actually. Her cousin

Dominic," Ada answered, a blush starting to creep up her cheeks until it was past her dimples.

"Ah, that's good. I'm sure he's a nice, respectful man," said Mrs. Storrow.

"Yes, he definitely is—"

"—very nice and respectful—"

"—of course—"

The four of us had all answered together, tripping over our words. We must have said *of course* three times each. If Mrs. Storrow had any suspicions, we had just confirmed them.

"Well, that is very reassuring to hear, girls," she answered, eyebrows raised. "And now, Caprice, you wanted to talk with me?"

"Yes, please, Mrs. Storrow. Is now a good time?" I asked.

"Yes, yes, it's fine," she said. "Why don't we go across the hall?"

Mrs. Storrow started walking, and I grabbed my business plan from underneath my chair and followed her. Ada squeezed my arm, and I turned around to see my best friends all smiling and mouthing words of luck and good wishes to me.

It was time to put Sal Valenti out of my head and focus on the task at hand.

Mrs. Storrow and I sat across from each other at one of the small tables set out in the smaller assembly room. As usual, she was well turned out in a stunning emerald-green skirt with a fashionable slot seam down the middle and an ivory shirtwaist.

"So, Caprice, my curiosity is piqued," Mrs. Storrow said as we sat down. "What would you like to discuss?"

When I had envisioned it, I had thought I would be terrified to present my proposal to her. I had thought I would be intimidated and insecure and on the verge of vomiting. But as I sat down across from her, a calmness came over me that I didn't expect. I put the rest of the evening out of my mind and started to speak.

"Mrs. Storrow, a year ago you made the suggestion that I open my own hat shop in the North End. That suggestion—your belief in my ability to do something like that—well, quite frankly, it changed my life. I realized that the expectations that my family has for me— that the world has for me—are too low. I want independence. I want to accomplish something professionally. If it weren't for you, if it weren't for the S.E.G., I'm not sure I would have ever come to that realization."

Mrs. Storrow was listening to every word, her eyes on my face. I took a deep breath and continued talking before I lost my nerve.

"The reason I'm saying all of this is because, as you know, I now hold the dream of a hat shop, *my* shop, very dear. Saving money has proven difficult, because even though I'm now paying

238

board to my parents, I have a great deal of family obligations, financially. So I'm here tonight to show you my business proposal. I've laid out all the details of my shop.

"I'd like to present them to you—not to ask you for money, because you've already done enough by just allowing me to work here. But, because no bank is going to give a loan to a poor immigrant girl, I thought you might have ideas for other ways I could find investors. So I can finally make Caprice's Millinery a reality."

Mrs. Storrow glanced down at the documents I had brought to the meeting and looked back up at me, giving me a slow nod. She leaned over, put her elbows on the table, clasped her hands together, and said, "Okay, let's hear it, Caprice."

I explained to her my entire vision for the shop—the business plan and everything I had been working on, including the designs and dreams that had kept me going for the last year. I laid out my figures, my fabric samples, and my designs. Mrs. Storrow occasionally stopped me to ask a question about how I had come up with something in my budget or where I had gotten the idea for a certain hat design. I talked about my dual role as shop owner and designer, hiring and training Fabbia and Vita as makers and, eventually, as trimmers when I felt they were ready. When I finished, I felt exhilarated. I felt like even if she had no ideas of how to help me, I had still accomplished something.

"Well, I must say I'm impressed," said Mrs. Storrow, tilting her head to look over some of the sketched hat designs. "You've certainly thought of everything, Caprice. And you had a solid answer to every question I asked."

She leaned back in her chair, and I thought I saw a glint of a tear in her right eye. "You're right, I've always believed in you, Caprice. Always believed you could do this . . . be an entrepreneur and help the economy of your own neighborhood." She smiled at me and shook her head as if she were a bit surprised at what she saw.

"I'm so proud of you. I can't tell you . . . I've known all of you girls since you were thirteen years old. And to watch you grow into these wonderful, bright *American* women—going to college, opening businesses, having professional careers—it's . . . well, it's truly something to see."

"Thank you," I answered, feeling my cheeks grow warm.

"I need to think about this and to talk to Mr. Storrow and some of my friends," she said. "Let me do some research, see if there's some way we can figure out a plan for you to get that initial investment that you need. Mind you, I cannot promise you that I'll find it. But I promise I'll have an answer for you in a couple of weeks."

She stood up and came around the table to give me a hug.

"Thank you, Mrs. Storrow," I said into her ear as we embraced. "No matter what happens, thank you for listening to me and taking me seriously. Thank you for everything."

"You're most welcome, Caprice," she answered as we pulled back from each other.

As we exited the room, she stopped and touched my elbow.

"Oh—one more question. How are your parents with this idea?" she asked.

"I'm working on that, Mrs. Storrow," I answered, giving her a smile and a sigh. "I'm working on that."

CHAPTER 16

God could not be everywhere, and therefore he made mothers.
—Jewish proverb

Sunday, February 28, 1909

"The war of silence between you and your father ends tonight, Caprice," my mother said. She was standing in our kitchen, hands on her hips, saying this to me as I was putting on my hat and coat. I opened my mouth to talk, but she held up her hand and continued, "Enough is enough. After the festival, I'm sending Frankie, Fabbia, and Vita to Arthur and Cecilia's for Sunday dinner. You and I need to talk to your father and sort everything out."

There was a simmering pot of marinara sauce on the stove behind her that had been made from the tomatoes we canned last summer. The smell of tomatoes and herbs permeated the air around us, and her cheeks were flushed a shiny pink from the stove's heat.

I was about to leave to meet my friends at the Santa Maria di Anzano Society Festival on Hanover Street. My father had already left to take Fabbia and Vita. Frankie had also left right after

243

Mass and was most likely standing on a corner flirting with some girl by now.

I had known this moment was coming. It had been three weeks since my father and I had really spoken to one another. We couldn't go on like this forever.

"Mama, before Papa and I had our argument," I said, trying to keep my voice quiet and calm, "I told you on Thanksgiving about my plans for opening a shop."

"And I told you I had reservations about it and needed to think," she said. "But you couldn't be patient. You *had* to tell your father about it, and now you aren't speaking to one another. You couldn't wait."

"Well, have you thought about it?" I asked. "And if you have, what in the world can you do about it?"

My mother shook her head at me, pulled out a chair, and sat down at the kitchen table.

"Caprice, don't you understand? I know how to handle your father, more than you'll ever know. If you have a husband someday, hopefully you will know how to manage him as well as I manage your father. Now sit. Your friends can wait."

I pulled out the chair across from my mother and sat down. She looked at me, studying my face.

"So about this"—she waved a hand in the air—"hat shop idea you have. If you really want to do this, how are you going to raise the money to open it?" she said. "I know you're paying board now, but you can't be saving that much."

"No, I'm not," I said. "It's been almost impossible to save a penny. I was going to tell you this tonight. The truth is I've asked Mrs. Storrow for advice about finding potential investors. She's going to let me know in the next week or so." My stomach flipped when I said this, because what if Mrs. Storrow couldn't help me? Then what in God's name would I do?

My mother's eyes were wide. "You asked . . . Mrs. *Storrow* . . . about finding investors? Mrs. Storrow of Beacon Street?"

"Yes, that very one," I answered, taking a deep breath. "She was the one who gave me the idea of opening the shop in the first place. You heard her at the holiday party. She believes in me. I wish . . ." I took a deep breath and grabbed my mother's hand across Christopher Columbus's face. "I wish you would too."

My mother studied our hands and was quiet for a moment. My jaw clenched. I was waiting for her to again start talking about why I, Caprice Russo, daughter of Sicilian immigrants, shouldn't do this—shouldn't *want more*. Why I should be thinking about marriage and babies and living a life just like hers. She pulled her hand away from me, leaned back in her chair, and looked me in the eye.

"Here is my problem with this shop plan of yours, dear daughter," she said. "This house, this family: this is where I have power. The family is where women are in control. They make the decisions . . . even if the men don't always realize this." She shook her finger at me, then pointed to the window.

"That world out there, that world is ruled by *men*. It will *always* be ruled by men. If you own a shop, you will always have to deal with that. Every. Single. Day. Men charging you more money for supplies because you're a woman. Men being slow to deliver something because you're a woman. Men trying to intimidate you on prices because you're a woman. It will not be an easy road for you. It is a path most women don't choose because it's very, very difficult."

"I know it's not going to be easy," I said. "But I'm not going to give up my dream because it's going to be hard. This is what I want to do with my life. I think . . . no, I *know* I can be an excellent shop owner, and I'm not afraid of the fact that it won't be easy for me. I need to at least try."

My mother and I sat there in silence for what felt like hours but in reality was only a couple of minutes. She finally raised her eyebrows.

"Okay. Okay," she said with a huge sigh. "So, tonight, we will talk to your father about it. But you have to let me guide the conversation. No more—"

Before she could continue, I jumped out of my seat, knelt down next to her, and wrapped my arms around her in the tightest embrace I could muster. I couldn't believe she was going to take my side.

"*Grazie*! Thank you, thank you, thank you!" I said into her hair, smelling the faint scent of lemon.

"Wait, wait, Caprice, let me finish." She got up from her chair, and I stood up with her. She picked a piece of lint off my coat, grabbed my shoulders, and gave me a stern look. "You *must* let me guide the conversation. I might be able to get him to accept this idea of your shop. He'll never agree to it without me. I know you're an adult now, but understand, he is still the head of this family."

I just nodded and smiled.

"And you must still be open to meeting some nice Sicilian young men now and then—just be *open to the idea*. Because that will give him *something*. He needs to feel like he's getting something out of this conversation."

I nodded my head about twenty times. "Yes, whatever you say."

If she had told me I had to meet two hundred Sicilian men in two days, I would have agreed. All I could think of was the shop, and if my parents gave me their blessing—well, all I needed was the loan. *The loan* . . .

"Just . . . thank you—you have no idea," I said as I recalled our conversation at Thanksgiving. "If . . . no . . . *when* I open this shop, I promise you I won't fail. I won't disappoint you or cause you heartache. I promise."

"You've never done any of those things before," she said, kissing me on both cheeks and giving me a hug. "I hope you won't start now." She laughed nervously and smiled, adding, "Now go. Go meet your friends. Tonight we talk to your father."

CHAPTER 17

Love, a cough, and smoke are hard to hide.
    —Italian proverb

I hurried down Charter Street to meet my friends in front of St. Leonard's. The Santa Maria di Anzano feast was the first festival of the year. It signified that winter was nearly over. It was the perfect Sunday afternoon for it—bright and sunny, warm for February. There was a light, salty breeze coming off the harbor, but I didn't even need to button my coat.

Of course, as I walked through the crush of people, I couldn't help but keep a lookout for a head that was taller than most of the crowd, one with a boyish face and light-brown eyes. I wanted to see Sal so much that it physically hurt, and yet I didn't want to see him because I knew it would be even more painful when I did. I had managed to avoid him since the night Maria had told me he was engaged. The same night he had kissed me. Although it had been *so* easy to avoid him—leaving the pottery shop at odd hours, frequenting Carmen's Butcher Shop on Hanover Street—I was beginning to wonder if, like my father, he was also avoiding *me*. Maybe he knew I had discovered he was engaged. That I had learned he was a skirt chaser after all.

"Caprice! Caprice—wait!" I heard a deep voice from behind me and I jumped, thinking it might be Sal. But it was Dominic, running to catch up with me.

I frowned and squinted my eyes at him, "Excuse me, sir, do I know you?"

"What?" he said, smiling when he reached me. He tried to plant a kiss on my cheek, but I pulled back from him.

"I said, do I know you?" I answered, still walking. "I have a cousin who looks a bit like you, but he's hardly talked to me in weeks."

"Caprice, come on, don't be like that," he answered, giving me an exaggerated pout as he adjusted his wool cap and tried to keep up with me. "I know we haven't talked much lately, but . . . well . . ."

"But you've been too busy falling in love with one of my closest friends?" I snapped, a little too loudly.

"Keep your voice down, cousin," he whispered, placing his hand on my arm. "Come on, look, I know you and Ada have talked about it . . . it's true, everything she told you." He stopped and looked me in the eye. "I feel the same."

"So are you eloping? Have you made any plans I should know about?"

He shook his head and stared ahead of us at something I couldn't see. "No, no. Of course we haven't . . . not yet. It's complicated."

"Yes, it's complicated!" I said, before I remembered to keep my voice down and whispered, "God help you if your parents find out."

"Caprice, what can I say?" he answered, a pleading look in his eyes. "I don't know what the heck to do. I never expected this. I never expected I'd fall in love with *Ada*." The way he said her name sounded like a promise.

We were rounding Hanover Street. This was not the place to talk, and we would part ways soon, so I just said to him, "Dominic, she's one of my best friends. Just promise me you'll be careful . . . careful with her heart, okay?"

"Of course I will," he answered, tipping his cap at me.

"I have to go meet my friends now," I said. "I suggest you avoid us today. Too many friends and family around in the light of day, too much risk for you two. You can see the heat in your eyes as soon as you and Ada are near each other."

"Yes, Ada and I agreed on that already." Dominic gave me a kiss on my cheek, and this time I let him. "I'm going to meet Frankie and some of the guys. I'll see you later."

We parted ways and I headed down Hanover Street. I could hear the sound of trumpets blaring from a few blocks away, and I knew the procession for the Madonna di Anzano had begun at the other end of the street. People were dressed in their Sunday best, talking and laughing with one another, enjoying the sun on their faces and an excuse for a few hours of leisure and socializing. Children ran by me yelling and throwing *ciceri*—beans—at each other from the little bags their parents had bought them for a penny off the pushcarts.

I spotted Thea first. Then I saw that Ada was standing on one side of her, and I was surprised to see Joshua standing on her other side, holding her hand. She looked relaxed and happy and seemed to be standing taller. Maria was there too, telling them all a story. Her face was pale, and she still looked like she could gain a few pounds. I hadn't seen her do much eating since her father passed.

"Friends! I'm so sorry I'm late, but I have a *very* good reason why," I said, putting my arms around Ada and Maria.

"Hello, Caprice," Joshua said, tipping his hat to me. "Now that the whole gang is here, that's my cue to go." He squeezed Thea's hand and gave her a kiss on the cheek.

"Have fun this afternoon, ladies. I'll see you for dinner at your house later, okay?" he said to Thea, smiling.

"Okay, I'll see you then," she replied, her eyes sparkling as she grinned back at him. We all said good-bye to him as he headed into the crowds.

"So, Caprice, now tell us the reason why you're late," Thea said, her round cheeks flushed pink from more than just the cool breeze.

I relayed the conversation I'd had with my mother, finishing my story just as the procession passed by our spot on Hanover Street. We all turned and quietly observed the group of men, women, and children as they marched by. The Santa Maria di Anzano Society was composed of immigrants from the province of Foggia, Italy. In the middle of the procession, four men carried the nearly life-size statue of the Madonna di Anzano on their shoulders. She was surrounded by blue and white flowers and covered in dollar bills, offerings to the Virgin. A marching band brought up the rear of the procession.

"Caprice, good luck tonight," Maria said, hooking elbows with me and squeezing my arm. "Please let me know how it goes. Now, if you'll all excuse me, I've got to go meet Mark."

"What? Oh, Maria, I thought we were all going to be able to spend time together this afternoon," said Thea, frowning with disappointment. "I feel like I haven't seen any of you lately. Please stay. I have so much to tell you all. About my job, about the wedding. Can't Mark wait?"

"Maria, we planned this time for the four of us," I said, unable to hide the annoyance in my voice.

"I'm sorry, ladies, but I really can't stay," Maria said, glancing above the crowd. "I promised Mark I would meet him in ten minutes."

Maria looked down at the ground, her curls blocking her face. "I'm sorry, I really am," she said. She whipped her hair back over her shoulder and tucked a few strands under her hat just as two longshoremen walked by us, transfixed by Maria's blonde halo of hair.

That's when I noticed the familiar young man standing on the corner across the street, openly staring at us. He caught my eye and I frowned at him, but he just tipped his hat and gave me a creepy grin. I noticed a deep scar above his eye, and that's when I recognized him. It was Rocco, Mark Toscanini's *college,* I had met at the dance. I felt an unnatural chill when I realized he had been standing there this whole time, waiting for Maria.

"Maria, is that really Rocco across the street, waiting for you?" I asked, disgust in my voice when I said his name. Now Ada and Thea turned to look, and he gave a small wave.

"Maria, are you ready to go?" he yelled, his hands cupped over his mouth.

"Just tell him you'll be late or something," I said. "So we can all walk and talk together for a little while. We'll walk you over to meet him later."

"Yes, that's a perfect idea," said Ada, nodding. "We'll walk you later."

"Look, I'm sorry," said Maria. She started to fidget with the buttons on her coat so she didn't have to look any of us in the eye. "But Mark . . . well, he wouldn't understand. He wants me to meet some friends of his from Charlestown today. He's thinking of running for political office—he said I can help. I promised . . ."

"You promised *us*. Come on, Maria, Mark can wait—the politicians from Charlestown can wait," I said, growing more frustrated that my strong-willed friend was acting so subservient to Mark Toscanini. I gave our linked elbows a little pull, and I was surprised when she jerked her arm away.

"Ladies, I'm sorry but I have to go," Maria said, a look in her eyes that was a mixture of regret and something that might have been fear. "I can't tell him I'll be late. I . . . I *can't* be late for him. I should actually go with Rocco now."

She gave us each a quick hug and started backing away before we could say any more to her. "I'll see you all soon, really, but I've got to go. *Ciao*." She turned and hurried across the street to join Rocco. He didn't say anything to her; he just started walking, and she did the same. The two of them ducked down a side street and disappeared.

Ada, Thea, and I just stood there for a few seconds, looking across the street.

"What is going on? I never thought I'd see the

day that *Maria Santucci* would let any man tell her what to do," said Thea, shaking her head as we started walking toward the waterfront. "What's gotten into her? She's usually so . . . well, honestly, she's usually pretty conceited when it comes to men."

"I know," I answered. "But . . . I think she feels she owes him."

I finally explained to Thea and Ada how Maria's father had ended up in debt to the Toscanini family because of his gambling habit. Though I had promised Maria I wouldn't, now that her father had passed, I felt it was okay to tell our two closest friends. I needed them to know how she had become mixed up with Mark in the first place. They needed to understand it all in the proper context.

"So that's how this whole mess with that *gavone* started," I said in conclusion. "And now I'm truly afraid that she's convinced herself that maybe she *should* be with him because of his money. It's the security her mother never had."

"All this time I've been wondering why she would even give him the time of day," said Ada, sounding as worried as I felt. "But Maria, of all people, would *never* end up like her mother. I really can't believe she thinks she ever would, Caprice."

"Me neither," Thea added. "And I don't care how much money and supposed power he has;

Maria is way too good for Mark. He is such a *schmuck*."

"Thea!" said Ada as she burst out laughing.

"Well, come on, we all know it's true," said Thea with a shrug.

"I agree, Thea," I answered. "But now he seems to have this hold over her, like you said. And, now a part of her feels like she owes him. I don't know . . . I haven't talked to her much about Mark since the night her father died. But I'll try again to talk some sense into her."

I stopped talking as we tried to make our way across Hanover Street. It was too difficult to speak above the din of milling crowds and pushcarts.

"Why don't we cut down some of the side streets and around to get to the other end of Hanover? We could get some sweets at one of the pushcarts down there," suggested Ada.

We took a right down Prince Street to take a less congested route to the other end of Hanover. There were still people strolling on the side streets, but it was much quieter and we could walk down the middle of the cobblestone street and hear ourselves talk. Ada was telling us a funny story about her organic chemistry professor when all of a sudden I stopped in my tracks.

It was the "To Let" sign that caught my eye, sitting propped up against one of the grimy large glass windows. There in front of me was a storefront, on the corner of Prince and Garden Court Streets, next to a little barbershop near North Square. The window frames were cracked and peeling, and the door was desperately in need of a paint job. I ran over and peered into the dirty windows to get a better look. It was bigger than it seemed from the outside, going farther back than I expected. The ceiling was tin, and there were rows of dark oak shelves flanking the walls.

"Caprice, what are you doing?" I heard Ada's voice behind me. "We nearly turned the corner and left you behind. What are you—*oh*." And I knew she had also seen the "To Let" sign.

She started peering in the windows with me. Thea came up behind us, and we were all cupping our hands, trying to see through the filthy glass.

"This is it, isn't it?" said Ada, giving me a wide dimpled grin. "That's what you're thinking, right?"

I smiled and nodded, feeling goose pimples up and down my arms just imagining what this place could look like. "It certainly *could* be it," I said. "But, right now, it's almost too much to hope for, ladies. I feel like it's all so uncertain still . . ."

"This is what?" Thea asked. "What are you two . . . oh! Your shop!" she said, jumping up and down. "This is *your shop,* Caprice. It's perfect! Oh, the possibilities . . . I could help you decorate! And we could use some of the ideas we put in your business plan. A pastel green for the interior, with a creamy off-white for the trim . . ."

"Oh, it is totally perfect, Caprice," said Ada, tugging on my elbow.

We started walking again, all talking at once, imagining the possibilities—the paint colors, the window displays, and the location. I finally had to tell Thea and Ada to stop talking about it because I was superstitious. My stomach started churning. I had not heard a word from Mrs. Storrow yet, which couldn't be a good sign.

We had joined a long line at one of the pushcarts selling cannoli when I suddenly felt something small and hard hit the back of my head.

"Ow!" I said, grabbing my head and looking up into the sky. "What in the world was that? Ow! There it is again. Neither of you felt that? Something keeps hitting the back of my head."

We started looking around, and Ada whispered, "Um . . . I think *someone* is throwing beans at you."

And having avoided him for two weeks, I could now do nothing as Sal Valenti walked up and stood right behind me in line. My knees almost buckled and I felt a little dizzy at the sight of him. How was it that just seeing someone could cause a physical reaction? I told myself that I was going to be calm and cold toward him, and yet as soon as I looked into his eyes, I felt the heat creeping up my cheeks and imagined myself melting into his arms. I took a deep, quiet breath.

Sal exchanged pleasantries with the three of us and introduced his cousin, Vito, the owner of a dry goods shop, who looked like a shorter version of Sal. I managed to squeak a hello. I was thankful that Ada and Thea started talking with Vito, because Sal and I just kept staring at each other.

Finally he said, "Um, Caprice, can we step out of line so I can have a word with you?" When he said this, he touched me on the elbow and I nearly jumped. I nodded and kissed Thea and Ada on the cheek.

"Ladies, I need to talk to Sal, and then I better head home. My parents are going to be waiting to talk with me," I said. Thea and Ada tried to communicate with their eyes what they couldn't say in present company. I nodded at them to let them know I understood. They were there for me. Whatever happened, they were always there.

I walked over to a side alley with Sal. *He's engaged,* I kept saying over and over to myself. *He's engaged to Pupetta in Italy, and he didn't tell me.* It was over. Whatever had been started was over now.

"*Tesoro*, I've missed you. Where in the world have you been hiding?" Sal whispered when we were finally off to the side where we could talk quietly. He was looking at me, his eyes filled with concern and something more that I tried not to think about. I stepped away from him, needing distance between us so I didn't feel his breath on my cheek, the way he smelled of pine and sea salt. I crossed my arms over my chest and looked him up and down, trying to shore up some courage, trying not to think about how much I wanted to jump into his arms right now.

"Tell me, Sal, when you write to your fiancée, Pupetta, in Avellino, do you call her *tesoro* too, or do you have a different name for her?" I asked, my voice tight. I looked into his eyes, trying very hard to keep my expression blank and cold, even as my cheeks continued to burn.

Sal's face blanched.

"Caprice, I can explain—" he started, but I interrupted him, holding up my hand.

"What's to explain, Sal? Are you engaged to Pupetta Falcone in Avellino or not?" I asked, my jaw clenched. "Tell me right now, is what I heard true?"

"Caprice, it . . . it's, well, officially it is true but, please, let me tell you what—"

"That's all I need to know, Sal. There's nothing else to say," I answered, trying but failing to talk softly. "You . . . by not telling me . . . by *kissing* me . . . you lied. How can I believe anything you have to say now when all this time you've had this secret? It's like I was a joke to you. Just something to pass the time until your bride arrives in July."

"Caprice, how can you say that?" said Sal,

261

anguish in his voice. He reached for my hand, but I pulled it away before he could touch me. "Please," he continued. "At least give me a chance to explain."

"I gave you a chance," I answered. "I didn't believe the rumors about you being a skirt chaser when I should have listened to *all* of them! How *could* you? There's nothing else to say, Sal."

And before I could speak with my heart rather than my head, before he could see the tears in my eyes, I turned and hurried up the street away from him. I nearly broke into a run. I dodged a group of little girls walking together, laughing, and eating *torrone*. For a moment I wished that my friends and I were that age still, blissfully ignorant of heartbreak.

I reached the doorstep of my building and leaned against the steps to try to catch my breath, wiping the wetness from my cheeks. I looked up to the window of my family's apartment, where my mother and father were waiting for me. The day was not over.

Before I went inside, I said a quick prayer to the Virgin Mary and made the sign of the cross. I needed all the help I could get. I took a deep breath and opened the building door. My dream of being in love was over, but now I was more determined than ever to make my shop a reality.

CHAPTER 18

*A candle loses nothing by lighting
another candle.*
—Italian proverb

I trudged up the stairs to my family's home. My stomach churned and my heart pounded, and I didn't know if it was from my encounter with Sal or the fact that I had to talk to my father for the first time in three weeks. I kept picturing the look of sadness on Sal's face right before I'd turned away from him. What could he say, though? He was engaged, and Pupetta would be here in a few months. Sal Valenti had broken my heart, and shame on me for letting him get close enough to do so.

As I arrived at our floor, I tried to focus on how the talk with my parents would go. I hoped, as my mother promised, that she could guide the conversation, but I was afraid it was going to be more of the same: *What about marriage? What about babies? What about meeting a nice young Sicilian man? Who do you think you are to want to own a shop?* I was so weary of it all.

Our floor was uncharacteristically quiet, as many of our neighbors were at the festival. All I heard as I took slow steps down the hall was the Castellano baby squawking and the sound of conversation coming from my family's apartment at the end of the hall. I heard my parents' talking and other voices that sounded like . . . but it *couldn't* be . . .

"Mrs. Storrow. Madame DuPont? What a surprise. Hello, um . . . how are you both?" I asked as I entered. It was as if I had walked into a strange nightmare. I felt like I might faint.

"Ah, here she is. Caprice, good to see you," Mrs. Storrow said, giving me a warm smile. Madame DuPont looked me up and down and nodded in . . . approval? Disgust?

The two women were sitting at our tiny kitchen table. Mrs. Storrow's hair was pulled in a tight bun, and she was wearing a smoke-gray silk dress with a cream-colored lace yoke. Madame DuPont was in a burgundy silk dress, her hair in a low chignon. They looked regal.

Their appearance made me aware of the shabbiness of our little home. I noticed everything that I normally took for granted . . . the cracks in the yellowish plaster, the chips in the shabby white coffee cups they were drinking from. My parents were sitting with them, my mother in her usual black cotton dress and my father in a threadbare shirt and faded brown pants. It was so incredibly odd to see them at our table—with the horrid Christopher Columbus oilcloth—having coffee and biscotti with my parents.

I nodded, looking at my parents' faces, trying to understand what conversation had taken place before I entered the room. My father had a strange smile on his face, and my mother was giving me a look I couldn't quite decipher.

"And Madame DuPont, this is really quite a . . . um, surprise," I said.

"Yes, it is good to see you, Caprice," said Madame DuPont, placing her hands on her lap.

"As I said to your parents, I apologize for dropping in unannounced like this," Mrs. Storrow said. "On a Sunday, no less. But we have some news we wanted to share with you—with all of you."

"Oh?" I asked, raising my eyebrows.

"Yes, Caprice. Please sit down," my mother said in strongly accented English as my father pulled out a chair for me. "Mrs. Storrow and Madame DuPont were just telling us about how well known you were as a trimmer in Boston when you were working at Madame DuPont's."

"Yes," Mrs. Storrow said, nodding. "Many of my friends and acquaintances ask me where that trimmer from Madame DuPont's has ended up, because she made the most beautiful and unique hats they had ever purchased. Your reputation as a trimmer remains unmatched in Boston."

"It is true," Madame DuPont said in her French accent, nodding. "I still get questions about where you are now working—at what millinery.

When Mrs. Storrow told me you were working at your little club's pottery shop, I thought it was a horrible shame. A waste of a very rare talent."

I glanced at my father, and he was looking at me like he was seeing me—the *real* me—for the first time.

"Which brings me to the reason why we're here," said Mrs. Storrow. "Caprice, I know we discussed your business proposition a few weeks ago. Well, I want you to know, Madame DuPont and I have talked it over at length. We both agreed it is a sound and worthwhile investment."

"Caprice, I know firsthand how difficult it is owning a business," Madame DuPont said. "It is very difficult, especially as a woman." She paused and cleared her throat. "Now, I was not easy to work for, but having high standards was part of what made my business successful. And I pushed you. I pushed you more than the other girls in the shop, because, in all honesty, the rest of them were talentless nitwits."

I thought I heard my father suppress a laugh. What was she saying?

"I knew you had a gift, Caprice," said Madame DuPont. "And the more I pushed you, the more you proved that with your work. Now, I know you are wondering why on earth I am here in your home. I would like to invest in your hat shop, Caprice. The one that you plan on opening here, in the North End. I can offer you some advice and guidance also."

"I . . . I'm at a loss for words . . . I just . . . I can't believe it," I answered. Madame DuPont. Investing in me?

"After discussing it with Mrs. Storrow, I know it is going to be a success," said Madame DuPont. "I would like to help. As I said, it is shameful to see such talent wasted. I am back and forth between New York and Boston all the time. I can teach you everything you need to know. But make no mistake: it is your shop. I have no interest in being a shop owner again. We can discuss terms with my lawyer. So . . . the question is, are you interested in my offer?"

I was still trying to get over the shock of Mrs. Storrow and Madame DuPont sitting at the Christopher Columbus table. Now Madame DuPont was explaining how she wanted to be my investor. I was speechless.

I looked at Mrs. Storrow, and she gave me a small smile. My mother's eyes were glistening, and her hands were clasped tightly together. My father was still looking at me quizzically. Madame DuPont cleared her throat.

"Well, Caprice," she said. "What is your answer?" Abrupt as always.

"Madame DuPont, yes, thank you very much. I am interested in your offer," I said. "As long as it is, like you said, my shop, yes?"

Madame DuPont waved her hand and nodded. "Yes, yes, Caprice, I have no interest in working that hard again," she said with a dry laugh. "I am getting too old. My husband and I are going to the French Riviera for the summer. I would like to help you, but only as an advisor and investor."

"Okay," I said, taking a deep breath. "Okay, then yes, and thank you. I don't know how I can ever thank you enough. And you too, Mrs. Storrow. Thank you from the bottom of my heart."

"Oh, you're welcome, Caprice," said Mrs. Storrow, patting my hand. "I know it's going to be a great success."

I realized my parents hadn't said a word, and I looked over at them, praying that they would finally understand.

"Madame DuPont, thank you. This is wonderful news. Mrs. Storrow, thank you also. Thank you for doing this for our daughter," my mother said.

"Oh, I'm not doing it for her—she's doing it for herself. I would never do this if I didn't truly believe it would be a very sound investment," said Madame DuPont.

I looked at my father, and he was looking down at the tablecloth, scraping something with his finger that wasn't there. He looked up at me, gave me a small smile, sighed, and shook his head.

"You are so . . . so . . . *different,* Caprice," he

said. "Your world is so unlike where I grew up. A little peasant village in Sicily is not like America, not like this city. *La nuova maniera americana*—the new American way—is still hard for me to accept, even after living here all these years."

He rubbed his hand over his tired eyes. He sighed again and looked at Mrs. Storrow and Madame DuPont, then back at me.

"But then this. Mrs. Storrow, you come here, and Madame DuPont, you tell me you want to invest in . . . in my daughter . . . in *my daughter's* business. You both are ladies of society—you believe in my daughter." He paused, and I held my breath. "So I have to say—who am I not to believe in my daughter too?"

I jumped up and wrapped my arms around his shoulders, swallowing as hard as I could and trying not to cry for the second time in an hour. He got out of his chair and looked at me, studying my face.

"I am so proud of you, my American daughter," he said, touching my cheek. "I may not say it. But I always *know* it."

"Thank you, Papa," I said, giving him another hug. "Thank you so, so much."

We pulled away, and I sat back in my chair. My mother was smiling and giggling like a schoolgirl. Mrs. Storrow was grinning from ear to ear and looking at me, understanding my happiness, sharing the joy of this moment with me. Even Madame DuPont, ever reserved, gave me a small smile.

"So I give this shop my blessing—as long as you continue to pay board and continue to help out with expenses, Caprice," my father said.

"Of course, of course," I said, thinking that if he had asked me to buy Vita and Fabbia shoes for the rest of their lives, I would not have cared.

"And as long as you are still open to meeting a nice Sicilian man now and then," he said, pointing a finger at me, trying to remind everyone who the head of the house was. "Just because you are going to be a shop owner doesn't mean you can't be married someday, can't have babies."

"Yes." I just nodded. Just because I had to *meet* a nice Sicilian man did not mean I had to *marry* one. But that was a conversation for another day.

"So," said Madame DuPont, "it's settled. I will set up an appointment with my lawyer and bookkeeper next week, and we can discuss next steps with them. I will send you a note regarding when and where."

"And you're going to continue to work at the pottery shop until your shop opens," said Mrs. Storrow. "Are you prepared to work evenings and Sundays to get ready for your opening day?"

"Am I ready? Mrs. Storrow, I think I've been ready my entire life," I said with a smile.

"I knew you'd say that," she said, giving me a wink. Then, looking at her watch, she added,

"Edward is going to be waiting outside with my car momentarily, so we must go. My husband has an important meeting this week, and I promised I'd help him prepare tonight. And Madame has dinner plans."

We all got up with her, and my father got Mrs. Storrow and Madame's cashmere cloaks and helped the ladies put them on. My parents stood there smiling; my father smoothed out his shirt, and my mother self-consciously tucked a stray hair back into her bun.

"An exciting new chapter begins for the Russo family," Mrs. Storrow said. "Thank you, Mr. and Mrs. Russo, for letting us visit unexpectedly like this. And thank you for giving Caprice your blessing in this new venture. I know she'll make you so proud."

"It was a pleasure meeting you both," said Madame. "I am looking forward to working with you again, Caprice."

"Thank you for coming to our home," my father answered, "and for helping my daughter." His voice broke a bit on the word *daughter*.

I walked the two women toward the stairs. Mrs. Castellano and Mrs. Mineo were sitting in the hall, chatting in Italian, but they stopped and stared when they saw Mrs. Storrow and Madame.

"Good afternoon," Mrs. Storrow said, giving them both a warm smile. Mrs. Castellano gave her a shy smile back, and Mrs. Mineo nodded and actually did a sort of curtsy-bow.

"Now, Caprice, it was all right that we came to your home today?" Mrs. Storrow asked me in a whisper when we reached the stairwell.

"Mrs. Storrow, of course, *of course* it was," I said. "I am thrilled beyond words. Madame, thank you."

"You can thank me when your shop is a success, Caprice," said Madame DuPont. "Then we will toast with champagne. Until then, there is so much work to do."

"Yes, there is," I said. "And I couldn't be happier about it."

As expected, Edward was waiting with the shiny black touring car, looking rather out of place. A crowd of little boys had gathered to sit on the steps to stare at it.

"I will be in contact soon, Caprice," Madame DuPont said as Edward opened the car door for her.

Before Mrs. Storrow got in the car, I gave her a tight hug and whispered in her ear, "I'm not sure I'll ever be able to thank you for all that you've done for me. For Ada. For so many of us. We're so blessed to have you in our lives, Mrs. Storrow."

She pulled back and held both my hands. "Caprice, as you know, James and I have one wonderful son," she said in a soft voice. "We desperately wanted a big family, and I wanted a daughter so very much. But that was not God's plan for us. You—all of you Saturday Evening Girls—you are my daughters. And I am just as blessed to have *you* in *my* life." She patted me on the cheek with her hand, brushing away the tear that was sliding down it.

"Thank you," I replied, because when someone said something like that, there were no other words.

"I'll see you soon, Caprice," she said as she stepped into the car.

"Good-bye," I said with a wave.

I stood on the steps of my building, surrounded by little boys waving to the car as it went down our street. I was still stunned by the day's turn of events. When the car turned the corner, something came over me, and I just started jumping up and down on the steps, whooping and hollering and pumping my arms in the air. All of the little boys started laughing and copying me, and it was a little impromptu party on the steps of 53 Charter Street.

CHAPTER 19

Love rules without rules.
—Italian proverb

Saturday, March 13, 1909

I had never been so exhausted in my life. But it was an elated sort of exhaustion. After Mrs. Storrow and Madame DuPont's fateful visit to my family home, my life had become a whirlwind of work—the pottery shop by day and working on the plans for my shop by night. Now that my scribbles on scraps of paper were going to become a reality, it was all I could do not to work twenty-four hours a day. My mother and father had insisted I try to eat dinner with the family most nights. But after dinner I had often gone back to the quiet peace of the pottery shop, working late into the night on *my own* inventory lists and sketches, as well as studying up on bookkeeping practices. It was all so exciting, sometimes I had trouble sleeping.

On those sleepless nights, I stared at the ceiling, listening to Fabbia's soft breathing and Vita's snoring and thinking about the shop. Of course, my mind had also gone to a certain young butcher whom I had not been able to get out of my head. Despite my efforts to throw all my physical and emotional energy into opening the shop, Sal always hovered in the back of my mind.

It had been thirteen days since I had seen him at the festival. I hadn't gone anywhere near his shop on Stillman Street for fear of bumping into him. But every time the bell jingled late in the day at the pottery shop, my heart jumped and I looked up from my sweeping or dusting or bookkeeping, hoping—but at the same time, fearing—that it might be him. The sad truth was that I had fallen in love with him, despite the fact that he would be marrying someone else. Only love could hurt this much. Sometimes I would imagine him and Pupetta walking out of St. Leonard's hand in hand on a sunny July day, and my heart would break all over again.

I was thinking about all of this as I put a beautiful midnight-blue vase on display at the S.E.G. shop. All I could hope was that someday soon I would get over Sal so I could simply focus on my business plans. The shop was my future. Sal was my past.

I glanced up at the clock and realized that everyone would be arriving for the meeting soon. I had started cleaning up my paperwork on the counter when I noticed a thick cream-colored envelope with *Caprice Russo* written on it in Madame DuPont's script. I ripped it open

276

and unfolded the papers inside. There was a handwritten note on top of some official-looking documents.

Caprice—Enclosed is the contract for the storefront on Prince Street. Please sign and give to Mrs. Storrow to return to me. My driver will drop off a key to you by next week. I will be in contact to schedule another meeting soon. – M. DuPont

At the top of the first page it read, *Lease for commercial space, 1 Prince Street.*

I read over the note three times. The shop on the corner of Prince and Garden Court Streets—the one I had seen the day of the festival—was going to be *mine*. Caprice's Millinery—just as I had imagined the first time I had laid eyes on it. It was almost too good to be true.

I sat on my stool behind the counter and started reading the lease. Just as I was signing it, the door jingled and Ada was standing in front of me, ghostly pale and shaking.

I felt chills up my spine. After Maria's father's death, my thoughts turned to the worst possibilities.

"Jesus, Mary, and Joseph! Ada, what happened? What's the matter?" I asked, grabbing her by both arms.

Then the door jingled again, and there was

Dominic, wild-eyed and frantic as he walked up to Ada.

"Ada, please, I'm begging you, just *please* talk to me about this!" He tried to grab Ada's hand, but she pulled it away.

"Dominic, I've said all I have to say," she said in a whisper, looking up at him with sad dark eyes. "I'm sorry, I'm *sorry*. Now, please, you have to go before people start arriving for the meeting. Please . . . just go."

"Dominic, I'm afraid she's right," I said. "We don't want everyone in the S.E.G. to see you two like this." I glanced at Ada, and her hands were gripping the wood counter, fingernails digging in. She was barely holding her composure. I whispered in Dominic's ear, "I'll talk to her."

"But, Ada, I . . ." His voice cracked, and then he put his head down and nodded. "Okay. Okay. I'll go for now. For *now*. This conversation isn't over. *This* isn't over . . ."

He stepped toward her, presumably to kiss her good-bye, but before he could, she ran and disappeared into the kiln room. The look on his face was so desperate, it brought tears to my eyes. He didn't even say anything to me before turning and heading out the door.

I hurried back to the kiln room, and there was Ada, leaning against the wall, covering her face with her hands. I walked over and gave her a hug, and she collapsed into me, sobbing on my shoulder.

"Ada, sweetheart, what happened?" I whispered.

Ada took a deep breath and tried to get control of her sobbing for a few seconds. "It's . . . it's over, Caprice," she said, breaking away from me and attempting to wipe her nose with her sleeve. "He met me a little while ago, to walk me to . . . to here . . . and I just ended it. I ended it with him, Caprice, and I'm . . . I feel like my heart has been shre-shredded."

I wrapped my arms around her again as she started sobbing so hard she was practically convulsing.

The kiln room was warm and had the earthy smell of just-baked pottery. There were two stools sitting among a number of biscuits—sand-colored pottery pieces—that had just been unpacked. I walked Ada over to one of the stools and sat her down on it. I pulled the other one next to her, taking my handkerchief out of my skirt pocket and handing it to her so she could wipe her face. Her sobs had calmed down, and she was now just softly sniffling.

"Ada, do you want to tell me what happened? What made you do it?" I asked, thinking about where Dominic had gone and how *he* was doing. I wished there were some way I could contact Frankie.

"I've been praying about it, thinking about it for days. Trying to decide what to do—what *I* really wanted," Ada said, looking at me with her swollen eyes. "I love him. Oh, do I love him. But, in the end, I couldn't give up school to be with him. I couldn't leave school, my family . . . my friends . . . it's too much of a sacrifice. Even . . . even for him."

She started to cry again, and I nodded at her and took her hand. She composed herself after a minute.

"I've always wanted more than this . . . this life that I was born into. I wanted more than to just get married and have babies and live in the same building in the North End for the rest of my life. You understand, right, Caprice?"

"Oh, Ada, you know I do," I said with a sad smile.

"My education, this gift that I've been given— it's the beginning of something *more* for me. And I need to hold on to that," she said. She blew her nose into my handkerchief before adding, "Do you know that one of my professors actually suggested medical school to me the other day—*medical school*. At Boston University. They accept women, and there's even a state scholarship fund that would pay for it all. Me, a doctor! Can you imagine?"

"You're about the only person I know who I could imagine becoming a doctor, Ada," I answered, squeezing her hand, feeling sympathy and pride for my brilliant friend.

"All this time I've been trying to figure out how to reconcile my goals for myself, for my future, with my love for Dominic." She paused for a minute, smoothing down her hair. "I just finally realized it couldn't be done. I had to choose. I can't elope. I can't give up this dream, this education. Even though I love him, it can't . . . it's impossible.

"If I'm truly going to consider medical school, then I have to focus on that alone. And there's so much I have to do. My mother and I have to finally reveal this secret to my father, and I have to plan and prepare and take more courses . . . and there's no possible way for Dominic to be in my life if I'm to pursue this dream. You were right all along, Caprice. I should have ended it before it started," she said, looking at me as her eyes filled up with tears again.

"Oh, Ada, I wish I were wrong. I wish it *weren't* impossible. I hope you know I didn't mean to seem judgmental; I just love you both so much and didn't want to see either of you hurt like this."

Ada just nodded and blew her nose into my handkerchief again. I decided it was hers to keep. I heard the front door jingle for the fourth time since we had been in the kiln room.

"I hate missing meetings, but I think we should

skip this one," I told her. "You're just going to get a lot of questions about something you don't want to talk about."

"I don't know," she said. "I always feel so guilty when I miss a meeting."

"Me too, but under the circumstances, I think we need to go get some air," I said. "I'm going to go leave a note for Maria and Thea to tell them what happened and to meet us on the roof of my building. It's unusually warm for March. It'll be nice up there tonight."

"Oh, Caprice," she said, "but what if we run into Dominic? I just . . . it's too hard to see him right now."

I shook my head. "I know, but we'll go up the back staircase. And I'm willing to bet money he's at the Sicilian Club for the rest of the evening."

She nodded, staring off in a daze, no doubt thinking of Dominic sitting at the Sicilian Club with Frankie and the rest of his *compaesani* . . . trying his best not to look sad in front of them. Trying his best not to think of her.

CHAPTER 20

No one can take the one who is
destined for you.
—Italian proverb

There was the sound of a distant mandolin being played by some old man on a stoop somewhere below. A breeze blew up, and I could smell the salty ocean air off the harbor, strong and clean. And even though it was close to seven o'clock, it really was warm—a particularly comfortable evening that held the promise of the days and months to come. I had not been on the rooftop of my building since the previous summer; my friends and I would occasionally come up here at night in the warmer months. The best time was August, when the tomato and basil plants were strong and tall, and their mingled scent was better than any perfume I had ever smelled.

I was surprised to find that our stash of candles and matches hidden next to the stairway was untouched. I lit a few so that we could see a little better just as Thea and Maria opened the door and walked into the fresh night air.

"Ada, how are you doing?" Maria asked as the two of them rushed up to her and wrapped her in an embrace, which made her dissolve into tears all over again.

"Thea, can you please help me grab some of these crates so we can have something to sit on?" I asked as they broke apart and Maria wiped Ada's face with her own handkerchief.

"Of course," said Thea, running over and taking two crates out of my hands. We arranged them in a circle, and all of us sat down.

"The candles make it feel like this is some sort of secret ceremony," said Maria with a devilish grin.

"Yes, it's called the 'purging of a broken heart ceremony,'" I answered.

"Thank you for doing this instead of the meeting," said Ada, looking at our faces in the candlelight. "I've missed the roof. I've missed all of you. I feel like we see each other less and less these days and I . . . well, if I'm going to have to nurse my broken heart, there are no other people I'd rather be with."

"And we're happy to be with you," said Thea.

"And I brought us some wine," said Maria, and we all started laughing. "I did—it's a homemade bottle that your family gave my family at Christmas, Caprice. I've been keeping it under my bed. I think this is the perfect night to open it."

"I agree," said Thea, the candlelight flickering off her freckled face. "Here, Maria, you pour and I'll pass out the coffee cups."

"Maria, have you seen much of Mark lately?" I asked. I couldn't resist. I was worried about her. About her and him. I needed to know what was happening.

"Uh . . . well . . . yes, I've seen him," said Maria. "I'm so sorry I had to rush off on the day of the festival. It was just really important that I meet these people from Charlestown. Friends of his family."

"Speaking of his family, didn't his cousin Carmen get arrested last week for taking bribes?" Thea asked, frowning. She asked the question rather innocently, but I knew she was now as concerned about Maria and Mark as I was.

"Oh, yes, but Mark said he's innocent," Maria said with a wave of her hand. "The charges will probably be dismissed. So, Caprice, what's going on with the shop?" As usual, she was eager to change the subject. I would let her—for now.

"Oh—well, this calls for a toast, girls," I said. "I signed the lease on the shop on Prince Street today. I think I'll be able to open in about three months!" The three of them all started congratulating me at once, and we stood up and clinked our coffee cups of wine together.

"That's really wonderful, Caprice," said Thea, glancing sideways at Ada. She was sitting down again, staring into the distance. It was like she was in a trance. But we kept talking, hoping it would help somehow.

"Now what about Sal?" asked Thea. "Have you seen him since the festival?"

I shook my head and took a sip of wine, trying to dull the now-familiar pain in my chest at the mention of his name. "No, not a glimpse of him."

"Do you want to see him?" Maria asked, clearly grateful to be talking about my mess of a love life instead of her own.

"I do," I answered. "But at the same time I don't. And I think it's probably best that I don't see him."

"Are you sure?" Thea asked. "Maybe you should hear his side of things?"

"I think I heard all that I needed to, Thea," I replied with a sigh. "Truly. Now, bride-to-be, how is that sweet fiancé of yours?" I knew we were supposed to be keeping Ada's mind off of Dominic, but I realized I didn't want to discuss Sal either.

"You know, I have an announcement of my own to make tonight," said Thea, taking a gulp of wine. "I wasn't sure if it would ever happen, but . . . I am falling in love with my fiancé. Can you believe that? It's two weeks until our wedding, and I'm *actually* falling in love with Joshua Robinowitz."

"Cheers to that," I said, holding my cup up to toast her. "I could tell you were at the festival."

"*Per cent'anni!*" Maria added.

"*Mazel tov*," Ada whispered, clinking her cup with mine.

"And you know that thing I was so nervous about—that happens in the bedroom?" Thea said, letting out a giggle. "I'm still nervous, but I'm . . . I'm actually . . . well, I'm kind of looking forward to it." Her cheeks started to take on a pink hue in the candlelight.

Maria and I started laughing, thinking about the night of her engagement party. Thea buried her face in her hands for a second to try to control her laughter, which made Maria start doing her snorty laugh.

Ada stood up and put her coffee cup down on her crate. "Girls, I'm sorry, I . . . I thought this would help, but . . . the truth is nothing can help me tonight," she said, her eyes about to spill over again with tears.

"Oh, Ada, I'm so sorry—I hope it wasn't me carrying on . . ." Thea looked like she was going to cry too.

"No, Thea, of course not, really. It's just—it's just so new, it's hard for me to focus on anything else but how I'm feeling," Ada replied, taking small backward steps toward the stairs. "Thank you for doing this. Thank you for all being here for me, but I'm just going to . . . I've got to go . . ."

She turned and ran down the stairs, and we

heard the break of a sob echoing from the stairwell.

"I'm going to go after her," Thea said, frowning. "I'm supposed to meet Joshua in front of Hull House soon anyway."

Maria and I nodded in agreement. "That would be good, Thea," I replied, walking over to give her a hug. "Would you please stop by the pottery shop in the morning and let me know how she is? I'm going to be there after nine-thirty Mass for a couple of hours."

"Of course," Thea said, nodding before giving Maria a kiss on the cheek.

When Thea left, we started picking up the vegetable crates and stacking them in the corner.

"Poor Ada," I said with a sigh.

"Yes, I do feel bad for her—but, you know, I think we all realized that this was doomed from the start," Maria said in a condescending tone. "She really should have known better than to get herself involved with him."

"Yes, but Maria, you can still have some sympathy for her," I said, feeling myself get tense. "Ada and Dominic fell in love almost despite themselves."

"All I'm saying is she should have used her head and not her heart. Then she wouldn't be feeling the way she does now," Maria answered with a shrug. She walked over and placed the bottle of wine near the piled-up crates. "I'm going to meet Mark now," she said, walking back over to me, buttoning up her coat, and putting on the purple velvet Charlotte Corday hat that I had made for her the year before.

"What?" I looked at Maria like she had lost her mind. "You're meeting Mark? When? Where?"

Maria adjusted her curls under her hat and didn't meet my eyes. "At a tavern his family owns, down by the waterfront."

"Well . . . is anyone walking you down there?" I asked.

"Um . . . no, no, but it's right down the street, for God's sake," said Maria, looking down and brushing some imaginary dust off of her coat.

I couldn't help myself. I was too worried about her to stay silent.

"Maria, honestly, I don't even know who you are lately. Aren't your father's debts to the Toscaninis paid? It's been months now."

"Yes," she said. "Yes, they're paid. Of course they're paid. We resolved that shortly after my father died. Thank God."

"Then why in the world does this guy still have such an influence on you? In the past, you never would have agreed to meet *any* man at *any* tavern! Even if it were ten in the morning. But almost eight o'clock at night? It's not safe. And it's no place for a respectable woman like you to go."

"Caprice, first of all, I'm going with Mark

Toscanini—I'm *with him,*" she said, her voice rising with anger. "So how dare you say it's not respectable of me. And to say you don't know who I am anymore? Well, that's just ridiculous. I'm still me."

"Well, the Maria Santucci I know wouldn't let any man tell her what to do. She would never be at his beck and call," I answered, my voice rising to match hers. "The Maria I know is way too smart for a guy like that. He is *poison,* Maria. How many rumors are you going to dismiss? How many excuses are you going to continue to make for him before you finally realize what he is? I'm shocked that you continue to spend time with him."

"Caprice, I have *not* changed!" she said, looking out at the Old North Church steeple instead of at me. "I just happen to be seeing a young man who has money and power and . . . well, if you must know, I'm . . . I'm eloping. With him."

My mouth fell open in shock, and I heard myself let out an enormous gasp.

"I am," said Maria, tilting her nose up, cold defiance in her eyes. "I'm eloping with him sometime soon, in the next month or so. I'm going to marry him."

"No! Maria—you can't do that!" I said, raising my voice. "Maria, I know you're so afraid of ending up like your mother, but—"

"Caprice, you cannot tell me what I can or cannot do!" Her eyes caught the light, and they were scorching. "We've been through this before! How dare you! How dare you judge me! You're damn right I'm afraid of ending up like my mother—of rattling pots and pans around behind closed doors at dinnertime so the neighbors think we have enough food to eat. She cries herself to sleep every night, mourning a husband who, when he was alive, was too drunk most of the time to notice her or his own children or anything else. You have no idea what my life has been like."

"No, I don't; that's true," I said quietly, trying to calm my voice. "I know you're scared of ending up with the life your mother has. But let me tell you something, Maria: it will *never* happen. That will never be you. Or me. Or Thea or Ada. We are all destined for better things. For better lives than our mothers have had.

"But you don't have to marry someone like Mark for a better life. He's not good enough to breathe the same *air* as you, and deep down you know that. You can do anything. You're a gifted dressmaker. You could open your own shop too. And you're really smart; you could take colleges classes like Ada. You're an amazing, beautiful, intelligent young woman, and Mark Toscanini will never be good enough for all of the things that you are!"

Maria looked at me and was silent for a moment. Her eyes were angry, but she looked like she might cry too.

"Maybe someday you and Ada and Thea will understand this decision," she said, her voice a hoarse whisper. "Understand why I am doing this. For myself. For my family. I'm done talking about it tonight. I'll . . . I'll see you later." She turned and opened the door to the stairway, and I heard her practically running down the stairs.

I threw my hands up in the air and looked at the stars.

"What a night," I said to the sky. I wrapped my arms around myself. The air had turned, and it was feeling chilly again.

I heard footsteps coming up the stairs to the roof door, and I felt a sense of relief. Maybe she was coming back to talk more, maybe she was having doubts, maybe I could convince her to change her mind.

"Hello?" I heard a baritone voice that made my stomach flip. "Hello? Anyone up here?"

His frame took up the entire doorway, and he was squinting as his eyes adjusted to the dark.

It was just me and Sal, standing ten feet from each other, alone together on the roof. A breeze came up, and I heard someone yelling from the street below. Somewhere in the distance the mandolin was still playing.

"Um . . . hi." I opened my mouth to continue

but then closed it again because I really didn't know what else to say.

"Hello," Sal said again, walking over to me. He didn't give me his usual smile, and I was glad because it would have been even harder to control my emotions. "I saw Maria. She said you were up here. Little party tonight?"

"Something like that," I answered, pressing my crossed arms against my stomach, trying to quell the jumpiness.

"So, Caprice Russo," he said, walking ever closer to where I was standing. "I am here because I need to explain something to you. And since you have taken great steps to avoid me over the last couple of weeks, I finally decided that I had to come find you."

"Oh?" I said, and I started to think about his engagement and how betrayed I'd felt when I heard the news, and my jaw started to clench and I held my arms even tighter around me.

"Yes," he said. "You see, a few years ago, my parents made an arrangement with another family still living in Italy, in Avellino. The Falcones— *compaesani* from their village. Dear friends. It was an arranged marriage between me and the Falcones' daughter, Pupetta. She's quite a bit younger than me; she just turned seventeen years old."

"Sal, I *know*. I know all about it. Why are you telling me things I already know? Do you want my blessing or something? Fine, you have it," I said, turning away to look out over the rooftop. What he was saying hurt too much. I didn't want to know any more about Pupetta-with-the-bad-skin.

He walked over to me, tapped my elbow, and looked me in the eyes when I turned back around. "Caprice, *pazienza*. Please. Just let me finish. It's important that you understand."

I sighed and finally uncrossed my arms, leaning up against the brick wall on the edge of the roof.

"Okay," I said, trying to sound calmer. "Finish."

"So, I have been engaged to this person, who I have never met in my life, for a few years now. I always had mixed feelings about it. Not as many of us, of our generation, are marrying like this . . ."

"Thank God," I answered, thinking of my father's ridiculous attempts.

"Yes, thank God," he said with a small smile. "Caprice, my reputation, well, it was somewhat earned before I met you. I did spend some time with a few women only to move on because I was always engaged to Pupetta. But I never, ever disrespected those women or made any promises I couldn't keep. I *never* did, Caprice. You must know that."

"I still don't know why you're telling me all of this," I said. "You never disrespected those women, you're engaged to Pupetta . . . so . . ."

"So when I saw you at the festival, I *was* still

officially engaged to her," he said, interrupting me, talking quickly, his eyes not leaving mine. "But I had been going back and forth with my parents for several weeks, trying to make them understand that *they* had to—*I* had to—break it off. They finally agreed. But during the festival they were still in the process of writing to the Falcones and making it final. That was what I wanted to explain to you before you ran away from me."

He took his hat off, and I really looked at his face for the first time since he walked through the door to the roof: the light-brown eyes, the dimple in his cheek. My heart was beating so hard I wondered if he could hear it.

"So, it's over. Why are you telling me this?" I asked, trying to brace myself for more bad news. Did he just want to clear his conscience? Apologize to make himself feel better?

Sal gave me a small smile, looked down at the ground, and started kicking the gravel.

"I knew you weren't going to make this easy for me, Caprice." He looked back up at me, and he stepped even closer. There were only inches between us now.

"I am telling you this, because . . ." He sighed and let out a nervous little laugh, coming so close I could smell the sweet warmth of his breath. "Caprice, don't you know? *You* are the reason I broke off my engagement. I've never felt like this about any woman before you. You. Your gorgeous smile is the reason. Your red hair is the reason. Your beauty and your intelligence and your stubbornness . . . and . . . and your silly laugh, and the way your eyes crinkle up when you're angry . . ."

He grabbed both of my hands in his and said softly, "My engagement was over the first day you walked into my shop last fall, Caprice. Don't you know that by now? I was . . . it was *over*. Because the only woman I could think about from that moment on was you."

I was speechless. I swallowed hard to keep from crying, and as I looked into his eyes, I was overcome with all the emotion of not seeing him for weeks, thinking he was not the man I thought he was, and realizing with enormous relief that I was wrong.

"Are you okay, Caprice?" he whispered, putting his hand under my chin and wiping away a lone tear that was sliding down my cheek.

"My hair is auburn," I whispered to him with a smile just as he put his lips on mine. That feeling I thought I might never experience again welled up inside me as he put his arms around me, and I fell into him with happiness and relief. He gave me a long, sweet kiss that made me forget where we were, what time it was, and all the things that had happened earlier in the evening. All I could think about was Sal and how good it all felt and how I couldn't believe it was happening and how I didn't want it to end.

And I wasn't sure how many hours we stayed up there on that roof, but we kissed and talked and laughed until long after that mandolin stopped playing.

CHAPTER 21

Forbidden fruit is the sweetest.
—Italian proverb

Saturday, March 20, 1909

"Fabbia, have you been practicing what Caprice has been teaching you?" my father asked poor Fabbia just as she was taking a big bite of brown bread. He'd been asking her this question at least once a day.

"Yes, Papa," said Fabbia with a sigh when she finally swallowed. "Of course I'm practicing every day, making hat shapes on the wire molds she made for me. I'm learning everything I can from her. Caprice, will you *please* tell him?"

"Papa, she's a really great student," I said. "Fabbia is going to be an excellent maker."

"And me too, right, Caprice?" Vita asked, looking up at me, her eyes hopeful.

"Yes, Vita, of course you too," I said. "Now I have to—"

"And Frankie, you're going over to do some painting at Caprice's shop tomorrow afternoon, right?"

"Yes," said Frankie. "As I said yesterday,

I'm going over there to paint it that girly green color. I'm bringing Dominic with me; he needs something to do." Frankie gave me a pointed look. Dominic and Ada had both still been acting miserable and heartbroken. Although I thought my cousin was the worse off.

"Well, maybe I should come over too," my father suggested. "To help. What do you think, Caprice? Do you need more help with the painting?"

"No, Papa, I think they'll be fine," I answered. "Besides, you have your own shop to worry about."

My mother was standing behind my father at the stove, and she gave me an amused look over his head. *Be careful what you wish for,* she said with her eyes.

"Okay, well, let me know," he answered, sitting back and taking a sip of wine, surveying all of us at the table. For some reason the hairs in his right eyebrow were sticking straight up today, which was a little distracting. "Do you think you'll still be ready to open by June?"

"Yes, Papa," I said, trying to reassure him for the hundredth time. "If everything goes according to plan, if I can get all the used furniture painted and refurbished, if all of my inventory has arrived, if my wire frames and model hats come in, if all my materials and ready-to-trim hats are delivered on time from New York, and we have the shop ready . . . it will be a great deal of work, but I should be open by June seventh."

"Caprice, sweetheart, aren't you going to be late for your meeting?" my mother asked. God bless her, she was trying to save me from what had now become a regular interrogation about my shop. *My shop.* I still couldn't believe it sometimes.

"Oh, yes," I said, jumping up from the table and grabbing my coat and hat off of the rack. "Thank you for reminding me. I better hurry." I went around the table and gave my father and siblings kisses on the head.

My mother was walking me out to the hall when my father called out, "Oh, Caprice, I meant to tell you, there's a young man coming over for dessert tomorrow night. His name is Tony, Tony Langone. His father is Tony too. You know, Mr. Langone, who has the newsstand?"

"Okay, Papa. Sounds good." Some things had changed. Some had not. I hadn't told my parents about Sal yet. I didn't know when or how I was going to manage that, but I didn't care. We were together. Sooner or later, my parents would have to understand.

" 'Sounds good'?" my mother said, her eyebrows raised and her lips pursed in a smile. "That's the first time I've ever heard you say that when your father tells you he's invited a young man over for dessert."

"Mama, I'm so happy about my shop that nothing he does could upset me right now. Besides, it's just dessert."

"Yes, yes. It's just dessert," she said with a small laugh, kissing me on the cheek. "Okay, my sweet, go see your friends. You've earned it."

Before I went to my meeting, I walked up to the rooftop to look for Thea's hat, which she thought she had left there last Saturday night. When I opened the door to the roof, I was surprised to see a man standing at the edge of it, his back facing me as he stared out at the harbor. In the next instant I recognized the curly dark hair and tall stature.

"Hey, Dominic, this is my place to go for a quiet moment," I said, teasing him as I walked over. "This is *my* roof. Don't you know you need my permission to come up here?"

He turned to look at me, and his sad, shadowy eyes told me he was in no mood for joking. He looked terrible even in the faint light. His olive skin was abnormally pale, and there was black scruff on his face.

"How're you doing, cousin?" I said, grabbing his elbow and leaning up to give him a quick kiss on the cheek. "I've been trying to get you alone all week just so I could see how you are. I've been worried about you."

"Well," Dominic said with a sigh, "I'm in love with a woman who I'm no longer with. And everywhere I go I'm reminded of her, of us when we were together. I go by alleys where we kissed, St. Leonard's hall where we danced. I swear I can smell her damn perfume in the air. It's torture, Caprice. I've even thought about going to Sicily to get away from all of the memories . . . but then I really don't want to ever be that far away from her."

"Dominic," I began, trying to be gentle with my words. "You know I don't want you to go to Sicily, but saying you don't want to be far from her when you can't be with her . . . well, that doesn't make sense. What do you—" I said, but he held up his hand.

"But that's the thing," he said. "She can't be with me right now, and that's what tortures me. But you know, Caprice, I've also made up my mind about something this week. I don't want to be too far away from her, because I've decided . . . because I've decided that I'm going to wait for her."

"What!" I asked, incredulous. "What do you mean you're going to *wait for her?*"

He shrugged and looked out at the harbor. Then he said very softly, "I'm going to wait for her. For as long as it takes. Forever, if I have to. I don't think falling in love, the way we fell in love—I don't think it happens twice in a lifetime. So I'm going to wait. She's a smart girl. At some point she'll figure out what I already know."

"Well, I just worry . . . I don't know if it's ever going to work for you two—the religions, her plans for school . . . everything . . . You know that, right?" I asked this, feeling a pain in my heart for my cousin and my friend. He was even more besotted with Ada than I had ever realized.

"Yes, well . . . we'll see. I disagree," he said, kicking the roof with his shoe. "Don't think I'm going to do anything now, mind you. I'm not going to follow her around or even talk to her. No, just be in the same neighborhood with her. See her gorgeous face once in a while," he said, nodding. "That will be enough. For now."

"Okay, cousin, if you say so. I just worry that you won't ever get over her. What if you can never really be with her? Please . . . please just *think* about what you're saying."

"I will, Caprice," he answered. "I have."

"I've got to go to my meeting." I kissed him on the cheek and turned to go. I was about to open the door to the stairs when I looked back at him. He was already lost in his thoughts again, staring out at the sea.

"Is it because you can't have her? Because she's Jewish?" I asked. "Is that why you love her?"

He looked at me with a sad grin. "No, Caprice, it's not like that. I love her because she's Ada."

I nodded and gave him a sympathetic smile before I headed downstairs.

CHAPTER 22

Whoever finds a friend finds a treasure.
—Italian proverb

I walked down the cobblestone streets alone because Maria was presumably somewhere with Mark. I hadn't even thought to ask Frankie or Dominic to walk me.

I knew it was nearly spring because many of the tenement windows above were open, and women had draped towels on the sills and were leaning out, idly gossiping with one another and enjoying the fresh, cool evening air on their faces. Elderly men and women had pulled out chairs on the sidewalks and sat, enjoying cups of coffee and talking with one another about the old country. The smells of Saturday night dinners mingled in the air. Tonight garlic, lentil soups, and marinara sauces overpowered the more unpleasant smells of the streets.

I was about to turn the corner when I felt someone grab my elbow, and I was yanked into the nearby alley before I could even see who it was. I turned and opened my mouth to scream, but before I could, Sal had put his hand on my mouth and was holding a finger up to his own, signaling me to be quiet.

"Salvatore Valenti, you scared me to death!" I said in whispered admonishment.

"You shouldn't be out walking alone this time of night," he said, looking at me with tenderness and lifting up my hand to kiss it, which gave me goose pimples up and down my arms. "Next time, tell me and I will meet you a block from your home to walk you. I was going to meet you at Hull House to give you these."

He opened his coat and pulled out a small bouquet of purple daffodils.

I took the bouquet and brought it up to my nose to inhale its perfume. "No one has ever given me fresh flowers before. Thank you."

"You're welcome," he answered, clearly pleased that I liked them. "I thought you could keep them at the pottery shop. I know you can't bring them home."

"Yet," I answered. "I'm still working on that. I just need some time."

"I know. Right now you should concentrate on getting that shop of yours open. I know how much work that is."

"I know you do," I said, my voice soft. I knew it wasn't considered ladylike, but on impulse, I stood on my tiptoes and kissed him right on the lips. When I stopped, he looked at me with surprise, smiled, and pulled me into his enormous arms and gave me a kiss that was both tender and passionate. We continued kissing in the alleyway until I realized I was going to be late for my meeting if I didn't start walking.

"I have to go," I whispered, feeling his breath on my cheek, wanting to kiss him more. Not wanting to leave him, but knowing I had to. "I'm sorry, but I really need to see my friends. To see how everyone is doing."

He nodded. "Okay, but let me walk you the rest of the way."

We couldn't hold hands. I wished we could, but the North End was too small. If we did, this would no doubt be the night I would run into my aunt Cecilia's best friend or my neighbor, Mrs. Castellano, or someone else who would go straight to my mother and tell her they saw me holding hands with Sal Valenti, the butcher.

So we walked together, our elbows brushing once in a while. I held my bouquet with both hands, and I talked to him about what was happening with my hat shop and my friends, and he talked about his butcher shop and how he had to go to a cousin's christening on Sunday.

"Caprice, I wish you could come with me to the christening," he said just as we reached Hull House. "But, with my parents still getting over the fact I'm not marrying Pupetta, it's just not the right—"

I held my hand up to stop him from finishing his sentence. "I know. It's like we said, not the right time yet."

"Yes." He nodded, grabbing my hand. "Have fun at your meeting. Do you need me to walk you home?"

"I would love for you to walk me home, but I think I should walk home with Maria. I need to talk to her," I answered. "Thank you, though. And thank you for my beautiful flowers."

"Good night, Caprice," he said, stealing a quick kiss on my cheek after checking to make sure the street was empty. "I'll see you soon." He winked and walked away as I headed into the shop. My heart was still beating hard in my chest from our stolen moment in the alley.

The shop was empty, but I heard the sound of muffled voices from upstairs, so I knew most everyone was there. I left my hat and coat under the counter in the shop, and I placed my purple daffodils in an ochre-colored vase, making a mental note to put water in it before I left.

I walked into the assembly room, and Thea, Ada, and Maria were standing at the front of the room with Miss Guerrier. Thea's face was tear stained, and there were familiar red blotches on her neck. I rushed over to them.

"Thea, what in the world is wrong?" I asked, giving her a hug. "What happened? What's going on?"

"The hall next to our synagogue at Baldwin Place flooded last night—some pipes burst or something. I'm not even sure exactly what happened," Ada said. "Anyway, the hall is a mess, there's water and . . . sewage . . . everywhere," she added, making a sour face. "It's going to take at least a month to clean up. And Thea's reception was supposed to be there next week."

"Oh, God. Oh, I'm so, so sorry, Thea," I said. "I can't believe that happened."

"Me either," said Thea. "And we're not getting the money back that we paid for the hall, so it's not like we can rent anywhere else for the reception . . ."

"So we have just decided we are going to have our first Saturday Evening Girls wedding reception right here, in this assembly room," Miss Guerrier said, putting her arm around Thea's shoulders.

"Yes, Caprice. You, me, and Maria will decorate it beforehand, right, Maria?" Ada asked, nudging Maria.

"Yes, yes, right. Decorate," Maria said in a quiet voice, cracking one of her knuckles. I looked at her, feeling tension in the pit of my stomach. We hadn't talked since last Saturday night on the roof. I wondered if she had made any more plans with Mark. Or if by some miracle she had changed her mind completely and decided not to elope. I almost didn't want to know the answer.

"That's wonderful, just perfect," I said. "Thea, I promise you we'll make it absolutely beautiful in here for your wedding day."

"Thank you all. Thank you," said Thea, the blotches on her neck already starting to fade. "When I walked into that hall this morning, I was just devastated. Joshua, our families— everyone will be so happy when I tell them. Thank you."

"You're welcome," said Miss Guerrier, and then laughing, she added, "It's not like anyone was going to be here for the meeting next week anyway. Now if you'll excuse me, I have to get a couple of things from upstairs before we get started."

My friends and I took our usual seats at the back of the room and talked about the preparations for the wedding. Maria was much quieter than normal, and though she talked to all of us, she never said anything directly to me. While Maria was telling Thea about some fabric remnants we could use to decorate with, I tapped Ada on the elbow and whispered, "How are you? Are you doing okay?"

Ada looked at me, the deep sadness in her eyes telling me what I already suspected.

"I still love him, Caprice," she whispered back. She frowned, tugging at her braid. "I'm not sure how I'm ever going to get over him. But I know I have to."

Miss Guerrier came back and started making announcements, so we had to stop talking and turn our attention to the front of the room. I noticed that Mrs. Storrow had snuck in and was seated near the fireplace.

"And for our next announcement, a warm congratulations to Gemma Ianelli and Naomi Goodman for getting accepted into the evening program at Wheelock College," said Miss Guerrier. "We know you'll make us so proud.

"Okay, one final announcement. This one has been a long time coming. Ladies, I'm thrilled to announce that we have our very first entrepreneur in the ranks of the S.E.G." Miss Guerrier smiled, her eyes dancing. "Caprice Russo will open her own hat shop on the corner of Prince and Garden Court Streets in just eleven weeks! Caprice, please come up and say a few words."

The room erupted in applause. Despite the heat creeping up my cheeks, I got up and walked to the front of the room.

As I joined Miss Guerrier, Thea, Ada, and even Maria started whistling and hollering like grammar school boys, and everyone started laughing and cheering even more. I was so overcome, so touched, I just stood there, taking it all in.

The room was finally quiet, my face crimson, as I cleared my throat. I looked around at all the faces—Fanny, Albina, Naomi—but then my eyes focused on the three people in the back of the room, with the seat next to them reserved just for me. Ada, Maria, and Thea. My dear friends.

And I knew exactly what it was I wanted to say.

"Thank you, thank you all. So, so much," I began, my voice a little shaky. "Mrs. Storrow and Miss Guerrier, I think I could thank you a thousand different ways and it still wouldn't be enough. But . . . let me at least try to articulate what this moment—and what this club—means to me.

"Lately I've been thinking about the choices we make, particularly the ones that can, in an instant, alter the course of our lives forever." I turned my gaze to Maria. Our eyes met for a few seconds. She was the first to look away.

"Seven years ago, I made the choice to go to that first meeting Miss Guerrier organized at the library. Over the years we've learned together and laughed together and sometimes cried together. Through it all, through the camaraderie of this club, I changed my mind about my future. I know I'm not the only one in this room that feels this way . . ." I saw girls nodding from around the room as I kept talking.

"Miss Guerrier, Mrs. Storrow, both of you. *This club*—all of you," I said, sweeping my arm across the room. "You changed my mind about what I, the daughter of Italian immigrants, could accomplish in life," I said, swallowing hard and squinting my eyes to keep the tears in. "You made me change my mind . . . and, in doing so, you changed *my life*. Forever. And I'll be forever grateful."

Everyone in the room stood up and started clapping. I looked toward the back, and Ada and Thea were wiping their eyes. Maria was looking everywhere but at me. I gave Miss Guerrier the tightest hug I could muster, and when I pulled back, I saw her eyes glistening too.

And then I walked over to Mrs. Storrow, and she took my hands and said in my ear above the clapping, "Caprice, I know your shop is going to be a great success. And I want you to know that I will be forever grateful for knowing *you*." I just nodded and threw my arms around her in thanks, smelling her French perfume.

CHAPTER 23

If a link is broken, the whole chain breaks.
—Jewish proverb

"We can just take a quick look; I know it's getting late," I said this as Thea, Ada, Maria, and I cut across Hanover Street together and walked to my shop. Thea had asked to see how it was coming along, and when Ada discovered I had the key in my pocket, she suggested we go see it after the meeting. I had been surprised when Maria agreed to come too, since she had barely spoken the whole night.

"I can't wait to see the most beautiful hat shop in the North End," said Ada.

"Ada, it's the *only* hat shop in the North End," I said with a laugh as I opened the door.

"Details, details."

We walked in, the bells I attached to the door signaling our entrance. I hurried over and turned on one of the kerosene lamps.

"I probably should have brought you in for the first time during the day," I said. "It's hard to tell what it's like when it's so dark in here."

"Oh, no, Caprice, don't be silly," Thea said, clapping her hands together. "It's perfect."

"We've really only just cleaned up so far.

Frankie and Dominic are going to paint it for me. It's going to be pale green with a cream-colored trim, just as you suggested, Thea. All of the furniture will be painted cream too," I explained. "Here in the back, there will be a few work stations—for me, Vita, and Fabbia for now. I'm going to have a screen to partition them from the front of the shop. The front will be like a parlor, with a long mirror, a chair, and a little table and a glass case. I'll display my latest hats in the window with sashes and lace curtains behind. The shelves will store supplies, and the hats will be arranged according to style and price. I'm sorry, I'm going on and on."

"Talk about it as much as you want, Caprice. It's *us,*" said Ada. "And you've waited a long time to ramble about this place. Don't you agree, Maria? Maria, is everything okay? How come you've been so quiet tonight?"

"Thea . . . I . . . there's something I have to tell you," Maria said. She was still standing at the front of the shop, separated from the three of us. Her hat was shading her eyes, and it was hard to see the expression on her face in the lamplight.

"What is it, Maria?" Thea said, taking a step toward her.

"Caprice . . . well, you probably know what I'm going to say. I told you part of this news on the roof last week. As it turns out . . ." Maria paused before continuing to speak. "As it turns out, I'm eloping with Mark next weekend. I'm eloping to New York City with him. We have it all planned out. I . . . I can't change it now. I'm sorry."

I heard Ada gasp beside me, and I glanced over at Thea to see a stunned look on her face.

"Maria, I . . . you're not going to be at my *wedding?*" Thea said, heartbreak in her voice. "But you've known about it for months. You . . . you have to be there. All three of you. You all *have* to be there."

"Is this really what you want?" asked Ada.

"I honestly can't believe you're going through with it, Maria," I said, unable to hide the disappointment and disgust in my voice.

Maria raised her head a bit, and I could see her big blue eyes now, cool and steady, but her voice wavered and gave her away. "I told you before, maybe someday you will all accept this decision. I'm doing it not just for me, but for Antonetta and Richie too. For my mother. It's the security that we all need. That we've . . . that we've *never* had."

"But Maria, it won't be the same without you there on my wedding day!" Thea said, her voice cracking. "How could you do this? It's more important to me that you, Ada, and Caprice are there than my own family, for goodness' sake. I need you there. Can't you wait? Why next weekend?"

"Or the more important question, why are you

doing it at all?" I asked, though I knew it was probably futile.

"Yes, that was my *next* question," said Thea. "Why do it at all?"

"Yes, Maria," Ada said. "Really, Mark Toscanini? Do you even love him?"

"Oh, Ada, be serious. I can't afford love!" said Maria, anger and something like sadness in her voice. "Love is a luxury. I'm doing this to survive."

"Maria, you're not going to end up like your mother, no matter what," I said, my voice rising. "What more can I say to convince you of that?"

"Caprice, stop. Just stop!" Maria said. "If you were in my shoes, you might do the same thing. You have no idea."

"We have some idea, Maria," Ada said quietly. "And we know *you*. We know who you are. You're too good for him."

"But, Maria, couldn't you at least explain to Mark that you have to attend my wedding—he could even come," Thea said, clearly devastated.

"I'm sorry, Thea, but this is the plan," Maria said firmly, as if she had no say in the matter. And I realized that she probably didn't.

Maria walked toward Thea to give her a hug, but Thea pushed her away.

"No. No!" Thea said, her voice choked with emotion. "I can't forgive you for this, Maria. And I think you're making an *enormous* mistake."

Maria stepped back. "I'll be there in spirit, Thea," she whispered, giving Thea a weak smile. Her eyes were glistening in the dim light of the lamp. "Now if you will excuse me, I just . . . I'm going to go home and make sure my mother is feeling okay. I . . . I hope you all can understand someday." She turned and ran out the door.

Thea, Ada, and I stood in shocked silence for a minute, taking in what had just happened.

"I can't believe she's doing this, Thea. I'm sorry," I said, putting my arm around her shoulder. "I'm sorry she ever laid eyes on Mark."

Ada added, "I am too."

"Well, more than anything I'm just upset that she's going to be married to that absolutely awful man," said Thea. "Of course I'm so disappointed she's not going to be at my wedding, but to think she's going to spend the rest of her life as Mrs. Mark Toscanini. That's just horrible."

We were all quiet for a moment, pondering our gorgeous, vivacious, smart friend being married to the biggest *cafone* in the North End.

"Well, we still have a week. Should we try to talk some sense into her one more time?" asked Ada.

I shook my head. "I don't know. It might make her even more stubbornly determined. But then, maybe we should. I need to think about it. At this moment, I have no idea what to do. I just desperately don't want her to become

Maria Toscanini—Mark Toscanini's Maria," I answered. "If she marries him, it's like he'll *own* her."

The three of us stood in melancholy silence, wanting to save our friend from herself but unsure how to do it.

CHAPTER 24

Heaven and hell can both be found on earth.
—Jewish proverb

Friday, March 26, 1909

On Friday I arrived at the S.E.G. Pottery before six o'clock in the morning to try to get some work done on my own shop plans before the start of the workday. It was going to be a busy day. In addition to working at the pottery shop, Ada and I had planned on getting the assembly room decorated for Thea's reception. It was hard to believe the weekend of her wedding had arrived. It was more difficult to believe that Maria would not be there for it.

I was sitting at the shop counter going over some of my hat designs when the jingle of the door made me jump.

"Hi, Caprice."

I looked up and there was Maria, holding a large sack in both hands. Her skin looked even paler than usual, and there were dark circles under her eyes. Her curls were pulled back loosely, and she was dressed to the nines, wearing a cream-colored shirtwaist and black skirt under a gorgeous silver-gray cloak that I had never seen her wear before.

"Oh, hi," I answered, clearing my throat. "Where the heck have you been hiding? I've been looking for you all week. I wasn't sure I'd see you before . . . before you left tomorrow. Have you been avoiding me?"

"No, no, of course not. I've just . . . I've been busy," she answered, bringing the bag over to the counter and sitting down. It was a poor excuse. "I brought these things for you to use, to decorate for Thea's reception. I bargained with every pushcart from here to Haymarket, trying to find the perfect fabric remnants." She opened the bag, and there were beautiful swathes of pink and cream chiffon and two enormous cream-colored tablecloths. I gasped in spite of myself.

"These are . . . these are all so gorgeous," I exclaimed. "Better than anything we have. Maria, thank you. Can't you stay to at least help decorate? Miss Guerrier is going to have someone fill in for me down here late this afternoon. And Ada is coming over to help after work, and you could . . . you could too."

Maria shook her head. "I'm sorry, I have to pack," she said, and I knew it was another lie. "Our train leaves at five a.m. from North Station. I've got to be up very early."

"Does your mother know?" I asked, wondering for the first time how Mrs. Santucci was feeling about this, if she was supportive of her daughter's decision to put security above love or reason.

"No," she sighed. "I'm leaving her a note tomorrow morning. We'll be back in a few days. I figure that will be enough time for her. And then I'm going to talk to her about having Antonetta come live with me . . . with us, to take the burden off of my mother. Richie will be fine, but Antonetta . . . well, it would be tough for her to not be with me."

I looked into her eyes. They were filled with a sad resignation, and for the first time in my life, Maria looked like her mother to me. We sat there for a moment, just staring at each other, before I quietly asked, "I'm sorry, but I just have to ask one more time. Are you sure you really want to do this?"

There was another pause, and I searched her face for an answer. Just as I thought she might say no, she said, "Caprice, I'm as sure as I'll ever be." She looked away, her voice soft and pained. "This is an offer that I think I need to take. That will help secure a future for me and my family that we might not otherwise have."

"But how do you know that?" I said. "This *is* America, and you are smart and talented and beautiful. How do you know you couldn't have a better future without Mark? I don't know how you got caught up in all of this with him . . . how it got this far . . ."

"Look, I'm sorry," Maria said, taking a step toward the door. It was like she suddenly closed a curtain on her emotions, and she had the same cool look in her eyes that she had the night she'd first told us the news. Her voice still wavered. "I'm sorry I haven't been able to make you understand. And I'm sorry I won't be there for Thea tomorrow. Please tell her that. Tell her I love her and I'll see you all soon. I have to go."

The door of the shop jingled as Maria ran away again—away from me, away from my friendship, and away from all of the things that Hull House symbolized.

"So that's it then?" Ada said. She was standing on a stepladder, tacking some of the pale-pink chiffon bunting onto the assembly room wall. "She's leaving tomorrow first thing in the morning?"

"That's what she said." It was four in the afternoon, but I was still feeling physically ill about Maria.

"Well, should we try to do something about it? Is there anything more we can do to convince her she's making the biggest mistake of her life?" Ada asked, stepping down from the ladder.

"Ada, I've thought about it all day, and I don't know if there is," I answered with a sigh. "I've thought about talking to her mother, but she hasn't had any influence over Maria for years.

I've tried so many times to talk some sense into her, but she's so stubborn. And I think . . . I think when her father died, she just made up her mind that this is what she *had* to do, no matter the consequences. It's crazy. I thought she'd come to her senses by now. I thought she'd tire of him and see him for the *bastardo* he is, but she hasn't."

"Well, I'm just sick over it," Ada said. "And Thea is still so upset too. And then, to be honest, I'm a little angry with Maria. This is Thea's weekend, tomorrow is supposed to be Thea's day, and . . . Maria's being a bit selfish. Really, of all weekends to elope."

"Of all weekends," I answered.

"So, again, what do you think? Can we do anything more?" Ada asked.

"I honestly don't know."

"But—" Ada said, just as I heard a baritone voice I knew all too well.

"It's a pink palace in here."

I turned around and there was Sal, drenched from head to toe, wearing no coat, just a hat and a butcher apron over his clothes.

"Hello, Sal," Ada said. "Caprice, I'm going to get some more of that fabric and those votive candles downstairs." She gave me a wink and headed out of the room. As soon as Ada left, I ran over and jumped into Sal's arms.

"Shouldn't you be working?" I teased him after he kissed me hello.

"Shouldn't you be?" he teased back, kissing a drop of rain that he had left on my nose.

"Miss Guerrier is having someone cover for me so I can help get this room ready for the reception tomorrow," I said.

"Ah," he said. "My cousin is covering for me for a few minutes. I had to see you, Caprice. Four days is too long."

"I agree," I said, holding his hands. I didn't even care that he smelled like damp butcher shop. I just loved being near him.

"Sal, listen, I know I've said it before, but I'm truly sorry you can't come to the wedding tomorrow," I said, looking up into his eyes. "I would love to be there with you, with you *by my side*. But my father has finally accepted the idea of me as a shop owner. And now to reveal to him that I'm secretly seeing a young man from Avellino . . . I just want to wait a bit longer. I'm sorry we need to continue to keep this a secret . . . I'm—"

Sal interrupted me as he touched my cheek. "*Tesoro*, it's *okay*. It's really okay. I can wait. For as long as it takes. As long as I know that you're mine, it doesn't matter to me who knows or doesn't know it. Yet."

"Thank you for understanding," I answered, and I stood up on my tiptoes and gave him a soft kiss on the lips.

"Look, I need to get back to close up my

shop," he said. "I'm sorry this was such a quick visit, but my cousin, Vito, could be passing out free chickens at this point. He's not so bright." He tapped a finger on his head, which made me laugh.

"Okay, you better go then," I answered, and he wrapped me in his enormous arms one more time to give me a hard kiss on the lips that almost made my knees buckle. And with that, he whispered a good-bye and left.

"So things are going well with Sal?" Ada asked as she walked back into the room, her arms piled with decorating supplies.

"Yes," I said, hurrying over to grab some of the candles from her. "Ada, I feel bad; I haven't even asked how you've been doing. How are you feeling about things? About Dominic?"

"I'm . . ." Ada began as she put all the fabrics and votives down on the floor. "I'm keeping as busy as possible at my father's shop. I'm throwing myself into my schoolwork in the hopes that something will take my mind off of Dominic, but it hasn't really worked. Instead of missing him less every day, I'm missing him more. It's like the more I try to stop thinking about him, the more I think about him. It's insane."

Ada knelt down on the floor and started sorting through the fabrics, shaking her head before adding, "But despite that, I think . . . I know I made the right decision. For my future, for my plans. My mother and I met with my chemistry professor, the one who told me about the state scholarship for the school of medicine at Boston University. He thinks I'll have no problem getting one. We're going to tell my father next week. My mother is so proud, she actually can't wait to tell him at this point."

She paused and sighed. "I love Dominic with all my heart, truly. I told you before, I never knew what it was to love someone until I fell for him. But I have never wanted anything more in life than an education . . . and to be a *doctor?* Well, it's beyond my wildest dreams, Caprice. It's a dream I never believed could even be possible until now."

"Oh, Ada." I knelt down next to her and gave her a hug. "I couldn't be prouder and more happy for you. That is the most amazing news. But I'm just so sorry about you and Dominic too. I wish there was a way that it could work out for you both. I'm sorry it can't . . . but because of all of the things you just said, I think you're right. I think it's the right decision."

Ada nodded. "Thank you. And, as much as it still pains me, I think so too. I just hope that one of these mornings, I'll wake up and my heart will hurt a little less. And that maybe someday I will actually not be in love with him anymore. And that he'll be able to move on from me too."

She looked at me, and her eyes still had that

same look of heartache they had the night she had ended things with him. "How is he doing, Caprice? I have to ask. I need to know he's okay."

"He's doing about the same as you, Ada," I answered. "Maybe a little worse off, to be completely honest. I wish there were some way I could help you both. More than anything, I wish there were some way you could be together."

"Me too," Ada said, giving me a sad smile. "Me too."

CHAPTER 25

Friendship remains a faithful anchor.
—Italian proverb

Saturday, March 27, 1909

I have to see her off. I have to say good-bye.

Those were the thoughts running through my head the moment I woke up. It was pitch black in my room. Vita and Fabbia were both in a deep sleep next to me. I swung my legs over the edge of our bed and put my feet on our hard, cold wood floor. I felt around for my clothes, nearly tripping over a pair of Fabbia's shoes in the process. I heard Vita mumble something about cheese in her sleep.

Judging from the darkness, I was hopeful that it wasn't too late to get to North Station before five o'clock in the morning. I had to see Maria before she left. At this point she probably wasn't going to change her mind, but as a friend, I wanted to see her off, even if she was making the biggest mistake of her life.

I tiptoed around Frankie snoring loudly on his bed in the sitting room, grabbed my coat and hat, and headed into the kitchen. The tiny clock on the shelf read three thirty. Still time.

The streets were as quiet as I had ever seen them. I walked down the cobblestones quickly, nodding to the few longshoremen who walked by me on their way to the waterfront.

Before I even realized it, I was standing in front of Ada and Thea's building. It was like my feet knew where to walk before my mind did. I knew I had to go in and at least give Ada the opportunity to go with me. Even if her father thought I was insane for knocking on the door at this hour. I was going to let Thea sleep. Her mother would probably start screaming at me if I dared knock this early on the morning of her wedding day.

I walked as quietly as I could up the stairs to Ada's floor. I stood in front of her door for a few moments, dreading the consequences of knocking but knowing that I had to do it. Just as I raised my fist, the door opened and there was Ada, smiling and fully dressed, her long hair flowing under her hat. She held a finger to her lips.

"If you didn't come get me, I was going to come get *you,*" she whispered, grabbing my hand as we headed toward the stairs.

"I thought we should let Thea sleep though, yes?" I whispered back.

"Definitely," Ada said, nodding. "She has a long day ahead."

We hurried down the stairs on our tiptoes. We were going to need to run to North Station in order to make it with any time to spare. I pushed open the front door of the building and nearly let out a scream, because there was a figure standing in the shadows at the bottom of the stairs. And then I realized it was Thea.

"You two didn't think you were going to leave me behind, did you?" she asked.

"But how did you know?" I said.

"I heard you going up the stairs, Caprice," she said as we all started walking as fast as possible. "I knew it had to be you. Ada told me Maria was leaving at five this morning. I was sitting in bed wide awake, thinking of the wedding, Joshua, and Maria leaving . . . when I heard you, I threw on some clothes and came down here to wait."

"Thea, I just wanted to give you a chance to sleep," I said. "Today is your wedding day . . ."

"Yes, really, Thea, you should go back to bed," Ada added.

"Thank you for your concern, ladies. But, like for you, Maria has been one of my best friends since I was thirteen years old. I don't care that it's my wedding day; I want a chance to say good-bye to one of my best friends before *she* gets married," Thea said. "I need to see her before she goes."

"Well, ladies, if we're going to make it to say our good-byes, we need to walk a little faster," Ada said, and we all broke into a run.

There were more people out on the streets as we got to North Station. It was 4:35 a.m., and I knew Maria and Mark would be boarding their train any minute. I spotted the board and hurried over.

"It's track two, the train to Providence," I said, as I started walking in that direction. "They have to get off in Providence and get on another train to New York City."

When we reached track two, crowds of people were already giving the conductors their tickets and boarding the train. Ada, Thea, and I searched frantically through the crowd. I finally spotted a head of familiar blonde curls about fifteen feet away, and I cupped my hands and called out, "Maria! Maria!"

Maria whipped around, and her face grew even paler when she saw us. Mark held her elbow tightly and gave the three of us a menacing look.

Maria whispered something in his ear. At first he seemed to disagree with her, but then he let go of her elbow, and she made her way through the crowds of people to us.

"What are you doing here?" Maria said, frowning at us. She looked tired and . . . scared. Her eyes were glistening; they were no longer the emotionless shields they had been in recent weeks. "Thea, it's your wedding day. What . . . ?"

"We came to say good-bye. We had to see you before you left," Thea said simply, with a shrug. Maria threw her arms around her. And Ada and I threw our arms around the two of them.

"We love you, Maria," I said into her hair. "I'm sorry I've been so judgmental. Whatever you do, I love you, and you'll always be one of my best friends."

When we pulled apart, Maria wiped her eyes with her hand, and I noticed she was trembling a bit. Thea blotted her eyelashes with a handkerchief.

"Thea, no crying. Your mother will kill you if your eyes are puffy for your wedding day," Ada said, and the four of us tried to laugh.

"Maria! Maria, we have to go!" Mark yelled.

"Well, I'll see you all soon," Maria said, giving us each a kiss on the cheek. "Thank you. Thank you for coming to say good-bye."

"You're welcome," I said, swallowing hard. "Be safe."

"Good luck," Ada said.

"And, Thea, I'm so sorry I won't be there today. You know that, right?" Maria asked.

"Maria, get over here *now!*" Mark screamed.

"Yes, yes, I know," Thea said. "You better go."

Maria was already walking backward. She turned, and when she reached Mark, he grabbed her elbow again, pulled her over to the conductor, handed him the tickets, and got on the train. Maria blew us all a kiss just as she got on.

Ada, Thea, and I all stood there in silence for a moment, staring at the entrance of the train where Maria had just disappeared.

"Come on, Thea," I whispered, hooking arms with her and Ada. "We have to get you home before your parents think you made a run for it."

We turned and started walking home.

"This is awful," Ada said. "I just can't believe it."

"I know," I answered with a sigh, a pit of sadness in my stomach. Thea unhooked arms with us to blot her eyes again.

North Station was starting to get more crowded, and we walked slowly through the throngs of people coming and going. It smelled like grease and soot and some other unpleasant, sour odor I couldn't identify. We walked out of the station, elbows still linked.

We were about to cross the street when I heard a voice shouting, "Wait! Wait, friends! Wait for me!"

We all turned, and there was Maria, running toward us with her travel bag. She was wild eyed, and her face was streaked with tears.

"I'm coming with you," she said as she crossed the street. "I'm coming b-back." When she reached us, she collapsed into us and started sobbing.

"Oh, Jesus," she said, her voice still trembling. "I thought I could be that woman. That *kind* of woman who marries for . . . for money. But . . . but I am not a woman who can marry any man for that . . . especially *that man*." She started sobbing again, and we surrounded her and walked as fast as we could. I knew Ada and Thea were just as afraid as I was that Mark would be coming after her.

"Caprice, you were right. I was choosing to ignore things. A lot of things," she said.

"But, Maria, I was too judgmental. And I'm truly sorry for that," I answered, so relieved that she was there with us.

"Well, you were," Maria said with smile. "But I know you—I know it was out of love. And you have to understand, I was flattered by the way he paraded me around, the money he spent on me, introducing me to all these people. But the closer we got to this day, the more I asked myself, how much could I ignore his business dealings? Or the types of characters he associated with all of the time? Most importantly, how could I put up with the way that he *treated* me—so controlling, like he owned me.

"Could I put up with all of that *forever?* For . . . *for money?* And then exposing my little sister to that kind of life too." Maria shuddered. "The truth was, I would have been trapped in a marriage as much as my mother was trapped in hers, just . . . in a different way."

"Oh, Maria, I'm so incredibly relieved you changed your mind," Ada said, wrapping her in a hug as we made our way back to the North End.

"Me too," Thea said. "And I'm sorry for our

argument last week. More than missing my wedding, I was afraid of your decision . . . I'm just so relieved."

"So am I," Maria said. "I started vomiting when I woke up this morning. I wasn't sure how I was going to get out of it, but I knew I couldn't marry him. I knew that I had made a huge mistake ever getting involved with him. But you see how he is; he's been watching my every move. He's tough to get away from. I was afraid of what would happen if I didn't show up this morning . . . so I stashed money in my brassiere. When we stopped in Providence, I was going to lie to him and say I was going to the bathroom and then get off the train just as it was leaving. He would have been on his way to New York City while I was on my way home.

"But then I saw the three of you standing there. You'll never . . . you'll never know what that meant. When I got on the train with him, I sat down and started to cry. Just as we were about to pull out of the station, I jumped up and started screaming that I had to get off. I just had to get away from him. Mark was literally holding onto my left arm so I couldn't leave."

"So what the heck did you do?" I asked, imagining the scene in the train car.

"I swung my bag as hard as I could, whacked him over the head with it, and jumped off the train," Maria said with a devilish smile.

We all gasped.

"Oh, what I would have paid to see that," Ada said, laughing.

"You and me both, Ada," I added.

"But, Maria, aren't you afraid, you know, of what he might do now? Now that you left him like that?" Thea said.

"*Un bastardo*!" Maria said. "I dare him to touch me. I could have most of the young men in the North End protecting me by tomorrow. In fact, I'll make sure of it."

"Oh, Maria," I said with a laugh, putting my arm over her shoulder. "You're back. I'm so happy you're *really* back."

"I am," she said, giving us her dazzling smile. The one we hadn't seen in a very long time. She linked arms with Thea. "Now, this is a very big day, ladies. Let's go get Thea married!"

CHAPTER 26

Count your nights by stars, not by shadows;
count your life with smiles, not by tears.
—Italian proverb

In the dim light of the temple, Thea looked luminous in her ivory satin foulard dress and long white gloves. Her green eyes twinkled in the candlelight, and her hair was in a romantic bun under a simple tea-length veil. The first thing I felt when I saw her walk down the aisle of the Baldwin Place Synagogue with her parents was overwhelming hope and happiness for her.

Joshua Robinowitz was watching and waiting for her under the chuppah, the ceremonial canopy that was a stitched quilt of meaningful fabrics—lace from her mother's wedding dress, her grandmother's apron, her baby gown. Among the many pieces, there was, of course, a piece of cream-colored table linen with *S.E.G.* embroidered on it in large letters; in smaller letters, there were forty sets of embroidered initials. Ada, Maria, and I had etched ours close together in bright-pink thread.

The second thing I felt when Thea walked down the aisle was a pang of bittersweet sadness, because even though we all said it wouldn't change things between the four of us, I knew that was a lie. When Joshua crushed the glass under his right foot at the end of the ceremony, Thea would be the first one of us to be married. It was a milestone in the history of our friendship. Whether we wanted to admit it or not, I knew somewhere, very soon down the road, another one of us would be getting married. The question is, would we choose rightly? Had Thea chosen rightly, marrying a man who was picked for her? She fell in love with him, so maybe she had. I hoped so. Only God knew for sure.

When the ceremony ended, Ada, Maria, and I gave Joshua and Thea a kiss and hurried over to Hull House to make sure the assembly room was ready for the reception. Some of Thea's aunts and cousins were going to bring the kosher food for the buffet. Frankie was going to help with drinks. I had asked him to help so that Thea's relatives could relax and enjoy themselves.

The three of us gasped when we walked into the assembly room.

"Where did you two get all the flowers? It must have cost a fortune!" Maria asked. "It looks absolutely stunning in here."

"I have no idea where the flowers came from," said Ada. There were small fragrant bouquets of pale-pink and cream-colored roses everywhere, filling the air in the large room with their sweet, subtle perfume. It completed the decor Ada and I had worked so hard on the day before.

"I don't know how they got here either," I answered.

"Oh, Caprice, there's an envelope on this bouquet with your name on it—here. I think this will solve the mystery." Ada handed me the envelope, and I opened it and recognized the thick ivory stationery:

Caprice. Please tell Thea I'm sorry I'm unable to attend her wedding festivities. These flowers are my gift to her and Joshua. Please give her my love and congratulations. – H.O.S.

I looked up at Ada and Maria, showed them the card, shook my head, and smiled. "Helen Osborne Storrow."

"Of course," Maria said with a smile.

The door jingled and the first of Thea's female relatives began to arrive, carrying delicious-smelling food and marveling at the wonderful setting we had created. Ada knew most of them and started directing them over to the buffet.

I was setting up the Victrola when Frankie entered. I nearly fell over when I saw Dominic walk in behind him. Hurrying over to them, I glanced at the buffet to see that Ada hadn't noticed their arrival yet.

"What are you doing here?" I whispered, feeling my face grow warm.

"Frankie said he needed a hand," Dominic said, giving me a wink. "Relax, cousin; I'm not going to cause any problems. I won't even talk to her."

"Yeah, Caprice, you know Dominic. He'll behave," Frankie said, patting me on the shoulder. "You should be more worried about me. A lot of pretty ladies from your club are coming to this reception."

"Just please, Dominic, don't do or say anything to upset her," I pleaded. "Your presence will be upsetting enough."

"Of course I won't," Dominic said, clearly offended and with heartache in his eyes. "I just . . . I just wanted to see her face again."

"Okay, I trust you," I said with a sigh. "Frankie, the bar is over there in the corner opposite the Victrola."

Frankie tipped his hat to me and headed to the corner with Dominic. I walked over to Ada, who was setting up even more food on the buffet table on the far wall.

"Are you okay?" I asked in her ear. She looked up at me with a small smile. Her cheeks were bright pink.

"Am I *okay?* I'm shaking I'm so nervous and . . . and so happy to see him. I wish he hadn't come, but I'm thrilled he's here. Does that make any sense at all?"

"Yes and no," I replied, laughing.

But then she stopped smiling, and her expression got very serious.

"Caprice, to be completely honest, I know that someday, very soon, I will have to have another very hard, very heartbreaking talk with your cousin about why we can't ever be together," Ada said, her voice filled with sadness. "But I know I made the right decision, the one I had to make. I know I can't sacrifice my dream of medical school, even for love, as much as it hurts me and Dominic." She sighed. "But, today is Thea's wedding day. It is not the day to have that talk with Dominic. Today, I just want to celebrate with Thea and enjoy seeing him again, even if I can't dance with him. Does *that* make sense?"

"That makes total sense to me, my friend," I said, giving her a long, hard hug. "I'm so sorry it can't be different for you and Dominic, but at the same time, I am so proud of you I can't even begin to tell you."

A huge cheer erupted as the bride and groom entered the room, and minutes later, Thea and Joshua rushed over to us.

"Caprice, Ada, this is so amazing! I can't . . . I'm so touched by what you all . . ." She gulped, and her eyes were watering.

"Ladies, thank you. It's the most beautiful wedding reception I've ever seen. Really."

Joshua took his eyes off Thea for a brief second and kissed Ada and me each on the cheek.

"You're welcome; we loved doing it for you," I answered.

"Oh, but Thea, before I forget," I added, "I was wondering if you could help me with something in a little while." I whispered my plan into her ear.

She started laughing. "That sounds perfect. Of course I'll do it."

"Okay, well, whenever you're ready, you let me know," I said.

"Come on, Thea. I think people are waiting for us to dance," said Joshua. And she nodded at me before they took to the dance floor. They didn't take their eyes off of each other the whole time. I caught sight of Dominic in the corner of the room, having a beer and talking to Frankie and my father at the bar. He couldn't keep his eyes off of Ada. Ada was talking with Miss Guerrier nearby and trying hard to pretend she didn't notice his stare.

"Ah, they are a beautiful couple, aren't they, *tesoro*?" I jumped as I heard Sal's unmistakable whisper in my ear. My heart leaped, and I tensed as I looked back toward my father. But he wasn't looking in our direction.

I turned around and Sal said, "It's okay, Caprice, I promise. I was invited."

"Invited? But I told Thea . . ."

"Oh, Thea didn't invite me," he said with a sly

346

smile. "A very good customer of mine invited me, with Thea's permission, of course."

"Who? Sal, what are you talking about?"

"Rosina Russo invited me," he said.

"Rosina Ru—my *mother?* My mother invited *you?*" I said in disbelief.

He laughed, "Caprice, you're so shocked. I'll admit, I was a little surprised myself, but why don't you go ask her? She's right there talking to Mrs. Goodman. And then come back over here and dance with me." I gave him a look but went over to my mother, who was enjoying a glass of wine and laughing at something Mrs. Goodman had said.

"Mama, did you—" I started to say, but she finished my sentence.

"Invite Salvatore Valenti? Why, yes, I did," she said, clearly proud of herself. And then while Mrs. Goodman turned to say something to someone else, she raised her eyebrows and whispered in Italian, "Hey, at least he's not Jewish, yes?" My eyes grew wide, and one look into hers told me she had known about Dominic and Ada for a while.

"But Papa . . . what if—" I said, and she stopped me again.

"We will work on your Papa and his old ways," she said. "He thinks Sal is a very good butcher— that's a start. Now go have fun—go *dance.*" I gave her a hug and walked back over to Sal, who immediately took my hand and brought me onto the dance floor. This time I did spot my father, who was chatting with Joshua's father. He did a double take when he saw who I was dancing with and went back to his conversation, but I wasn't fooled.

"So you're surprised?" said Sal.

"Shocked," I said. "Although my mother has definitely surprised me a lot this year, so you'd think I would be used to it. I think my father just noticed us dancing."

"I wouldn't worry too much. For all he knows, it's just a dance," Sal answered, and I looked up into his eyes, and we both knew it was so much more than that.

The song ended and Thea came up behind me and tapped me on the shoulder.

"Congratulations to you and Joshua, Thea," said Sal, kissing her on both cheeks. *"Per cent'anni."*

"Thank you, Sal," Thea said. Looking at me, she added, "Caprice, are you ready?"

"Yes, definitely," I answered.

"Okay, give me about thirty seconds," she said, and then disappeared into the crowd.

"Thirty seconds for what?" Sal asked, furrowing his eyebrows.

"Oh, we've just got a little something planned for the girls. I promise I'll be back soon. Go have a beer with my brother and Dominic." I almost leaned in to kiss him on the cheek but thought better of it.

I spotted Ada first; she was standing near the fireplace with a few people. I grabbed her by the elbow and whispered in her ear.

"We've got an emergency. It's Thea; she's on the roof. We've got to grab Maria and head up there," I said.

She nodded and followed me as we whisked Maria away from the three young men who were all trying to talk to her at once.

"What in the world is the matter?" Ada asked as we ran up the back staircase to the roof.

"It's Thea. She's an absolute nervous wreck," I told her. "I think she's having second thoughts. It's—she's nervous about tonight—the bedroom stuff, you know."

"But I thought she was okay with it!" said Ada, breathless.

"It's a little late to fall apart about it now, isn't it?" Maria said as we finally burst through the door to the rooftop.

"Yes, it's a little late to fall apart now," said Thea, beautiful, serene, and smiling as she handed Ada, Maria, and me glasses of wine.

She was standing in the middle of Miss Guerrier's rooftop garden—which was just starting to reveal its early spring splendor, with crocuses and columbines and the promise of other flowers starting to bloom.

"What is this? You mean you're not . . . falling apart?" asked Ada, looking at the wineglass.

"No, far from it," said Thea with a laugh, her face already flushed.

"This was my idea," I said, looking at the three of them. "I wanted to get us all up here for a few minutes, to have a couple of toasts, just the four of us. So if you will all raise your glasses, I will start."

I held up my glass of homemade red wine and looked first at Thea. "To Thea. I think I'm speaking for all of us—to see you so happy makes us happy. *Per cent'anni* and *mazel tov*!"

"*Per cent'anni* and *mazel tov*!" Maria and Ada said in unison as we clinked our glasses.

I held up my glass again. "I also want to toast my three best friends in the entire world. To a hundred more years of friendship."

"Cheers to that," said Maria, and we clinked our glasses again. "Can I add to that sentiment? A toast to the three of you, my priceless family of friends. Thank you for helping me be brave enough to not settle for less than I deserve."

"Oh!" Thea said after she took another big sip of wine. "I also want to toast to finding passion in every aspect of your life. *Especially* in the bedroom." We all collapsed into laughter, and Maria let out one of her snorts.

"Okay. I would like to give one more toast," said Ada after our laughter calmed down. She looked at all of us and said, "To following our dreams, whatever direction the wind blows us."

We quietly clinked glasses again.

"Oh, I nearly forgot one," I said. "I'm sorry, this is the last one, I promise." I held up my glass one final time. "To the Saturday Evening Girls, without whom none of us would be here, together, today."

"To the Saturday Evening Girls!" we all hollered into the night sky, clinking our glasses one last time.

And the four of us stood side by side at the edge of the roof, sipping our wine, laughing and talking, and watching the stars glimmer over the harbor in the distance.

ABOUT THE RESEARCH

This novel is a work of fiction, but the Saturday Evening Girls Club was very much a real club in Boston's North End in the early- to mid-twentieth century. It originally started in 1899 as a book club run by North End librarian Edith Guerrier. With the financial patronage of prominent Boston philanthropist Helen Osborne Storrow, the book club evolved into something much more. By the 1910s, in addition to the Saturday Evening Girls Club, there were additional clubs for younger girls, each named after a day of the week. At the height of their popularity, the clubs had over 250 members collectively.

The Saturday Evening Girls (S.E.G.) Club pottery, or Paul Revere Pottery as it is also referred to, is a fantastic example of the creativity of the Arts and Crafts Movement. Today S.E.G. pottery is quite valuable and highly sought after by collectors. In addition to information I found online and in a few books that focus on the pottery itself, the Schlesinger Library at Harvard University was a great source for primary research materials. The author Kate Clifford Larson's thesis paper on the club, published by the University of Chicago Press, was another incredibly valuable resource. The more I learned, the more I wanted to write a novel about these smart, sassy, enterprising young women who wanted more out of life than society expected of them.

Whenever I finish a historical novel that is based on a true story, I always want to know, who is real and who is not? And did any of these events actually happen?

As I mentioned, Edith Guerrier and Helen Osborne Storrow were the actual founders of the club. I must also note that there was one other founder: Edith Brown, Guerrier's partner, was the artistic director for the club. I did a great deal of research on all three of these remarkable women, in an effort to capture who they were and what they meant to the young women of the club. I could not find as much research on Edith Brown, and though I included her in earlier drafts, having two Ediths serving the same role in the story was just too cumbersome. Isabella Stewart Gardner was a prominent member of Boston society and lifelong patron of the arts. She lived on the fourth floor of Fenway Court, which is now the Isabella Stewart Gardner Museum.

Finally, the following women were actual members of the club, and I included them in the story really just to honor their memory. Though they are very minor characters in the book, they deserve special mention: Albina Mangini, Sara Galner, Fanny Goldstein, and Lillie Shapiro.

Some of the stories in this book are based on real events that I came across in my research. The scene in the novel at Fenway Court is based on an actual event—the girls did in fact perform *The Merchant of Venice* for Isabella Stewart Gardner and her friends. The way they were received there is based on firsthand accounts by some of the club members in attendance that evening. The scene that features Caprice and her friends delivering pottery in Mrs. Storrow's car is also based on a true story I discovered in my research.

For more information, please visit my website: www.janehealey.com.

ACKNOWLEDGMENTS

The road to publication for *The Saturday Evening Girls Club* has been long and winding, and I need to thank the many people who helped along the way.

To Charlie: My husband, best friend, and the love of my life, thank you for always believing in me and my writing. This story never would have happened if it weren't for you.

Thank you to Ellie and Madeleine, my daughters and cheerleaders. I love you more than words, and you are my greatest accomplishments.

Thank you to my parents, not only for the free babysitting, but also for your unconditional love, support, and belief in me and this project.

Thank you to my mother-in-law, Magee, and the late Tom Ungashick, for their love and support. Magee, thank you also for our serendipitous trip to the movies!

To Tammy Inman, Susanna Baird, and Rebecca Delaney, my dear writing group. For the early reads, edits, feedback, for everything. You ladies are my kindred writing mamas!

Thank you to the lovely author Haywood Smith for reading my very first draft and seeing *The Saturday Evening Girls Club*'s potential despite that draft's many, many flaws.

Thank you to the wonderful instructors at

Grub Street Writers. A special thanks to the terrific author and Grub Street instructor Emily Franklin for also seeing the potential of the story and taking time outside of class to help me get it right.

Julie Gregori Cremin, you were a critique partner extraordinaire, and this would not have happened without your fantastic editing. Thank you.

To my cousin the author, David Healey: I am incredibly grateful for your support and advice.

To the amazing greater Melrose community: For blowing me away with your support and enthusiasm during the book's Kindle Scout campaign. There are too many of you to name, but I am so thankful to each and every one of you.

To the family, friends, and strangers all over the world who voted for *The Saturday Evening Girls Club* during its Kindle Scout campaign: a thousand thanks.

I am eternally grateful to Megan Mulder, editor at Kindle Scout, for walking down the hall and telling Danielle Marshall, editorial director of Lake Union Publishing, about this book during its thirty-day Kindle Scout campaign.

Finally, an enormous thank you to Danielle Marshall; my terrific editors, Miriam Juskowicz and Faith Black Ross; and the rest of the wonderful team at Lake Union Publishing. It is truly a dream come true, and I couldn't have asked for a better home for "the Girls"!

ABOUT THE AUTHOR

Jane Healey was inspired to write *The Saturday Evening Girls Club* after learning of the group's history while researching an article on their namesake pottery, also known as Paul Revere Pottery. She became fascinated by the relatively unknown stories of these smart, sassy, enterprising young immigrant women living in Boston's North End at the turn of the twentieth century.

In addition to being a fiction writer, Jane is a freelance journalist and consultant. Her publishing credits include the *Boston Globe*, *Boston Magazine*, AOL / *Huffington Post*, the *Street*, *Publishers Weekly*, and *New England Home*.

Jane holds a bachelor's degree from the University of New Hampshire and a master's degree from Northeastern University. She shares a home north of Boston with her husband, two daughters, and two cats. When she's not writing, she enjoys running, reading, and cooking. For more information on the author and her work, visit www.janehealey.com.

Books are produced in the United States using U.S.-based materials

Books are printed using a revolutionary new process called THINKtech™ that lowers energy usage by 70% and increases overall quality

Books are durable and flexible because of Smyth-sewing

Paper is sourced using environmentally responsible foresting methods and the paper is acid-free

Center Point Large Print
600 Brooks Road / PO Box 1
Thorndike, ME 04986-0001 USA

(207) 568-3717

US & Canada:
1 800 929-9108
www.centerpointlargeprint.com